PRAISE FOR

"Steamy, romantic, mouthwatering story was delivered just right, penned to perfection, and kept me hypnotized cover to cover."
-Natasha is a Book Junkie

"Undeniably explosive, flirty, and addictive... We were hooked!"
-The Rock Stars of Romance

"Get ready to be hot and bothered because Nikki Sloane creates the perfect erotic storm and you will love getting caught up in it!"
-Agents of Romance

"Hot, sexy, steamy, and so much more, Nikki delivers a story that will keep you begging for more!"
-Bella from PBC

"A love story with a side of sexy-as-sin foreplay, erotic exploration, and characters who know how to excite and pleasure. A scorching hot read!"
-Roxy Sloane, *USA Today Bestselling Author*

"A slick, captivating, and incredibly sexy book. Sloane injects humor and depth into a compelling story, and ensures readers will be back for more."
-SM Book Obsessions

"Three Simple Rules is a smoking hot read that will have you hooked from the first page. Nikki Sloane is a hot new erotic author to watch for."
-The SubClub Books

THREE little MISTAKES

NIKKI SLOANE

Text copyright © 2015 by Nikki Sloane

Cover photograph © Tomasz Zienkiewicz Photography

All rights reserved. Except as permitted under the U.S. Copyright Act of 1976, no part of this publication may be reproduced, distributed, or transmitted in any form or by any means, or stored in a database or retrieval system, without the prior written permission of the publisher.

The characters and events portrayed in this book are fictitious. Any similarity to real persons, living or dead, is coincidental and not intended by the author.

Cayenne Edition

ISBN 978-0-9983151-2-6

for my husband

chapter ONE

JOSEPH

What the fuck was this girl doing at my club?

She looked like she couldn't be a day over twenty, which meant I had an issue with the door. Someone wasn't checking the IDs, or not looking at the photos close enough. I'd have to talk to my manager about that, *again*.

The girl stood in a semi-circle with her friends, a half-empty drink in her hand while she surveyed the selection of men nearby. From my vantage-point on the second floor balcony, I saw the dark roots of her hair, giving way to pale, dusty blonde streaking down that glowed in the low light pulsing from the DJ booth.

She laughed and touched one of her friends on the arm. Calm. Casual. Like she had every right to be here, and wasn't jeopardizing my club's liquor license simply with her presence. Annoyance flared and made my skin hot. Perhaps I should have given my staff the benefit of the doubt. Maybe her fake ID was fucking amazing.

I turned away from the balcony and glanced back at my tiny, disorganized office. My manager had ordered too much of some import and now the cases were stacked in a corner, and the result was claustrophobic. Dune, a nightclub, used to be the favorite of all my properties, but in recent years there'd been a turn in clientele, and another club began to dominate my focus.

So dark and illegal, the smell of that place didn't wash

off for days. I fucking loved it.

The blonde finished her drink, tilting the glass back and obscuring her face. I didn't like that. It was hard enough to see her across the expanse of the dance floor. Pretty, with a cute, up-turned nose and high cheekbones. Maybe a designer nose. I'd spent the last few years studying women and their quest for beauty. Was the girl lucky in genetics or lucky with rich parents?

The clients at my blindfold club would eat her up. The younger, the better, for some of them. I didn't judge my clients' tastes, as long as the girl was old enough and wanted it. Besides, I'd met plenty of thirty-year-old women with less maturity than ones who were eighteen.

Hairs lifted on my arm and the back of my neck in hyperawareness. Movement to the left of the girl was too abrupt and aggressive to be dancing. Shit. A couple of douchebags were getting heated. A hand flung in the other guy's chest and shoved backward.

If he wanted space, he got the opposite. The offended man was all over the guy who'd shoved him, getting in his face. Stiff posture. Hands balled into fists and, as if sensing the impending fight, the area around the men cleared.

Except for the blonde.

Her friends scattered and she tried to follow, but she was the last one to get out of the way.

"Fuck," I said into the earpiece I wore. "Someone get on that mess and break it up." Where the hell were my bouncers?

The first punch landed on the guy's jaw, knocking him askew, but only for a second. He reared back and unleashed his own attack, the thick rope of muscle in his neck straining, visible from all the way up where I was.

THREE *little* MISTAKES

The only thing I valued was being in control, so my hands tensed on the balcony railing as I stood powerless to stop what I sensed was about to happen. The smaller of the two men began to retreat, backing up and trapping the blonde behind him, pinning her to the wall.

"Move!" I ordered into the earpiece to my bouncer, although I really wanted to say it to the girl directly. *Move before this gets really bad.* Mario's enormous bald head worked its way through the crowd, struggling to get there in time, but his wide and impressive build made that difficult.

The bigger of the two men fighting launched forward, pummeling the smaller one. The girl's mouth dropped open, her face twisting in shock or pain. Maybe she wasn't receiving the blows directly, but she could sure as hell feel them.

Mario broke free from the crowd and grasped the bigger guy's shoulder, jerking him away, but a second too late. The final punch missed its intended target and struck the girl instead. Her head snapped away from the impact, and one of her hands flew up to cover her cheek, which was sure to start swelling immediately.

Fuck me. If I had any hope of her not getting busted in my club, it died with that assault.

Realizing what he'd done, the guy threw his arms up and backed away in a silent apology. An *"I didn't mean to hit a girl"* was plastered on his expression. Mario yanked the guy farther back as another bouncer appeared to collect the loser of the fight, releasing the girl from the wall. The last thing anyone expected, Mario included, was for her to spring forward at the man who'd hit her. Even over the pumping bass of the music that throbbed in my chest, I'd swear I heard the slap of her palm across the asshole's face.

Her friends flooded in, surrounding her and pulling her away. Despite everything, I wanted to smile at this victim who refused to play the part. What a tough bitch.

But I had to work fast if I was going to stay ahead of this. "Get an ice pack, tell the friends their drinks are paid for, and bring the girl upstairs."

I watched my orders executed one by one. All of the friends' gazes turned up to my balcony, and finally the girl's lifted too. Her hand fell away from her face to point at the balcony, maybe asking the staff member if that was where she was going or if I was who wanted to speak with her. This action revealed the spot that was already darkening on her pretty, underage face.

Fucking shit. I swore in my head the whole time she made her way upstairs. I didn't need attention on this club, because it might lead to attention on other things, and prison was about as appealing to me as it was to anyone else.

My hand flattened the front of my dress shirt, smoothing it down. I could be charming. My eyes were kind and my smile warm, or so I'd been told, and I played up the old southern accent I used to have when needed. I disarmed. No one suspected the wolf beneath my surface, and only a handful of people knew about him.

The door swung open and my manager escorted the blonde in, who pressed an ice pack to her cheek.

"Thanks, Alan," I said, dismissing him.

Her eyes blinked, drinking me in, and she seemed to study me just as intensely as I did her. I wasn't prepared for how . . . well, *adorable* she was. There wasn't a better word for it. Thick, glossy hair that went nicely with her fair skin, even though she wasn't a real blonde. Bright eyes. Lush, pink lips. Oh, yeah. The men at my other club would write blank checks for that face. And Heather had given her notice, which meant I needed to fill a spot . . .

Stop evaluating her and focus.

"Are you all right?" I asked. There was no need to force concern. I was genuinely worried about what had happened to her.

"I'm okay."

I wasn't expecting such a strong voice from a slight girl, but then again, I'd gotten a taste of some of her fire downstairs, hadn't I?

"I own this club, and I want you to know I take security very seriously. I'd like to apologize on behalf of my staff for the incident. If you need to see a doctor, someone can—"

"I said I'm okay." Her voice was clipped, as if annoyed. If she wanted to blame me for what happened, I understood and respected it. She should have been safe here, and I'd failed that obligation.

"Can I get you anything?"

She pulled the ice pack away and held it up. "Someone brought me this, I'm good."

But, oh no, she wasn't. The bruise was already bright red.

"That's gotta hurt like hell. I have Advil in my desk somewhere, for the swelling." I yanked open a drawer and rummaged through it.

The ice pack returned to the injury. "No offense, but I'm not interested in taking pills from a stranger. I've got some in my purse anyway."

The drawer creaked as I shut it and set my gaze on her once more, starting at her heels and working my way up. Petite frame and in good shape. A narrow waist that called for hands to latch onto it. To pull her backward onto my—

My head clouded with lust and left me disoriented. What was with me? What was this reaction?

"Do you want to call the police and file a report?" I asked. *Please say no.*

"No!" She made a face as if her own response had startled her. "No, I'm fine. Wrong place at the wrong time, let's not make a big deal out of it."

She was underage. Her alarmed expression said the cops coming here was the last thing she wanted. Yeah, me too.

"Look, Mr . . ."

"Joseph." It came out of my mouth before I thought better. Last name would have been more professional, but for some insane reason I wanted this girl to know my name. Normally her innocent, fresh-faced look wouldn't do anything for me, but the strong voice, her sharp eyes, and the unexpected slap had piqued my interest.

"Joseph," she repeated. "I'm not going to sue your establishment. To be honest, I'm not supposed to be here, and I'd kind of just like to go home."

The girl had given me an out, but I couldn't let it go. "Can I see your ID?" When she shot me a dubious expression, I added, "I still have to document this, in case something happens down the road or you change your mind about bringing charges."

I was sure the expression I gave said this wasn't negotiable. Her hand dug in the pocket of her jeans and pulled out the driver's license, extending it. I crossed the space to her, and now the full claustrophobic effect took hold. This girl in front of me was small, and yet she filled the room. Her gaze was fixed on me, and a fleeting emotion passed through her. Anxiety? Did I make her nervous, or had my request simply done that?

The ID was real, and most definitely not hers. I tightened the hold on the plastic card until the edges bit into my fingers. "I'm keeping this," I said, glancing at the name, *"Molly Givens."*

"What? Why?" Her expression didn't falter. Didn't change a hair.

"Because you shouldn't be in here when you're not twenty-one."

Her face soured. At first, I thought she looked pissed at being busted, but no. This was something else.

"All right, *Joseph*," she snapped. "Maybe that's not my ID, and I know I look young, but I promise you, I'm over twenty-one. I turned twenty-one two years ago."

"You're using a fake ID when you're twenty-three? That makes sense."

Her jaw tightened. "It does when you're me."

"Okay, I'll bite." She'd never know the truth there. "Who are you?" I scrutinized her once again. Were they filming some big blockbuster in Chicago right now and she was a rising star? She didn't look familiar. But the longer I stared at her, the more I began to think she might not be lying about her age. The hardened expression aged her dramatically. Didn't make her any less sexy, though. Maybe more.

"Don't worry about who I am. Do you have a back exit I can sneak out of?"

I let the commanding statement go, but countered with my own. "Sure. But I need one thing first."

She shifted uncomfortably on her heels, her body language hinting at her unease. "Okay, what?"

"Your name," I said.

She groaned. "You can't have it."

Oh, shit, that turned me on. I loved a puzzle, and everything about this girl was a contradiction. A legal drinker using a fake ID. A delicate-looking girl who shrugged off a punch to the face. The fact that my cock was twitching in my pants when she was way off my type, not to mention fifteen years younger than I was.

"Why not? I told you mine."

"No, forget it." Her expression was a mixture of annoyance and worry.

"You won't even tell me your first name? Am I asking something too difficult? Tell me." And . . . there it was. The edge to my voice that signaled I was about to shift into a more dominant persona. The one which craved absolute control. Demanded total submission. Her mouth dropped open at the order.

"My friends . . . call me M."

"Em? Short for Emily?"

She shook her head slowly. "No, my name is not Emily. Can you show me the way out?"

A dark voice in my brain whispered, *I can show you lots of things, little girl.* I wasn't quite ready to let this conversation be over. "You still haven't told me your name, though."

The ice pack came off her eye and slammed down on my desk. "Not going to happen." Defiant. Hot. I enjoyed her fire. Shit, I wanted another taste. What would she be like in a darkened room, bent over a bed? Would her eyes burn as I sank inside her, one of my hands fisted in her hair?

Why the fuck did I need to know so badly?

"All right, Madison," I said, assuming it was a name that

started with an M. "If you won't tell me your name, at least let me drive you home."

"My name's not Madison." Her expression went blank. It was unreadable, and I didn't like that. I was excellent at knowing what went on behind other people's eyes. "You want to drive me home? You look busy with those P and L statements."

What the hell was she talking about? I followed her gaze toward my computer, where like an idiot, I'd left Dune's profits and losses spreadsheet open. I minimized the window as quickly as possible, and when I straightened, I expected to see her halfway out the door.

Instead, she'd taken a step closer. One thin eyebrow arched as she scrutinized, peering at me like I was suddenly intriguing.

"I guess the reports can wait?" Her voice softened. I wouldn't have thought it was possible, but it sounded sexier like that.

"Yes, Mary."

"You can keep guessing all night, but you won't figure out my name."

I couldn't choke back the sarcasm. "All night, huh?"

The corner of her mouth twitched up in the faintest of smiles. "You offered to drive me home, didn't you?"

Just wait a fucking minute here. Was she hitting on me? I ignored the voice in the back of my head that warned no smart girl would get into a car with a stranger. "Is that a yes?"

The faint smile widened into a seductive one. "Sure, why not?

Alarms blared louder in my mind, but I disregarded

them. "I'm keeping the ID, Marissa."

"Good for you, Joe."

I tensed. "No, not Joe. That," my voice was firm, "is not my name."

Surprise swept across her face and left puzzlement in its wake. "Okay, sorry. Joseph." She brushed her hair back over her shoulder. "Thanks for the offer. That actually will be a big help. Is your car parked close?"

"Yeah. Did you check a coat downstairs?"

"I did. Let me grab it and tell my friends I'm leaving." She held up her phone and snapped a picture of me without warning. What the hell? "So they know what you look like in case I don't show up for class tomorrow," she explained, her fingers tapping rapidly on the screen, undoubtedly texting it to someone. "Although you look like a nice enough guy, Joseph what?"

"No way, honey. You haven't given me your first or last name."

Her face twisted into a scowl, even though her eyes never left the screen of the phone. "Don't call me honey. It's M." Her gaze lifted finally, rising up to meet mine. "Joseph Monsato. It's on your club's website."

When had I lost control of this conversation? From the moment she'd crossed the doorway, she'd been in charge, not me. Things would change once she was in the passenger seat of my Porsche. I tugged the suit jacket hanging on the back of my chair and slipped it on, striding over to her.

M had a stone-cold poker face, but her body betrayed her. The proximity to me *did* make her nervous. Her shoulders lifted in a breath, even as her eyes didn't widen or dart away. The tension in her shoulders and neck said she was on high alert, which was smart. I was interested in her, and already power was shifting my direction.

"Joseph Monsato." I used a warm tone. "Nice to meet you, M."

The poker face cracked a little. "Right, yeah. You, too."

"Do you want to introduce me to your friends? Would that make you feel safer?"

"You don't have to do that."

"It's no trouble."

She shook her head quickly, probably thinking about how strange that would be. "We can just go. I feel safe."

Did she? I smiled.

chapter TWO

M was waiting for me in the narrow hallway beside the metal back door, and the February wind howled outside. She cinched the belt of her long wool jacket tighter and flashed a hesitant look.

"You sure this is okay?" she asked. "Your bar will be closed by the time you get back."

"It's fine. I have a club manager, and I'm not usually here on Thursday nights anyway." I pushed open the heavy door and gestured for her to go through. It had begun to snow, and fat snowflakes wafted down on the alleyway. Her chin tucked to her chest as we went out into the cold, and I hit the unlock button on my keyring, flashing the lights of the Porsche. "That's me."

She paused as if uncertain when I opened the passenger door for her.

"Second thoughts?" I asked. If she said yes, would I be disappointed? Would I find a way to persuade? I was used to getting what I wanted, and this? Yeah, I wanted it.

"No, no second thoughts." She slipped into the passenger seat and her gaze focused on me. "How does this overpriced car handle the snow?"

I should have been offended, but instead I was thrilled to get attitude from her. The taste I wanted, although now I'd had it, I craved more. Most people didn't give me lip. They either worked for me or wanted something, so they were professional and respectful. "The Porsche does just fine, and don't worry, I know what I'm doing."

Did I? I'd come to Dune tonight to have a hard discussion with Alan about the covers at the door declining, and instead, I was leaving. Cold air blasted us as I started the car and flipped on the seat warmers. We'd been alone in the office, but the door had been open, and now with snow blanketing the windshield, we were trapped, sitting close beside each other on freezing leather.

Her fingers splayed out on her thigh, curled into a soft fist, and her breath went shallow. Nervous.

"Can I ask why you agreed to let me drive you home," I said casually, "if I make you uncomfortable?"

"I don't know. Why did you offer? It seemed like a strange thing to do."

"It was." I flipped the wipers on and watched as they brushed the loose snow from the windshield.

"You didn't answer the question." Her voice was just louder than the swipe of the rubber against glass.

"You didn't answer mine, either." She was lit by the soft light of my dash, casting shadows across her angular face. Goddamn, she was pretty.

M touched her bruised cheek, wincing slightly.

"I . . . think you're interesting."

My pulse jumped at the admission. "Yeah? Maybe I think the same of you." I wrapped my fingers around the gear shift between us, putting my hand closer to her body, and I could feel heat radiating from her. "Where are we going, M?"

"Lincoln Park."

The Porsche slipped out of the alleyway, snow growling beneath my tires. "Where do you go to school?"

"Loyola, for my MBA." After a few moments of quiet, she continued, "How do you like owning your own business?"

"It's great. Busy, though."

"I'm sure."

The wipers continued their slow, slick slide over the glass, generating the only sound between us. I stared at the glowing taillights ahead of me. In downtown Chicago you'll hit traffic at any hour, any day of the week, even Thursday at one in the morning. Technically Friday. And the snow didn't help, either.

"I haven't ever done this before," she said.

"Done what? Ridden in a Porsche?"

She paused. "Gone home from a bar with a stranger."

Is that where she saw this going? Was she going to invite me in when we arrived? "It's going to be a long drive," I said. "We don't have to be strangers, Martha."

"*Martha?*" Her laugh was light and warm. "You honestly think that's my name?"

"You could give me a hint."

She leaned back, relaxing into the seat. "Okay, here's your hint. You're not even in the ballpark. How do we get to know each other? Trivia questions? Or should we play 'would you rather'?"

Her teasing tone got me to smile. "Questions should work. Favorite sex position, go."

Her response was silence. I glanced over, catching the stunned expression on her face. I liked her off-balance and it only served her right, since she had been good at doing it to me.

"I'm sorry," I said, "but I know you won't answer any questions about your identity, so I chose to start there, with something fun."

More silence. She wasn't going to answer? I pressed too hard on the brake when the realization dawned on me.

"Don't fucking tell me a beautiful girl like you is saving herself for marriage." My stomach turned. Didn't she realize how short life was? All the pleasure she could be missing out on?

"No, I'm not a virgin," she said. "I appreciate the compliment, but the profanity, not so much."

There was no helping the grin that tugged across my face. "Did I offend you, little girl, with my adult language?"

"Hardly."

"Then, quit stalling and tell me your favorite position."

"Wow, you're ridiculous."

I wanted to push her buttons. She'd seemed so confident in my office, and now she was slowly unraveling. "Let me guess," I said. "Him on top."

Her head turned away so she could stare out the passenger window. "Sure, yeah. You got me."

Everything deflated. This wasn't as fun as I had hoped it would be, and now the silence was tense and uncomfortable, her posture stiff. I'd fucked it all up. "Hey, forget it, I'm sorry—"

"I like when he's behind me."

Her soft, almost guilty voice was a caress of leather cat o'nines across trembling skin. It got me hot. "Oh, yeah? Why?"

She paused, as if unsure whether to continue. "I like . . . when he's in charge."

My grip tightened on the wheel. "Do you? You like it when he's got his hands on your waist, fucking you?" She squirmed, so of course I had to go all the way to find her limit. "Or maybe," I continued, "you like one hand wrapped around your throat and the other touching your pussy, as he's slamming his cock inside you."

"Oh my God." Her face locked up in shock.

"That's how I like it."

I'd stuck the visual in her brain, and wondered if she was imagining me as the man with his hand wrapped around her delicate neck, the other stirring circles between her legs and making her moan while I slid my cock deep inside. She swallowed so hard I could hear it.

But my plan turned out to be a mistake, because now I was getting hard. I hadn't touched her. She hadn't taken off any clothes—in fact, she'd put her large coat on which criminally hid her figure. And yet my dick was swelling annoyingly against the fly of my pants.

I watched men worship the naked bodies of beautiful women every Friday and Saturday night at my blindfold club, using their mouths, their hands, their cocks . . . but I'd become desensitized. The scenes on the security footage did little to arouse anymore. But this girl with the shocked expression? She started a burn inside me and brought me to life. Dangerous and thrilling.

"Who talks like that to a stranger?" she asked breathlessly, although it seemed rhetorical. "Do you want me to jump from your moving car?"

"We both know you're not going to do that."

"Oh, yeah?" she snapped. "What makes you so sure?"

I laughed. "Because I saw your reaction, how your knees squeezed together, and your cheeks flashed red. It turned you on, little girl."

"Don't call me that."

It wasn't a denial. "Give me something else to call you," I said. "Like your name."

"It's Martha," she grumbled.

"Are you some sort of celebrity? Is that why you won't tell me?"

She sighed. "At this point I'm not telling you my name just because it bothers you."

The snow was getting heavier as I crawled onto Lake Shore Drive, but traffic was beginning to ease. "You like bothering me?" I asked.

"Perhaps."

I caught her glance for a fraction of a moment, and the gleam in her eye only made the situation in my pants fucking worse.

"Are you originally from Chicago?" she asked.

"Yes and no. I was born here, but I lived in Tennessee for a while, before coming back. And you?"

Her expression went serious. "Uh-uh. Pass."

Jesus Christ, she wasn't going to answer that? I yo-yoed between interest and irritation. Her withholding information was cute only for so long. "Fine. Why are you going for your MBA?"

"Because my family . . . wait, no. Pass."

"Pass?" I wanted to tell her to stop being a brat or I'd pull the car over, yank her out of her seat and into my lap so I could discipline her appropriately. I might have turned her on with some filthy talk, but aggressive actions were a whole different story. "Maybe we should just listen to some music."

My finger clicked over the radio controls on the steering wheel, but then her small hand closed around mine. Hers was icy cold, and yet burned against my skin.

"I'm sorry," she said. "I swear I'm not trying to be pain. What else do you want to know? My favorite color is blue. I fell off a dock when I was six years old and almost drowned, and now I have an abnormal fear of seaweed. Favorite ice cream? Mint chocolate chip."

My gaze went from the hand clasping mine on the wheel over to her hopeful expression.

"Better?" she asked.

"I didn't give you permission to touch me." My voice was guarded.

There was the quiet sound of her sucking in a breath, and she tried to draw away. No. She'd started it. I would press further, until I found out where this thing between us was headed.

"But since you did," I continued, "this goes here." My fingers wrapped around her wrist and tugged her hand down, setting it on my thigh. Not on top of my dick, which was throbbing, but not too far from it, either.

It was a test. She'd touched me in a friendly gesture, but I could read beneath the action. M was curious, but nervous.

"Tell me a secret," I demanded.

A long moment passed before she let out the breath she'd been holding. "I've lived kind of a sheltered life. Until last month, my parents were really involved, and that made it hard to do what I wanted. Tonight I decided to do things I wouldn't normally."

"Such as going home with a stranger."

Her light, tentative squeeze on my leg sent every drop of blood in my body surging south of my belt, and I clenched my teeth. *Jesus Fucking Christ, control yourself.* "What happened last month?"

"A lot of stuff. My . . . mom moved out." Her voice fell low as her hand inched upward. "And I broke up with my boyfriend."

"How long were you together?"

"Two very long years."

So her interest wasn't so much in me personally, as it was in a little rebound action. Fine with me. The longest relationship I'd had? Maybe two months. I didn't date because nothing lasted forever.

"So now you're off the leash and out from under your parents' scrutiny, and you came to my club looking for some fun." I took her lack of an answer as agreement. "Did you find it?"

The hand slipped further along the length of my thigh so it brushed just against my hard-on, her movement hesitant. "Maybe," she said in a shaky voice. "You tell me."

I let out half a laugh. She was trying so hard to be bold. "If you're going to touch me, honey, do it for real." I repositioned her hand. "Feel how hard I am? You did that."

She gasped. "Don't call me *honey*." Her scolding was whisper quiet.

Her fingers flexed, but once again, she didn't retreat. She wasn't backing down. Her hand brushed lightly, caressing me.

"Fuck, touch me, M." I guided her, dragging her hand down every goddamn inch, pressing her palm hard against me. I spun the wheel, turning off of the expressway.

"Where are you—?"

There was a parking lot just one block down, and I maneuvered through the slush up to the automatic ticket stand.

Snow battered me momentarily as I rolled down the window, stabbed the button, and yanked the ticket out of the feeder. The gate lifted and I pulled in.

"Joseph." There was a tremor in her voice that I ignored, guiding the car under the bridge of the El track that ran over the lot, keeping us secluded from the one lonely security light. I parked in the shadows, sandwiching my car between two that were coated in ice, as if they'd been there a while. The snow was blowing sideways, and we'd be hidden in no time.

Not that it mattered; not a soul was around.

I turned off my headlights and gave her my full attention. No, not true. She'd had it the moment I'd spied her on the dance floor of my club.

"What's going on?" Her cautious look was a warning, like she no longer felt all that safe.

"I can't focus on driving and what you're doing at the same time. This is what I want to focus on, don't you? What would you normally do?" Again I guided her hand to massage me.

Stuttered breath dragged through her parted lips as she feathered a single stroke over my zipper and the flesh beneath.

"Yeah," I encouraged. "Like that."

Her next stroke was more confident and I choked back a groan. The girl's effect on me was insane.

The interior of my Porsche wasn't built for comfortable fucking, if that was where this was headed, but I didn't care about comfort now. There was only the shocking need inside me. I wanted to extinguish it by sinking my cock so far inside M she'd forget everything else. So neither one of us would know her name.

The power seat slid back as far as it would go while she continued her teasing. "Take off your coat," I commanded.

Her delicate hands abandoned me to undo the belt at her waist, then release the buttons one by one, her gaze stuck to me like she couldn't look anywhere else. When her coat was off, I held out my hand.

"Climb over the console and get in my lap."

She stared at my hand like she was making a choice, even though we both knew she'd already made it. "Is there enough space for me?"

"You mean because of my enormous cock?" I teased. "Get over here and finish what you started."

I'd hoped the joke would break some of her tension, and it seemed to work. She put a hand on my shoulder, and after some maneuvering, she had a knee on either side of the driver's seat, the steering wheel just a few inches from her ass. I tipped my head to look up at her, pushing back the blonde hair that tumbled into my face, and set one hand on her hip, urging her to settle down on me.

"Are you going to kiss me?" she asked.

I gave her a smirk. "Do you want me to kiss you?"

"I haven't kissed anyone new in a long time."

"That wasn't an answer."

Her hips shifted down, setting her weight on my erection in a pleasurable and torturous way. "Yes," she said. "I want you to kiss me."

"All right," I said, thrilled with not just her request, but how her choked voice made it sound like a plea. Nothing compared to the sound of a woman begging. I tangled my hand in her hair and tugged her close.

Couldn't just go and do it, though. I teased, letting my lips hover over hers, enjoying the soft rasp of her hurried breathing. I skated my mouth over her cheek, sifting my hands through her soft hair that smelled really fucking good. A tremble built inside her, forcing her to vibrate.

She wasn't cold. I'd made her take off her jacket, but I also had the heat on high, and the windows were already fogged. Her shudder was in anticipation, and I savored it for one final moment more before I captured her lips with mine.

Holy shit.

chapter THREE

NOEMI

Joseph Monsato reeked of confidence, power, and authority. I'd spent my life around men like him, so I knew it in an instant, but his power was different than what I was used to. Persuasive and . . . sexual. He wasn't a model, but his body sold sex and sin, and I'd never seen a more fascinating creature. I was thrilled to let my responsible self fall under his spell.

He was a stranger, and yet I sat in his lap, making out with him in the driver's seat of his ridiculous Porsche. He held me steady with a firm grip on my jaw, while I was adrift from what his incredible mouth was doing to mine.

Ross, my selfish ex, in two years had never kissed me the way Joseph was doing now. Confident and skilled. Like an artist honing his craft, Joseph painted a new sensation with each brush of his lips or caress of his tongue. He didn't ask permission. No, this man took what he wanted. He possessed only my mouth, but it felt like my entire body was under his command.

He'd ordered me to take off my coat and get in his lap, and I'd done it. I'd made the decision tonight to do the opposite of anything normal, sensible Noemi would do. Get in the car with a beautiful, strange man I'd met five minutes before? Cautious Noemi wouldn't dream of it. This wild version of myself not only got into the car, but she flirted.

I wasn't sure how much credit to give myself about hitting on him. Even when I made a move, he was pushing me further, directing my actions. Weirdly, I'd liked it. Following his orders made it easier to throw caution aside.

His lips pressed against mine, firm and demanding, which made sense. Every inch of Joseph was demanding. He wasn't the most gorgeous man I'd ever seen, but he was beautiful. Tall and lean, as if efficient, compact muscle stretched on his narrow frame. Striking eyes beneath dark eyebrows, a long, straight nose, and a sexy mouth. The things that tumbled out of it were shocking, but I couldn't deny those dirty words played a factor in his overall appeal.

His hand on my jaw drifted to my shoulder, and then his fingers curled so he could drag his nails lightly down my arm, all the while kissing me. His mouth was addictive with its wicked, teasing movements. He drew my bottom lip in and bit down gently, forcing a startled noise from me. I sounded as if I needed air, panting and gasping like I was drowning on dry land. I was.

I was drowning in his kiss.

My hands moved independent of thought, pushing his jacket open and I set my palms flat on his chest. Beneath his dress shirt, I could feel the hard muscle and the rapid thump of his heartbeat, which was beating only half as fast as mine.

"Are you warm enough?" he murmured into the side of my neck.

"I'm fine." I was lying. I was going to rattle apart. I both did and didn't want his hands to touch me everywhere.

"You're shivering," he said.

"I'm fine," I repeated, stronger. I swallowed, although my mouth was dry, and closed my eyes when he sucked on my neck. The sensation surged through my center and the trembling intensified. Oh, God. I fisted his shirt in my hands and arched my back, shoving my breasts in his face.

He continued his wordless taunting. Joseph's hands roamed over my thighs, up my back, cupping my neck, but never strayed to where I made it obvious I wanted them.

"Are you going to touch me, old man?" I'd hoped it would irritate him like his *little girl* comments irritated me, but he chuckled.

"Do you want me to touch you?" he asked. "Then say it."

Couldn't he just take control? I'd fallen into a pattern with Ross not to speak unless I specifically didn't like something.

"I . . . want you to touch me."

"Where?"

The sound of frustration slipped out before I could gag it. Joseph pulled back from me, his gaze focused and intense.

"If I could read your mind," he said, "I'd have done it. I like communication, M. Tell me where you want me to put my fucking hands."

Oh my God. My brain emptied of thought. "Wherever you want," I blurted out.

His eyebrow yanked up, and his sexy mouth widened into a smile, like I'd just said the best thing he'd ever heard.

"Turn around. Put your hands on the steering wheel."

Turn around? His car had less room than a gym locker. Yet, I tried without question or protest. It was awkward. I moved clumsily and he got an elbow to the face, but with his help, I turned to sit in his lap, my back against his chest.

"Well," I said breathlessly, "that was sexy."

He laughed lightly, and then pulled the sides of his

coat around me, wrapping me in his arms. It was sweet and unexpected.

"I told you," I whispered. "I'm not—"

He tugged the neck of my shirt to the side and set his mouth on the newly exposed skin. I shuddered as warm breath washed over me. My head lolled back, resting on his shoulder while he feasted on my flesh, moving along the sensitive skin toward my ear.

"And I told you, hands on the wheel." His tone wasn't playful. It was controlling and exciting. The smooth, leather-wrapped steering wheel was cold in my fingers.

I moaned when his hands closed tightly on my breasts. His touch was confident, and why wouldn't it be? I'd given him permission. Beneath me, his hard-on dug into my ass.

"Is this where you wanted me to touch you? Your tits?"

My head spun at the unaccustomed word. I grew drunk off of the sensations as he pinched and massaged, the tip of his nose caressing the edge of my ear.

"Answer me."

"Yes," I gasped. I shifted in his lap and he groaned. The growl from him was sexy, and a muscle low in my stomach clenched.

"Fuck," he hissed when I did it again. The engine roared abruptly and a tight laugh rang out. "Whoops."

Because his foot had accidentally hit the accelerator. My face warmed, enjoying that I'd caused that reaction from him. Then, one of his hands abandoned my breast and shot between my legs.

"Oh!"

He bit down on my neck the same moment he stroked me through my jeans. His hand moved up and down in slow strokes, increasing pressure with each pass. I tried to close my legs but he widened his, and since my legs were on top, his action kept mine open.

"Is this where you really wanted me to touch you?"

I didn't want to admit it, but *yes*. His hand created a burning ache. A need clawed inside me, desperate to escape, and whispered this man was the key. I nodded quickly.

"Use words to tell me," Joseph commanded.

It came out breathless. "Yes."

"This was where I wanted to touch you." His voice was quiet, but loud in my ear. "This is where I want my cock to be."

I fractured as my brain disconnected from my body. I didn't do anything when both of his hands worked the button of my jeans. I stopped breathing as he inched the zipper down.

"Open your eyes," he ordered. "Watch what I'm going to do to you."

The amber colored light from the dash was just bright enough to see his fingers ease under the parted denim, slipping over the satin of my panties. Lower. And lower.

My hands clenched the steering wheel, going white knuckled when his probing fingers caressed me through the thin fabric. Sharp electricity fired across my nerves, making me jolt. Responsible, conservative Noemi began to freak out, while the wild side of me fought to keep her quiet. I liked it too much for him to stop, but I was sitting in the lap of a stranger, who had his hand down my pants. *Oh, God.*

"Wait, wait..." I let go of the wheel and grabbed his wrist.

"What's wrong?"

I could barely find the words. "I feel like this is getting out of control."

Joseph stilled, and beneath me muscles hardened. "There's plenty of control here. It just happens to all be mine."

I gasped as his hand moved again, stirring where I was damp and achy. I bit my bottom lip to get it to stop trembling. The responsible voice in my head screamed this was dangerous and stupid.

What he was doing felt wrong. Bad. So very good.

"Tell me you like this." He was the devil inside my head. "Tell me to pull your panties to the side and touch your wet, little cunt."

I squirmed, shifting away. The vulgar word broke the leash on sensible Noemi, and it was as if I was emerging from a fog of lust. What the hell was I doing? Being wild didn't mean I had to do something I might regret.

I grabbed the sides of my zipper and pulled it closed.

"Hey." His hands rested gently on my waist. "What are you doing?" When I rose up to climb back into the passenger seat, his hold strengthened. "Answer me."

"I don't like that word." There was a sharp edge to my voice. "Let me go."

Tension fell away as he released me and I clamored over the console, scrambling into the passenger seat where the air was easier to breathe. I needed space from his dominating presence before I completely gave in to his filthy mouth. I'd never heard anyone talk like that, and never had someone look at me the way he did now.

Joseph wanted to devour me.

I could feel his desire thick in the air, choking. His head tilted just a degree. "I thought this shocked and innocent girl routine was cute at first."

"It's not an act."

"I get it," he said. "Put your coat and your seatbelt on."

I pulled my coat out from underneath me and slipped an arm in the sleeve, hoping another layer would protect me against my attraction to him. I already had a tinge of regret about getting out of his lap.

"Where are we going?" I asked.

"I'm taking you home."

Wait, no. What would happen if he saw my building? "No, we can't go there."

He triggered the windshield wipers which brushed the wet snow from the glass that had us secluded from view. He set his focused gaze on me, and I felt exactly like his annoying barb, like a little girl.

"*We?* I'm not interested," he said, "in convincing you that you want to fuck me. I don't do halfway. Either you do, or you don't." My mouth fell open, but coherent thought failed me. "Communicate. Tell me if you want to fuck."

I cringed. "So romantic."

"*Romantic?* I'm talking about screwing you in this cramped front seat, where the steering wheel's going to be in the way, and it'll probably be awkward as fuck. But I promise you, once we get started, neither one of us is going to mind."

I was fairly certain he was right. Would he bark out commands the whole time, demanding I tell him every detail about how I liked it? Could he deliver on his promise when no other man had? I wanted to believe. A new wave of desire washed over me and left my mouth dry in its wake.

Joseph leaned toward me and softly curled his fingers under my chin, keeping my gaze tight on his. "I'm betting the good girl inside you is telling you to say no, but there's a part of you that wants to say yes."

My bottom lip twitched as he dragged his thumb lazily over it, then pushed it slowly into my mouth. Every inch of him was so sexual, even something as silly as slipping his thumb past my lips was erotic. He didn't have to tell me what to do. I closed my lips and sucked gently, giving him the innuendo of what it would feel like if I went down on him.

His eyes flared with heat. "Who am I getting tonight, M? Do you want to be bad?"

I did, but twenty-three years of doing the right thing was hard to shrug off. My chest tightened painfully.

I couldn't.

His thumb withdrew and he slid it down my neck slowly, leaving a damp trail in its path. Disappointment ringed his eyes, like he knew already. Joseph sighed and straightened, then put his seatbelt on. "Okay, good girl. Let's get you back to that sheltered life."

We barely spoke the rest of the drive, and the silence was so uncomfortable it was painful. Worse, the snow had grown heavier during the short time we were parked, and we were both tense as the car slid through a stop sign.

As we neared my block, I lied. "This is my building, you can drop me at the front."

"I can walk you." His voice was tight, like he both did and didn't want to say it.

"No, thank you, here is fine."

On the steering wheel, his grip tightened as if irritated, but he pulled into the snowy loading zone and put the car in park. I had the seatbelt undone and a hand on the door when he touched my thigh.

"Your name."

My breath caught in my throat. I felt like he deserved it. "Noemi."

"No-em-ee," he parroted back, no recognition of the name in his eyes. "Em."

"Yes," I uttered as he leaned over and took my lips with his.

This kiss was soft and restrained, as if he was kissing a girl goodbye after a date. My head spun. I'd made my choice, and while I didn't like this kiss as much as his other one, I was grateful for this version. His hungry, demanding kiss from earlier would have been impossible to refuse.

I stood on the snowy curb and watched his black Porsche 911 pull off, taking the beautiful man away. I'd turned him down so I wouldn't do something I'd regret, but a terrible thought flooded through me. You regret what you don't do, more than what you've done.

For being wild tonight, I'd done a terrible job. The disappointment formed fast and snowballed.

Why the hell did I say no?

chapter FOUR

JOSEPH

I could not stop thinking about the good girl I'd driven home last night and kissed goodbye like she was my fucking girlfriend. Who was she, and who did she turn me into? What would have happened if I'd gone slower to ease her in, or pushed harder? It fucked with my head.

I'd jerked off like a man on a mission when I got home, as if it could relieve the desire for her. Didn't work both times, or this morning, either. I'd imagined her pink lips wrapped around my thumb just like she'd done in the car, only while she rode my cock into fucking oblivion. We'd have vanilla sex the first time, but then the sheltered girl wanted to try something new. Something *dirty*. I'd show her how good it felt.

Tonight Payton was managing the blindfold club. It gave me a second chance to go to Dune and talk to Alan about the fading covers, although it would be a challenge. Fridays were busier. I arrived early and appreciated the flustered look from the staff. I was hardly ever here, and two nights in a row? It'd start rumors that something was happening, and perhaps it should. I didn't like any of my businesses struggling.

After the meeting was over, I closed myself in the office. Alan's indifferent attitude had left me grinding my teeth. His answer was to hire a club promoter, but that wasn't a realistic option. Throwing money at a problem typically only bought you time, not a solution. Plus, it was a risky investment. I'd used them in the past and had little results.

The cases of the imported beer were still here, stacked four high against a wall, irritating me. My skin was jumpy and itching for relief.

I knew the source of my frustration. Noemi. The total lack of control was ridiculous. How had ten minutes in my car reduced me to this? I poured myself into my chair, determined to get the numbers done for the month. I needed the distraction.

It was just past midnight when I pushed back from the desk, my work finished. I didn't feel the satisfaction I normally did when assessing my tiny empire. Four businesses in Chicago was a lot to manage, but I was open to considering more if it was the right fit. Dune was my least profitable, but my "members only wine club," my front for the blindfold brothel, more than made up for it.

I went out onto the office balcony, glancing at the VIP area where one of the tables had bottle service. A group of men in suits lounged on the red velvet couches, chatting with the women at the next section over. Every one of them was looking to get laid. You could taste it in the air, the sex and need. I could smell it on myself.

Shit. I should swing by and check on Payton after leaving here. She'd only been back from Japan for six weeks, and while I was checking on her, maybe I could scene with one of the sales assistants. Making the deal with the johns always put them in the money and got them hot. It was a great combination for power play.

My gaze scanned the crowd, looking for the good girl

who'd rejected me last night. Some of me wanted to find her and make her pay for what she'd done. What she was *still* doing to me, haunting my thoughts.

The same sensation from the previous night needled up my spine. Was she really there, or was it a figment because I wanted her to be? Noemi sat at a side table, her stare fixed in my balcony's direction. Two empty glasses rested on the tabletop—why hadn't those been cleared? She'd been there a while. Waiting.

As soon as she saw me, her face filled with surprise and she stood eagerly. She pointed to herself, then up to me, asking if she could come up. I shook my head, gesturing I'd come down. Putting us in the confined space of my office would turn my balls an even darker shade of blue.

Music thumped unrelentingly from the speakers on the main floor. I threaded through the crowd until I reached her. The bruise had faded to almost nothing—wait, it was makeup. She'd done a helluva job covering it.

The ends of her blonde hair curled softly on her maroon colored top, and the deep V showed off plenty of cleavage. Black pants with sheen clung tightly to her curves, and ended in black heels. Sexy makeup, big earrings, and an outfit that looked painted on. She still looked young, but the effort wasn't lost on me. Noemi wanted to look like she belonged here.

She looked fucking amazing. Thank God I hadn't let her upstairs. I'd have my hands inside that shirt in two seconds flat.

I leaned in close and yelled over the music. "How'd you get in? I took your ID."

Her expression fell. She'd expected a warmer greeting.

"I used my real one."

"Where are your friends? You're here alone?"

She nodded, setting a hand on my shoulder. "I came to talk to you. I . . . changed my mind."

My cock twitched, but the rest of me kept it together. "Oh, you want to be bad now, little girl?"

"Yes. Ask me when I changed my mind."

I was willing to play along. "When?"

"About fifteen seconds after I got out of your car." Her posture was confident, but her eyes were anxious.

I gave a hard look. "I don't believe you."

"Dance with me? I'll show you."

My curiosity spiked and overwhelmed my desire to stay off the dance floor. I motioned for her to lead the way.

The heavy bassline pumped onto the floor, flooding over the heaving bodies. Her arm hooked around my neck and she placed her other hand on my chest, over the buttons of my shirt. I trapped her hips. Fuck, I liked having her back in my hands. We fell into an easy rhythm, matching the pounding music.

Beneath the strobe lights, she came alive. Her chest rubbed against mine, teasing and making promises. Her hips swung side to side, brushing her lower body over my fly. I slid a hand lower, gripping her ass tightly, encouraging her. Her heated expression said she knew what she was doing.

My cheek tugged into a smirk. She thought she had the power in this situation. Not even close. I spun her around, yanking her back up against my chest. My hands settled low on her hips and I pressed against her ass. *Feel that. Feel who's in control.*

Her response was to grind on me. As the beat dropped,

her back arched and it pushed her breasts forward. The guy on our right grinned. He had to be receiving a great view of side boob. The crowd was undulating with the music in a hot, chaotic mess.

My hips matched the sway of hers as I began to test her desire to be bad. I inched my hand lower, closer to her center. I expected her to balk. Instead, fingers laced on top of mine, pushing our hands over her zipper. Her head swung my direction.

"This goes here," she said.

It didn't matter that she was nervous about delivering the line. Her daring move and hearing her echo back my command from last night forced me to reevaluate whether or not I had absolute control.

"Bad girl," I whisper-shouted to her.

I feathered a touch there and then slid my hands over her body, trying not to stay too long in the best places. There was a time and place for exhibition, and in front of my staff wasn't one of them.

Noemi was such a tease, and I loved it. It built torturous anticipation, and I couldn't wait to exact my revenge. I was going to make this girl wait all night. Excitement swept through me, leaving power behind. I'd never made a good girl beg and couldn't imagine anything sweeter.

Our movements were fucking with clothes on and synchronized to the song that was so loud it was hard to focus on much else. Only her body and the pulsing beat. Blonde hair splashed in my face as she turned back to face me and crushed her lips against mine.

Her kiss last night had been shocking. This girl was like mainlining Viagra. I wasn't a goddamn teenager anymore, but a taste of her lips was all it took and I was raging.

"I'm going to fuck you on my desk. Right now."

Her movements slowed to a stop. *Be patient*, I reminded myself. I wasn't going to blow it with her a second time. *Not everyone is as fucked up as you, Joseph.*

"You came here for that," I reminded. "Waited for me. Let's do what we both fucking want."

She blinked and nodded. "Okay."

I took her hand and led her upstairs.

My office door locked with a click. Noemi stood in the center of the room, her arms crossed over her chest, and she stared at the desktop like it was her doom. Wasn't this what she wanted? Her breath picked up with every slow step I took toward her. I'd be lying if I said her trepidation didn't turn me on, just a little. The rush of power made me strong.

"Put your hands on the desk." My tone was authoritarian. An order.

"Are you going to tell me what to do the whole time?" It wasn't snarky, it was a curious question.

"Yes."

She hesitantly leaned over and set her hands on the desk. "Why?"

"Because that's the way I like it."

Her arms were already trembling, and I hadn't touched her. Her breathy voice shot straight to my dick. "Why?"

"There was a time in my life when I didn't have control, and now I want it all. No more questions, Noemi."

I stepped behind her and pushed her hair over a shoulder. She shuddered as my fingertips trailed down the long curve of her throat, and skated inside the neckline of her shirt. They drifted over the flesh, seeking access beneath her thin bra. I leaned over her, setting my other hand on the desk for support.

A quiet moan slipped from her lips as I circled her taut nipple and tweaked it.

"You like that, little girl?"

Her shoulders trembled. "Yes."

"Mm. I can't wait to suck on these tits." I rolled my palm from one perfect breast to the other. "I can't wait to bite them. Would you like that?"

Her body filled with hesitation. "I . . . don't know."

"What do you say we find out? Stand up."

She didn't. Noemi remained as if frozen to the desk. "Wait." It came out exactly the same as last night, coated in fear.

No. We hadn't even started, and she was getting cold feet again?

"I think I've *waited* enough. What's the problem?"

She walked her hands back toward her hips and stood. "There's no problem, but I need a minute." Her scared expression was a bucket of cold water on me. "I want this. I do, I swear. It's just—"

"You need a minute so you can overthink this." Fuck it, I couldn't do patient. I lifted her and plunked her ass down on the desktop with a thud. I snaked a hand behind her to grab a handful of hair, yanking her head back so she had no choice but to look up into my eyes. Hers were startled and wild.

"I told you," I said, "I don't do halfway and I don't waste time. You want to be bad, let me show you how it's done."

I slammed my mouth on hers, cutting off the noise of surprise she made. I didn't ask for permission, I took. I possessed.

She fucking submitted.

When I'd sat her on my desk, I'd stood between her legs, and now they clamped around my hips. The rest of her seemed desperate to get close, too. Her breasts flattened against my chest and her hands tunneled in my hair, encasing me. She had no problem responding to the PG-13 stuff. My tongue filled her soft mouth, dominating.

When she grew greedy, I shoved her down until she was flat on her back. The whites of her eyes were enormous a split second after I pushed her full breasts together and squeezed roughly. My thrust slammed my throbbing cock against her body, insinuating what was going to happen.

"I like this shirt." I buried my face in her tits. I tugged both the shirt and the cup of her bra away, and latched onto her flesh. My tongue swirled, seeking the hardened nub of flesh, and once I had it, I bit down.

"Oh..."

It was impossible to tell what type of sound she made. Pleasure? Pain? Either one would work right now. I hadn't bitten hard. "You like it?" No answer. "Tell me." I did it again, pulling the flesh between my teeth and fluttering my tongue over it.

"Yes, yes..." Her back bowed off the desk.

I pushed up on my hands and stared down at the girl beneath me, her nipple just peeking out from where I'd pushed the shirt aside. "I want you topless, now."

The hesitation was in her eyes. "Joseph, I don't want to stop," she said quietly, "but can we slow down?"

I considered her statement. "Why?"

Her gaze shifted away. "I barely know you."

The top was adjusted to cover herself and I pulled her

back up to sitting, then cradled her head in my hands. "You don't have to know me to enjoy this."

Her hands settled on my shoulders. "But what if that's the way I like it?"

Lust still flooded in my bloodstream and my thoughts were cloudy. I lived detached to avoid distractions, so telling her personal shit wasn't appealing. But the fact was, I wanted to slide my cock eight inches deep into this distraction so bad I could fucking taste it. "It's better this way. The less you know, the less of me you can regret."

Her expression went south. "I don't know if I can be what you're used to."

I laughed softly. "Don't worry about that. Just do what you want."

"And what if what I want is to go slow?"

Shit, trapped in my own words. Every moment she remained on the desk, the further away she felt. Her shoulders pulled inward, as she shut down.

"Noemi." I kissed her slowly. "If you want to stop, tell me. But if what we've done is already too much, this isn't going to happen."

I watched the different emotions play out on her face. Anxiety, disappointment. Remorse.

"I shouldn't have come," she whispered.

Un-fucking-believable.

My phone buzzed in my pocket, interrupting an asshole comment from sliding past my lips. I dug the phone out and glanced at the screen. "Fuck."

"You swear too much," she muttered under her breath.

I ignored the comment. The text message was from Payton.

> Need you ASAP. Major issue with Mr. Red.

There wasn't any other option. "I have to leave. There's a problem at another one of my clubs." My emotions were all over the place. Annoyance that she was turning me down again, after claiming she wanted me, and concern about Payton's message. My dick was aching for Noemi, but once again, there'd be no satisfaction. "I guess we're done here."

"I'm sorry," she said, sliding off the desk. "Can I see you again?"

I left her, wanting to get away, and snatched up my coat. Couldn't let her see me in this weakened state of frustration. "See me again? For what?"

"Your sparkling conversation." The distance between us must have given her strength to dish out the biting tone.

"I don't date, if that's what you mean." I shrugged into my coat.

"So, this is it? We're done just because I wanted to go slow?"

She was being a brat again. "Don't put it on me. You made this decision, more than once, I might add. I know who I am and what I want." I shoved my office door open. "See you around."

chapter FIVE

I pushed open the glass outer door, and Julius nodded, buzzing me through the club entrance. He was part of the security team on tonight. A beast of a man who could crush skulls with one hand, but he was too smart to have to do that. Julius knew when to use his mouth to solve a problem, and when to flex his muscles instead.

Payton stood in the guest lounge, wearing a tailored black dress, an earpiece, and a determined expression.

"What's the situation?" I asked. I'd only had time to send her a text to let her know I was on my way. I needed to cool down and focus on driving in the snow.

She coursed a hand through her black cherry colored hair and set it on her hip. "Mr. Red saw me."

Payton was knock-out gorgeous and used to be my top girl. Hell, we'd started this place together, and for a time, Mr. Red had been exclusive to Payton. He'd been smitten with her, but as he was paying her to fuck him, the relationship was one-sided.

I trusted Payton. She loved sex, money, and had no problem selling pussy. She'd offered to step in a few nights a month to help me focus on my other businesses, and as much as I loved this place, having the option of a night off was necessary.

"What the fuck?" I said. "How did he see you?" She was supposed to stay in the office, watching the monitors.

"We had a problem with a walk-in."

"What kind of problem?"

"The kind where he wanted to renegotiate afterward." A dark look flitted over her. "Don't worry, I straightened him out. I didn't even need Marquis' help."

Marquis was another member of my security team—the opposite of Julius. Marquis was one mean son of a bitch. He boxed in the featherweight division and was always looking for a fight.

"I was leaving the payment room," she continued, "and Mr. Red was in the hallway. It was my fault, I should have remembered that he was done and checking out."

I don't know how much she knew about him. Mr. Red had been a mess when Payton left the club. He'd threatened to tear apart the city to find her, and when he couldn't, his threats turned on me. But they'd been empty threats, caused by a man in pain. He'd loved Payton. Her disappearance had been a tremendous blow, and it had taken months for him to form a relationship with a new girl. I'd tried everything. Mr. Red was my best customer, not just in cash, but in networking. Half my member list had come from his referrals.

"What'd he do?" It felt like I'd swallowed a stone. Everything could fall apart if Mr. Red decided it should.

"He was pissed." Her expression changed to sadness. "Well, he was upset. He demanded to talk to you, but I tried to explain—"

"Where is he?"

She pressed her lips together momentarily. "Holding room C. Should I go with you?"

"No." I hurried through the empty lounge toward the holding room. Nothing good could come from her being in the room. I followed the hallway, which housed the guest rooms, and turned to the door marked with a C in brass, rapping my knuckles on it. "It's Joseph."

"Come in," a muffled voice answered back.

His real name was Rosso. He was a media mogul who owned magazines, newspapers, and several first-tier cable networks. On top of that, he was branching into other industries, such as real estate. A lot of pokers in the fire.

Mr. Red was where I wanted to be in the professional world. I didn't meet face to face with any of the other club members after the first interview, but every once in a while, he'd see me. We'd talk vague business strategies over whiskey while Claudia prepared for him.

"Good evening, sir. I came as soon as I could." I always acted as if I didn't know who he really was, which perhaps made me look stupid, but I believed he appreciated it. Anthony Rosso was famous for his wealth and his outspoken personality, and a few years ago he'd participated in a reality show geared toward entrepreneurs. Rosso was a household name, like Zuckerberg or Murdoch. Certainly here in Chicago where Rosso Media Group was headquartered.

Mr. Red sat on the black leather couch with his head in his hands, paying no attention to the porn that was running on the plasma TV on the opposite wall. The gold wedding band on his finger glinted in the soft lighting.

"You told me she was gone." It was an even mixture of pain and fury from him.

"She was gone," I said. He stood abruptly, his eyes wild and unfocused. Fuck, had he been crying? I lowered my gaze to the floor and pretended not to notice. "She's only come back to Chicago recently."

"You told me you fired her." His voice gathered

strength and rage.

"Yes, I did."

Mr. Red was mid-to-late fifties with dark hair and graying at the temples. He wasn't the type of man who visited the gym, but he also worked himself to death like I did, which meant he didn't indulge much. Apparently, his only vice was my club.

It wasn't surprising that a man like him wanted to play here. He was powerful, rich, and connected, which made him practically untouchable. If he ever got caught, his legal department would have him out in twenty minutes, and the public relations machine would grind out a story about him being unaware that his favorite wine club was actually a high-class brothel. The public would buy it absolutely.

But Mr. Red didn't come to the club because he was a sexual deviant and got off on kink. He came because Anthony Rosso's wife was a frigid bitch who wanted nothing to do with him. He'd confessed to me one night a few months back that his wife not only knew about his visits, but *encouraged* him to go. After having a kid, she had zero interest in any kind of sex.

I almost felt sorry taking his money. *Almost.*

"If you fired her," he said, "what the hell is she doing here, running the place?"

"Please, lower your voice." I remained calm and collected, hoping he would feed off of my subdued state. "I don't know who could be in one of the guest rooms or in the hallway." Mr. Red was smart and would understand what I was implying. There were plenty of other powerful men in Chicago who were members here. Some of them operated outside of the law, and catching Mr. Red at the club would be advantageous.

"I trust her," I said, "to oversee things while I'm not here."

"You should have told me. I had a right to know that she's . . ." His gaze drifted away as he seemed to search for a grip on his emotions. "I've changed my mind. I want to talk to her."

"I think that's a bad idea."

He refocused on me, giving a look that probably made men in his boardroom feel three inches tall. "I didn't ask for your opinion."

"She's not the woman you knew last year. And she doesn't see clients—"

"Get her in here, now."

I took a breath. "She's getting married, sir."

Mr. Red wasn't equipped to handle a woman like Payton. That man's name was Dominic. One night with him was all it took for her to chase him to Japan, and a year later she came home with a massive engagement ring on her finger. The girl who'd been like me—uninterested in relationships—was getting *married*. I'd called her a traitor as a joke, but it was half-true.

The concept of Payton getting married was a visible slap, and the sting didn't ease for a long moment from Mr. Red's face. "Married," he repeated, probably for himself. "She said she didn't do love. All those times I asked . . ." He seemed suddenly aware that he was speaking out loud. Maybe he felt like I was judging him, because he scowled. "You can't be with someone, night after night, and not get attached."

I disagreed, but kept the opinion to myself. Back when Payton had been taking clients at the club, we sometimes fucked afterward, when her client couldn't get it up or had failed to get her off. Had I felt a connection to Payton? Sure, as we were similar. But I wasn't attached. Nothing lasted forever, and we'd both been happy with our casual relationship.

Sex was just sex. I didn't allow emotion to enter into it. It was about mutual pleasure.

"If that's true," I said quietly, "that you became attached, what about Clare?"

Her real name was Claudia, but I'd put a rule in place that the girls never gave their real name.

Mr. Red rubbed a muscle on the back of his neck. "I like her very much, but it's never been the same."

He didn't have to tell me that, it was obvious. Mr. Red never asked Claudia to come home with him after. He never offered to buy her a penthouse apartment. He never lingered, hoping to catch her leaving the club, as he had with Payton. But he'd been seeing Claudia exclusively for well over a year, and it'd gotten to the point that she only saw him now. Well, figuratively. Claudia still wore the blindfold. She didn't know who Mr. Red was.

He must have felt hope at the sight of Payton in the hall, and now crushing defeat. All his money and power wouldn't be able to get him what he wanted this time.

"I still want to talk to her."

He wanted closure, fine. I strode to the door, only to have it swing open. She must have been in the hallway, listening. Payton scanned the room and her gaze settled on the wounded man perched on the edge of the couch. Her posture was stiff and formal, but softened as he looked up at her.

Mr. Red's voice was heavy with remorse. "I'm sorry I grabbed you."

Shit. Payton hadn't mentioned any kind of altercation,

but I hadn't given her time to explain.

"I'm fine. It's not like that was the first time you've touched me." Her clipped tone gave the distinct warning that it would be the last time.

My pulse ticked up a notch. Payton was smart, but she could also lose her cool and burn a bridge that I needed. Mr. Red slowly rose to stand, and from the gaze that seared her direction, I was sure I no longer existed to him. There was only her.

"Where did you go? I tried to find you."

She was surprised at the reveal, but hid it immediately. "Tokyo. I needed a change."

"Japan?" He shook his head, perhaps in disbelief. "Mr. Monsato tells me you're getting married."

She shifted her weight on her feet and set a hand on her hip. Her icy tone was accusing. "Did he?"

"So you were just lying to me all those times we were together?"

Every alarm in my head sounded and the noise was deafening. *Fuck, Payton, don't say anything.* I expected her attitude to show in all its brilliant colors, yet she strolled confidently up to him, her expression shockingly empty.

"No, Mr. Red. I never lied. I'm sorry that you wanted more and I couldn't give it to you. Before Japan, I wasn't capable." The corners of her mouth lifted into a sad, half-smile.

The look he gave Payton was an uncomfortable mix of desperation and pain. "What's his name?"

"It doesn't matter. I'm happy, and you just had a great time with Clare."

"I want his goddamn name."

My shoulders tensed. Payton took a step back and her

gaze flicked to me, silently asking what she should do. The filter holding back what she really wanted to say could go at any moment.

"No," I said, playing the card I didn't want to. "I don't share client names with anyone who's not staff . . . Mr. Rosso." His body went stiff. "I'm sure you can respect that."

For a tense moment, no one moved.

I grabbed the lapels of my suit jacket and shifted it to hang comfortably on my broad shoulders. "I'm sure you're tired, Mr. Red. Let's not worry about any details tonight. Marquis will escort you to your car." I fished a business card out of my interior pocket and extended it to him. "Please call me if you want to discuss anything."

He stared at the card with disdain, which was the emotion I was feeling. I'd just offered to let him leave without paying, and the concept of men fucking my girls for free made me sick to my stomach. I'd have to pay Claudia out of club money, but it would be worth it. Mr. Red had to come back.

The card was snatched out of my hand, a final glare cast her direction, and Mr. Red stormed to the door, slamming it behind him like a spoiled child.

"Marquis," Payton said into her headset. "Can you take Mr. Red to his car?" She straightened and her attention went to me. "He looked for me when I was in Japan? You didn't tell me that."

"Honey, he went fucking nuts. When you quit, it put me in one fucked-up situation."

She raised an eyebrow, as if annoyed. "Pretty sure you fired me, or don't you remember, *suck my cock right now*?"

My jaw tightened. We hadn't discussed that night in

much detail. I didn't like thinking about it, or how I'd lost control. "Yeah, I remember. I also remember that I apologized for it, and it all worked out in the end. I'm sure your Dom would agree."

Her eyes narrowed at the subtext. Dominic wasn't her Dom. Deep down, Payton and I would never work. I was as dominant as they came, and she was a switch. Sex worked for us when she wanted to be the submissive, but she'd never truly submit. There'd always be that independent part of her who couldn't give in completely.

"What about you?" she said. "You think Mr. Red will be back?"

"I fucking hope so." Without him, the club wouldn't last long without fresh blood. "If he shows and you're here, you keep your ass in the office where it belongs, or get it back on the table."

She smirked. "There's only one man I'll get on the table for. And if I do? You're welcome to watch. Maybe we can show you how it's done."

I laughed, and it felt good to ease the tension. "I think I know how it's done. You get off on being an exhibitionist."

Her eyes gleamed with knowing. "Takes one to know one, Joseph."

chapter SIX

NOEMI

I'd wanted to be bad and failed. *Twice.*

Failure wasn't allowed in my vocabulary. I scoured the Internet for any detail about Joseph, but there was nothing. It took two days before I gave in to the dark thoughts whispering to find him. I returned to Dune, stalking a man I'd turned down. I would not do it a third time.

The man I found fascinating hadn't been at Dune all week. I'd struck up a conversation with the bartender and learned the owner didn't visit much. I'd need to look for him elsewhere.

The crazy ideas kept coming, like a train I couldn't stop, and I no longer cared. My regret over backing out the second time was so enormous I had a hard time focusing during class. I fantasized about lying on his desk in his darkened office while he commanded me to touch him. To tell him how good it felt. I wanted him to have total control over me. What would we have done if sensible Noemi hadn't been there? That shuddering, scared little girl was messing up my life, and I wanted her gone.

I'd destroy her, and use Joseph Monsato to do it. He was perfect, and I wanted him. I longed to know what he'd do to me, and what he'd get me to do to him.

Google said he owned two more establishments in the downtown area. One was a comedy club over on Wells, and the other was a restaurant that wasn't too far from my apartment.

I'd waited tables a few summers at a country club, so getting the waitress job there was easy. I didn't learn much from the staff about him. Mr. Monsato was as much of a mystery to them as he was to me, but I'd heard he liked to come in some mornings for an early lunch before the restaurant was open.

So I took every lunch shift I could get with my class schedule. Nine long days passed before the hostess flitted through the prep station and asked the chef if the owner's lunch was ready.

"Where is he seated?" I tried to sound casual.

She studied me for a moment. "Table twenty-six. You want to take it?"

Yes. *Hell yes.* "Sure, it's no problem."

She shrugged and gestured to the plate the chef set on the pass. "Have at it."

The ceramic was warm in my clammy hands and I gripped it tightly. Every day that passed without seeing him made the legend grow larger in my mind. He couldn't be as stunning and magnetic as I remembered, I warned myself while I made my way out of the kitchen.

Table twenty-six was a four-top tucked away at the back corner of the empty dining room. There he sat, his back to the wall and his attention buried on his cell phone screen. The legend I remembered didn't do him justice when he was wearing a three-piece black suit. A silver tie was knotted at his neck. The dangerous, sexual man I'd fantasized about paled in comparison to this one.

My chest tightened and it became hard to breathe as I

planted one foot in front of the other, willing myself across the carpet toward him. My heart slammed against my ribs as I set the plate on the table with a quiet thud.

Joseph didn't look up at the sound, and I froze. What now? This was the moment I'd been waiting for, and he was oblivious.

"Can I get you anything else, sir?"

"No," he said, glancing at the plate. "Thank—"

Our gazes locked and time slowed painfully.

He blinked. His expression was a total mystery. "Noemi?" He scanned the room once, then focused back on me. "What are you doing here?"

I'd rehearsed all of this in my head countless times, but now my mind was blank. "I work here."

Skepticism passed through his eyes. "You do? Are you aware I'm the owner?"

"Yes."

His phone was abandoned on the table top and he scrutinized me, considering my answer. "And is that why you work here?"

I swallowed hard. "Yes."

Joseph leaned back in his chair and his gaze drifted down slowly, taking in the uniform. The red button-down shirt and black necktie, which was tucked into the black waist apron, tied over my fitted black pants. Oh, no. Was I wearing something wrong? The gaze drifted back up to meet mine, and it was heated. No, better. It had a look I'd seen from him before, the look that made my knees go soft.

Lust. But it faded as quickly as it had appeared.

"As much fun as it is to see you," he said casually, "I'm not up for another round of your *wait* game right now."

I steeled my voice to sound strong. "I'm not here to play that. If *wait* comes from me, you should ignore it. I know what I want."

"Oh, of course." His patronizing tone was sharp, but it helped solidify my desire. "You think you're really ready this time?"

"Yes."

The conviction in my word gave him pause. "I'm sure you think so."

This was the moment I'd been desperate for. I'd be damned if I was going to back down. "Tell me what you want me to do. I'll do it."

A small smile grew on his lips. How did he make something so innocent look sinful and dirty? "All right, little girl. Take off your apron."

Easy. I fumbled with the strings in the small of my back and tugged the knot free, then tossed the black fabric onto a nearby table.

"Undo your belt."

This command was slightly harder to follow. Sensible Noemi raised a warning, but I ignored her. This was a test. I slipped the end of the belt loose from the buckle, feeling Joseph's dark eyes watching my every move.

"Good," he said, when it was done. "Unzip."

"Here?" I whispered. He nodded.

Maybe it wasn't a test. I tried not to falter or think. *Just follow his command.* I unbuttoned and unzipped my pants, but my hands trembled.

Pleased surprise streaked his face. I was sure I'd already made it farther than he thought I would. Joseph relaxed in his seat, throwing an arm on the back of the empty chair beside him, as if watching a show.

"Okay so far?" There was an edge of teasing, which I probably deserved.

"Yeah," I said between deep breaths.

"Pants down to your knees. Your shirt comes up, so when you lean over and put yourself face-down on this table, you'll show me your perfect ass."

My need to stay decent was swept away in a tidal wave of desire. *You're going to do it, Noemi.* I glanced around the empty dining room. The rest of the staff would be in the kitchen for another twenty minutes. I shimmied the waist of my pants over my hips and down my thighs until they were bunched at my knees. Cold air wafted over my newly exposed legs. My lavender lace panties barely covered my backside and I couldn't contain the shudder. I was nervous to be doing this where anyone could catch us, but the dark, bad part of me was excited. I was *doing* it.

I pushed the placemats and silverware out of my way, yanked up my shirttails, and did as ordered, lowering my upper body to rest on the veneer. I was bent over the end of the table, and Joseph shifted his seat to an angle to see me better.

The only sound was his clipped breathing.

"Goddamn. Pull those sexy panties down," he said, his voice hushed but no less sexy. "I want to see your pussy."

"Oh my God," I whispered. His filthy commands set me on fire, and created a line that sensible Noemi couldn't get across. My fingers clawed at the waistband and pushed my underwear down until it was around my thighs, leaving me naked and vulnerable. Showing Joseph a part of me that few men had ever seen. And I loved it.

"Look at you." It rang out like he couldn't believe it. "What would you do if someone walked in right now and saw this? With your ass bare, and your pussy waiting to be fucked?"

I had no thought in my mind, so I picked the only answer I could. "I'd . . . do whatever you told me to."

He snatched up his phone abruptly, typed out a message, and then dropped the phone back on the table. "I've told my manager not to let anyone disturb us. Here's hoping he can follow orders as well as you can."

I expected him to touch me, but he sat in the chair, watching. Silent, and unmoving. His dark eyes had me locked in place. I wanted his skin on mine, his lips on mine.

"Are you going to touch me?" I whispered.

His smile was triumphant. "When I'm ready, I will. I think you'll have to *wait*."

Oh, God. It was awkward lying bent over on the table while my legs shook, but it . . . did something. My craving for his touch grew enormous in a blink of an eye. He seemed unaffected. First, he took off his suit jacket, folded it, and set it on the seat of the chair beside him. Second, he unbuttoned his cuffs and rolled his sleeves back. Anticipation was heavy and suffocating. Then, Joseph shifted his chair back to the table, picked up his silverware, and set about cutting into his chicken marsala. He was . . . holy hell, eating? While I was letting it all hang out?

He was smart and calculating. While he ate, his attention was only on me. This was a test, to see if I would break.

I wouldn't. I'd spent my whole life being tested.

But the hunger for his dirty words and his touch built until it was almost unbearable. How long did I remain like this? What if this wasn't a test, but a form of humiliation? I was a heartbeat away from covering myself when he stood, picked up his chair, and disappeared from view.

"Hands behind your back." There was hardly a thump, but it sounded as if he'd placed the chair directly behind me, and sat down on it.

I clasped one hand around the other in the small of my back, which made the shiver in my shoulders more pronounced. I startled when his thumbs slipped under the sides of my underwear and tugged the fabric further down my thighs.

"Fuck, Noemi. You look good enough to eat."

I stopped breathing when something wet touched me. He licked. Again and again. His tongue teased between my legs where I was aching.

"Holy shit," I moaned.

"Oh, so the good girl can swear? Or is that only when I'm fucking her with my mouth?"

I clenched my hand tighter on my other, trying to ground the moment and not lose myself in the sensation. What he was doing felt amazing, and my already weak knees softened with every pass of his skilled tongue over my flesh.

Joseph was going down on me in the restaurant he owned, right out in the open. It was wrong, and I couldn't get enough of it. Warm hands closed on my ass cheeks and massaged while his mouth continued its assault.

"You taste so good." His tongue pressed deep inside, then slipped down, and his lips closed on the center point of my desire, sucking, causing me to moan quietly. "Do you like that?"

"Yes," I whispered.

"What do you like," I could feel his lips moving against my sensitive skin, "*specifically?*"

The muscle low in my belly clenched. In my fantasies he demanded I talk dirty to him, but the reality was both better and worse. I was excited to speak up, but nervous I'd say something unsexy and he'd laugh.

"I like what you were just doing."

The mouth was gone, but he lingered close. I could feel warm, hurried breath rolling over the backs of my legs. "You liked it when I sucked on your clit? Or when I put my tongue inside your pussy?"

I closed my eyes. "The first one."

"Say it, and I'll do it again."

I pulled air into my body, which felt like an enormous task. "I liked it . . . when you sucked on my clit."

I cried out as he rewarded me. Oh my God, it felt so good. His hands tightened on my ass, like an involuntary reaction to my sound of pleasure. But one of them released its grip and slid towards my center, down through the valley of—

I jolted as he brushed past the place that had always been off limits. My hands flew to the tabletop to push myself up.

"No," he commanded in a firm tone. There was a sharp sting of pain in my thigh, as if . . . did he just pinch me? His other hand flattened on my back and pushed me down, urging me to stay in position on the table. "I'm not going to remind you again. Hands behind your back."

I did as told, struggling to catch my breath but it was hopeless. He sank a finger deep inside my pussy, all the way until his knuckles pressed against me.

"Oh my God." The indecent movement of his finger was

intense. His slow thrusts made me shake uncontrollably and I spun out of control. My fingernails dug into my wrist as I clenched it tightly.

"I'm guessing from your reaction," he said, his voice confident and hypnotic, "no one's touched you there before?"

"No." I tried not to pant. Pleasure crept along my body, flooding from his finger.

"Let's find out how bad you're willing to be." Even though I couldn't see his face, I could hear the grin in his words. His hand withdrew, leaving me feeling empty. "Put your hands on that perfect ass."

I hesitated. What did he mean? Where was this going?

"Now." His dark tone forced me into action. I reached down and put one palm flat on each cheek. "Good. Like this." His hands wrapped around my wrists and pushed them away. Opening me to him.

"Oh my God."

He chuckled. "Stay like that."

It was an impossible request. I was going to shake apart. His thumb pushed inside my pussy and retreated, and began to move up. Before I could form words, two fingers drove into my pussy, and the thumb traced a wet path to my other entrance. Dirty. So *fucking* dirty.

The thumb swirled, spreading my arousal around. I had no idea it would feel like that. That there'd be pleasure from this shocking touch.

"You're not going to tell me to wait?"

"No." I struggled to keep guilt from my voice.

"You like it like this, don't you, filthy girl? Riding my fingers and letting me touch you where no one else has?"

I bit my bottom lip, but released it a second later.

I should lie and say it was too filthy, but I couldn't. "Yes. I like it."

He pumped his fingers faster, and heat spilled over, burning everything away except for the two hands working my body like a master. The chair creaked, just audible over my gasps, as he shifted.

"Oh my God!" I cried when his face was between my hands, his tongue swirling where it made the good girl in me scream.

"We've got to expand your vocabulary. We haven't even gotten to the fucking yet and you're already stuck on repeat."

He stopped talking and the sensations he gave me flipped the entire world upside down. His tongue traveled over my skin, licking where I shouldn't allow. It was terrifying, wrong, and so amazing. I clenched my hands, pulling them further apart to give him better access, no longer caring whether or not what we were doing was bad. Every cell in my body was tingling.

"Oh, fuck," I moaned.

"Better." He picked up the pace. The rhythm of his fingers was perfect. Not too fast to lose sensation, but not too slow that I needed more. They drove hard, tapping a spot inside with a steady beat. Every second felt better than the last. And his tongue fluttered, making me lose my mind.

I was about to orgasm for the first time ever with a man. I knew what the beginnings felt like. I could get myself there on my own, but no one else had been able to. There was something wrong with me, Ross had figured out. But here it was, the warm numbness working up my legs, threatening to erupt.

Had Ross been wrong? What if there wasn't something

wrong with me, but with him?

"Are you about to come?" Joseph asked.

"Yes." Yes, yes . . .

I yelped in pain as his fingers yanked out of me and he pinched my clit.

"Not yet." There was a crash which sounded like he stood so fast it knocked the chair over. Joseph's tone mocked. "*Wait.*"

"No," I cried as the orgasm faded with the sting of his pinch. *No!* I'd been so close.

There was a jingle as his belt was undone. Fumbling, followed by a crinkle. A torn condom wrapper fell onto the table.

"You'll wait until you can come all over my cock. Up on your elbows."

Maybe he didn't know just how cruel he'd been. He'd only meant to tease, but coming from sex wasn't possible. What had just happened was a fluke; the perfect combination of sensation and timing. It'd never happen again.

But I walked my hands across the table and lifted up onto my elbows as the head of his dick nudged me. Even without the orgasms, I still enjoyed sex. The feel, the emotion, and the connection. I took a deep breath when his hand settled on my hip, and he began to press inside.

I'd use Joseph to drive away the scared girl. That is, if his enormous dick didn't kill me first.

chapter SEVEN

JOSEPH

I'd jerked off so many times while thinking about this moment. It didn't happen at my restaurant in my fantasies, but this was even better. She'd been worth all the waiting and then some. Her soft moans were hot, but her submission was scorching. How she hadn't tripped the smoke alarm was beyond me.

I set one hand on her hip and stroked a hand over the round globes of her ass. I wanted to know what it would look like with my handprint welling red on it. Fucking gorgeous, probably, just like the rest of her.

The condom would dull the sensation, but I wasn't going to complain. It'd be a tight fit inside her, so a little less sensation might be good. I wrapped my hand around my cock and pressed it against her wet, ready pussy.

She took a deep breath, a signal that it was all right to continue. Noemi had found a way to embrace her wild, reckless side. Just when I thought she couldn't get any hotter, this version of the girl appeared, ready to play.

Her breath cut off when the tip of my cock pushed inside.

"Fuck, you're tight." I groaned and squeezed her hip to steady myself. *Go slow*. I didn't want to hurt her. It was one thing to tease, or cause momentary pain as discipline. A little pain was good as it heightened senses. Greater valleys meant stronger peaks, but this wasn't that kind of pain.

I gained another inch of her wet heat that gripped my cock like a vise. It was hard to think about anything other than the urge to drive and the need to *take*. I wanted to claim and own every inch, right motherfucking now.

Noemi groaned as I slipped deeper still.

"Good, baby girl," I said. "Take it."

Her shoulders tensed and her back bowed. A stuttering breath was exhaled when I was buried as far as possible.

Like an idiot, I just kept talking. "Yes, fuck. *Yes*."

I held still and let her catch her breath, needing to catch mine as well. I'd called her *baby* girl. Not *little* girl. Did she pick up on the difference? I was sloppy and out of control.

"You okay?" I whispered, sliding a hand up her spine to gently cup the back of her neck and turn her head toward me. She gazed over her shoulder, her face pale, but determined. She nodded quickly. "How many guys have you been with?"

"Just one," she said, breathless.

Every muscle in my body seized. "One?" She'd said she wasn't a virgin, but she was so tight—

"Two," she amended. "One, and now . . . you."

My cock twitched. "Such a good little girl before you met me. I'm going to ruin this tight pussy." I pulled back and gave her a thrust, her first taste of what it was going to be like when I fucked. "You want me to ruin you, Noemi?"

"Yes." Her breathless voice made my heartbeat pound in my ears and broke the wall on my restraint. Why didn't I have any fucking control around her?

I widened my stance so I could move. Retreat and advance. Faster. Harder. *Deeper*. Jesus, she was so wet, it was fucking insane. Every thrust sent a small shockwave rippling across her ass cheeks. Sexy.

"Oh my God, Joseph."

"Does it feel good? You like my cock inside you?" There was no answer. I twined my hand in her hair and tugged her head back, getting her attention. "Say it."

"I . . ."

My thrusts were hard and rapid now, slamming her body against the table. Her shallow, quick breathing matched my tempo.

"You, what?" I lowered until my chest was against her back and skated my lips across her neck. "Am I making it hard to speak?"

"Yes." She shuddered beneath my lips. Power surged strong in my veins. "I like your . . ."

I grinned, realizing what her hesitation was. "Use adult language."

"I like your *cock* inside me."

Yes, baby girl. Me, too. Thankfully I didn't say it out loud. Instead I latched my teeth on her earlobe and focused on my goal. It was time to make her come—she'd certainly earned her reward.

I wrapped my arm to band low across her hips, and set my other hand on the tabletop for leverage. The necktie she was wearing threw me for a moment. Next time we fucked, there'd be no clothes, at least not on her. She could wear the tie, though. She'd look sexy as fuck with something around her neck and nothing else, plus it'd give me another point on her body to demonstrate control.

Or maybe I could take her tie off right now, bind her wrists, and see just how far the newly uninhibited girl was willing to let me push. Putting restraint on a person eventually made them more wild and desperate. I had countless hours of video proof on my backup servers at the blindfold club.

But a fire that burned too hot didn't last all that long, and fucking her was like being inside a volcano. I was sweating, and my hand almost slipped on the table. The slide of my dick inside her snug body, paired with her quiet moans, was going to do me in before I was ready.

"Yes," I groaned. Her pussy clenched, squeezing me with pleasure. My balls tightened and tingled, aching for release.

Yet the cadence of her breathing didn't alter. Her moans didn't increase when I fucked her so hard the silverware rattled against the wood. Water sloshed in my glass, splattering on the table.

I switched tactics, rolling my hips against her ass, grinding. Her reaction was similar. Like it felt good, but not good enough. No mind-numbing orgasm was eminent. My hand on her waist drifted down through the small thatch of curls between her legs, seeking her clit.

Her tremble reverberated through her body and into mine. Better, but still not enough. I stirred her faster. She was slick, and her breath was a full-out pant, but her legs didn't tighten, and no muscles clenched in anticipation of her release.

"Are you close?" I asked, perplexed. True to frustrating form, she didn't communicate. "Tell me if you're close to coming," I ordered.

"No."

The asshole part of my brain was pissed. How could that be? This felt fucking amazing to me, how could it not for her? I had to force myself back from exploding inside before she got hers. My partner always came first when I fucked.

"Are you uncomfortable?" I asked, slowing, even though the Neanderthal in me wanted to pump until release. "Am I hurting you?"

"No, no." Her hand reached back and threaded through my hair, gently tugging me close until my nose was pressed against her cheekbone. "It feels really good. I just don't, um, get there."

Wait a minute. Icy pinpricks jabbed at my skin and I stopped moving altogether. "What do you mean, you don't get there? You don't come?"

She shook her head slowly, her gaze down at the tabletop, as if embarrassed.

"But you said you were about to, when I was tongue-fucking you."

Noemi's lush bottom lip was snagged between her teeth. "Yeah, that would have been the first time, you know, with someone else."

All thought vaporized, other than I'd made a little, terrible mistake. "Son of a bitch." It felt like I'd been hit by a truck. Her first orgasm that wouldn't have been self-induced, I'd pushed back in a moment of spite. How much damage did I do, when so much of the female orgasm was mental? I could have been the first man to get her off.

No, fuck it. I *would* be the first man. "I'm going to fix this."

She tensed. "Like I'm broken?"

Shit! "No, I didn't mean it like that." I pushed slowly against her, stealing her breath. "I meant I was a fucking asshole, and I'm going to make it up to you. Right now."

I slammed my cock inside her, building quickly to a punishing rhythm, using my fingers to tease and manipulate her swollen clit. I needed my other hand on her hip to keep myself steady, but it ached to be on her tits. "I want you to think about when I had you on your back on my desk." I ran my tongue over the tip of her ear, tracing it. "Remember when I was sucking and biting on your tits?"

She whimpered.

It made me throb painfully for release. For a time, I was excited at the idea of hearing her beg, and now I was concerned I was going to do the begging. I certainly deserved to. My fingers pressed hard on her flesh, rubbing back and forth furiously. Flames of pleasure licked at me, beckoning to the point of no return. *Wait*, I commanded myself.

"Doesn't it feel good?" I asked. "Let go, baby girl. Give it to me." Jesus, I had to get a lid on my runaway mouth. Pressuring her to try to come would only backfire. There was one way to get me to shut up. I slowed my tempo to a manageable one, but fucking her like this still felt much too good. "Kiss me."

It was a strange command, and it was like she knew. Her eyes widen in surprise, but she turned onto one elbow, and brought her lips to mine.

No, bad idea. I'd forgotten what happened when our mouths met. There was the delicious taste of her soft lips, and I wanted to get lost in her mouth. Her goddamn moan when I slipped my tongue over hers practically sent me overboard. I was drowning in this woman already.

Her tongue mingled with mine, but she broke the kiss abruptly. "I imagined this," she said between two hurried breaths, "every time I've touched myself since meeting you."

She'd blurted it out as if she'd had a momentary bout of courage, but now was scared of the consequences her admission would bring. Like I would judge her? Like it wasn't the hottest thing to hear?

"Fuck, I did, too," I said. "Every goddamn day, more than once. And, Noemi? My fantasies didn't come close."

"Really?" She squeezed her legs together, tightening her body's grip on me.

"Yes. Holy shit, do that again."

The clench of her already tight pussy made my vision go hazy. *Okay, time for a new strategy.* I couldn't maintain the fingertip's grip on the edge another second, so my goal shifted to coming as quickly as possible so I could focus all of my energy on her.

"This is what I wanted," she said. "God, it feels so good." She collapsed face-down on the table, her head turned to the side and hair fell over her face, fluttering on her rapid breathing. The change in angle catapulted me into the end sequence. Too late to pull back now. My hand latched onto her shoulder, holding her in place.

Every muscle in my lower body got involved so I could work like a piston. I fucked her as the wolf inside wanted to. Primal and basic. She cried out my name but it was dulled with my pulse screaming in my ears. My vision narrowed to a tunnel as both hands tensed; one dug into her shoulder and the other took a fistful of her long hair.

"Shit, oh fuck . . ." I groaned, and then there were no more words. I came, hot and hard in a fucking rush like nothing else. My body shook from the detonation of pleasure, vacating my mind.

Even as the orgasm began to subside, I struggled to bring my brain back online. Okay, her turn. You got yours and it was pretty fucking spectacular. Make this right.

Noemi lay still. Her glazed eyes blinked sluggishly as I slid out of her the final time. I took off the condom and folded in my paper napkin, then pulled up my pants. I tugged my zipper closed quickly. Meanwhile, she carefully pushed herself up to stand, and bent as if attempting to pull up her pants.

"What do you think you're doing?" I said.

She froze, her eyes growing wide.

"You think I'm done with you, little girl?"

Anxiety lingered in her expression. I was completely dressed again, and her pants were below her knees now. Her hands clasped together and she subtly pressed them over her legs.

"Are you trying to hide that pretty pussy from me?" I moved in close so I was a breath away, staring down into her hazel eyes. "You know I've already seen it. I've already *tasted* it." And I was about to do it again.

I lifted my foot and put it between her knees, pushing her pants down to her ankles. "Sit on the table and lie back."

Her expression shifted to alarm. "But we just—"

She didn't follow my directions, so I put my hands on her hips and lifted, seating her on the edge of the table with a thump that once again rattled the silverware. I used a sharp tone. "Lie back."

The veneer squealed faintly under her bare skin as she moved. I righted the chair I'd knocked over and sat, scooping my hands under the backs of her knees.

"Up," I urged.

She didn't understand my intention until her knees were above my head and I ducked down inside the circle of her legs. Her ankles were bound by the pants holding them there, resting behind my neck. She was spread open to me and her gaze darted to mine, nervous. She was checking to see my reaction to her being completely exposed.

I smiled. "You're so fucking sexy, you have no idea."

She pushed out the breath she must have been holding. I ran the pad of my thumb ever-so slowly down her slit, and she twitched from the touch. Sensitive. I shifted an inch closer in my seat, settling in, and got to work.

"Oh . . ." It was quiet from her, but rang loud as hell in my ears. My hands curled around her thighs while I used my mouth, running the tip of my tongue over every wet inch of her pussy, before zeroing in on the spot that would bring her home.

A hand crept onto the top of my head. There wasn't pressure in her touch, it was like she wanted to hold on. Her other hand found mine on her thigh, gripping my fingers. I squeezed her right back, and nuzzled.

A new moan slipped from her, verging on a whimper, which changed abruptly when I eased a finger inside her body. My tongue fluttered in a Z-pattern over her clit, and my finger searched for the spongy spot deep inside that created a more intense orgasm.

Fingernails raked softly over my scalp and the hand clutching my fingers went white-knuckled.

"Oh my God, that feels amazing," she whispered.

A fire was building in Noemi, it was obvious from the way she writhed on the table. But she seemed to reach a plateau of pleasure, never getting all the way to the apex. The rapid thrust of my finger, which was coated in her arousal, was hard to maintain. My tongue was starting to get tired and my jaw ached, but I wasn't going to stop. *Nothing lasts forever.*

"Look at me," I said, pulling back so I could catch my breath. I locked gazes with her from between her thighs, but continued to fuck her with my finger. "It's going to happen, baby girl, just relax and breathe. I'm doing this until you come. I don't care if this place opens and other people come in. Would you like that, if people watched me licking your sweet pussy?"

Her eyes hooded and a strange tingle warmed inside my chest. The good girl liked the sound of that, even if she wouldn't dare say it out loud. I shook her hold off and shoved my hand up her shirt, palming her bra-covered breast. Her back arched, as desperate as I was for the touch.

All the effort was taking its toll on me, because I was growing hard, *again*. Unreal. I found her nipple through the bra and rolled it between my fingers, pinching. Gentle at first, until I dipped my head back down and sucked her clit between my lips.

"Shit!" She bucked under my lips. Hearing the profanity from her good girl mouth turned up the heat. Christ, soon I'd be full-mast from going down on her, not ten minutes after coming harder than I had in forever. And then what? I was out of condoms. Why the fuck didn't I carry more than one?

I'd have to calm down and wait until later. I already knew once wasn't going to be enough with her, and that was before she'd revealed the boy she'd slept with was a selfish motherfucking prick.

The harder I pinched at her, the louder she got, encouraging me. Did she like a little sting of pain? This girl was a special order, made just for me. I touched her everywhere I could, moving two fingers inside.

Noemi had jumped when I tested her waters with anal play, but she'd also almost come when it had been my main focus. My third finger dropped down, rubbing her asshole while my first two fingers fucked her senseless.

Goodbye, plateau. Everything changed in a moment. Her chest heaved as she struggled to find air, and her legs trembled.

My face heated with a smile. "You filthy girl."

I put pressure on the finger, creeping inside.

"Whoa, wait . . ." she said. She'd told me to ignore it, so I did. Her head snapped up and she looked terrified, but I could see it was already too late. Her orgasm was in motion, heading for the finish. "Wait, wait . . ."

I played her body like an instrument, and finally, she started to make music. Her gasps turned to moans, increasing in volume as her body shuddered. Inside, her pussy pulsed on my fingers.

"Good girl," I said, kissing the inside of her thigh and slowing my fingers as she came. *Yes.* Her head fell back on the table with a bang, and she cried out, the muscles in her lower body quaking. Watching an orgasm roll through her was hotter than a month's worth of footage at my club. Hotter than a year's worth. Plus, I was seeing something no one else had before. Her gasps, her hands that seized my head, every last drop of her orgasm, was only for me.

I let her ride the final seconds out, savoring it. Her recovery was slow, but it also seemed like it had been an epic eruption.

I wanted her again. Instead, I ducked out from between her legs and stood, placing a hand on the table beside her head, leaning over her. Her eyes were closed, and aftershocks of pleasure seemed to ripple through her still.

"Have dinner with me tonight," I commanded.

chapter EIGHT

NOEMI

Holy hell, Joseph had done it. He'd fucking done it. My body was tingling and weightless in the aftermath of my first orgasm that hadn't been caused by my own hand. Was it always like that? The euphoria had lasted forever and a day.

I stared up at him and his demanding eyes, which were gorgeous, and tried to pull myself back together. He'd asked me to dinner, and was waiting on my answer.

"I thought you didn't date." I was still breathless, but it could have been his intense stare that was causing it.

"It's not a date." He bent down and pressed his lips to mine, and the world spun again. He was like a drug, at least I assumed, as I'd never done drugs. Sensible Noemi, who was presently shell-shocked, wouldn't have allowed drugs to mess up any of her parents' carefully laid plans.

"Not a date," I repeated, skeptical. He put his hand on my shoulder and helped me sit up.

"It's a job interview."

I rose onto my shaky legs and scrambled to pull my clothes back up, knowing it was ridiculous to hurry given what we'd done. "Technically, I already work for you."

He laughed softly. "No, you're fired. I'm not employing a waitress who has sex in the middle of the dining area with a customer."

Oh, holy crap. I'd never been fired before, and the

business side of me was horrified. "Joseph—"

"Do you need this job? Because I'm under the impression you came here to get to me." The side of his mouth twitched up into a smile. "And now you've had me. Do you want to be done with it?"

That was the ideal scenario, so I pressed my lips together. Even though my clothes were back in place, I still felt naked, and a large part of me wanted to strip everything off and climb back on the table. "What's the job?"

"We can discuss it tonight."

I frowned. "No, we can't. I have a meeting about a case study I'm working on."

He wiped a hand over his mouth, as if considering alternatives. "Tomorrow."

"Sure." My heart fluttered. Tomorrow I'd go out to dinner with the man whose dirty mouth made me feel like a new person, one who actively lived her life instead of following the plan her parents had given her.

"Six o'clock?" he asked and I nodded. He lifted his suit jacket off the seat, slipped it on, and pulled his phone from an inside pocket, extending it to me. "Your number."

I tapped it out on the screen, and when I passed it back, he caught my hand in his. He used his hold to draw me close, slipping an arm around my back. His warm breath on my neck made me shiver. His power over me was intoxicating.

"Think about what we just did when you touch yourself tonight." His tone was non-negotiable, a strict order.

If I was brave enough, I would have told him there was a one hundred percent chance of that happening, but I couldn't work up the nerve. Instead, I nodded quickly. He glanced at the screen of his phone as if checking the time, and he scowled.

"I've got to go." He crushed his mouth over mine, then his mouth traveled to my ear. "That was easily the best meal I've ever had."

I turned my apron in and the manager waved me off, mumbling something about a text message from Joseph, and it was all right not to come back.

I should have felt guilt about my total lack of professionalism, or shame at what I'd done, but I didn't. All I could think about was doing it again. The wrongness felt good on me, an odd, new sensation.

My phone rang as I plodded through the snow to the CTA stop closest to the restaurant, and I sighed when I saw the name on the screen. I'd just doubled the number of men I'd slept with, so of course he would call.

"Hey," Ross said. "What are you doing tonight?"

"I've got a group thing, that case study for MacKenzie's class." I didn't bother to point out that I had it every Monday night since the beginning of the semester. Ross couldn't remember when we were dating, he wasn't going to start now. "Why? What's up?"

"Can you blow it off and help me out? Gillian's having a wine tasting with a bunch of alumni tonight and invited us."

Us. I ducked into the stairwell, grateful to be out of the wind, but instantly irritated. Gillian was the professor that Ross was a TA for. There'd be opportunity for networking for Ross. I'd have gone if I was his girlfriend, and I'd have been bored out of my mind. But we were *friends* now, nothing more.

"I can't, sorry."

"Come on, Em, please? This could be really important for me."

For a moment, I considered caving. He'd been trying so hard to get his foot in the door somewhere, either an interview or an internship. But I shook my head, not that he could see it. I'd turned down dinner with Joseph tonight. I was trying my hand at being bad now, and sticking with my studies was as far as I was willing to go with being good.

"You can't go by yourself?"

He hesitated. "It's a couples thing."

The train rail rattled overhead and I hustled up the stairs to the elevated platform. It was loud enough I thought about asking him to repeat it, but I knew what he'd said. "We're not a couple anymore."

"I know, but we could fake it if we had to for one night."

Joseph had unleashed something inside me, and the words tumbled out. "No, I've faked it enough times with you."

"Wow," Ross said, his tone harsh and condescending. "That's fair."

The train clattered to the platform and I darted through the open doors, finding an empty seat. "I'm sorry," I muttered, although I didn't really feel sorry. "I get that this thing tonight is important to you, but you've got to understand my grades are important to me."

A noise like he'd scoffed echoed through the phone. "Yeah, like your dad's not going to find you some cushy job, no matter what."

What the hell was he talking about? He'd known my family his whole life. "Um, have you not met my dad?

Because if you had, you'd know how likely that is." This conversation needed to be over. "It doesn't matter, Ross. You said we should focus on ourselves. So you should go do that."

"What the hell's gotten into you?"

Joseph Monsato. "I'm just doing what you told me to. I've gotta go. Good luck finding someone to fake it with." I ended the call and tucked the phone in my purse. It had to look ridiculous, me sitting alone on the El, grinning like an idiot.

The rest of the day dragged, but I did my best to stay active in the case study group. A text message came through late in the evening, when I'd gotten back to my apartment, shed my winter clothes, and put on my most comfortable pajamas.

> It's Joseph. Dinner at the Italian Village okay?

I sighed in relief. I'd struggled with paranoia that I'd never hear from him again since I'd already slept with him. At the time, a tiny, bitchy voice whispered his dinner invitation had been the fastest way to brush me off.

> Yeah, sounds good.

> I'll pick you up in my overpriced car at six.

I laughed, and then realized he didn't know what building I actually lived in. I wasn't about to get into it through text messages, so tomorrow I'd have to hang out in the atrium of the building one block over.

> **Don't be late. I don't like to be kept waiting.**

> I won't be.

> Send me a picture of your wet fingers after you've fucked yourself with them tonight.

I almost dropped the phone. Even in text messages, he was commanding and it was thrilling. Where was the shame in what I'd done? In what I was doing? I'd slept with a man I knew almost nothing about, and I'd let him take me right out in the open. Who could I become beneath him?

I curled up under the covers in the bed Ross and I had made love in, but I'd never felt an inkling of what I'd had on the table with Joseph. Being wrong and bad was just as I'd hoped it would be. It was so, so good.

A job interview, not a date, he'd said. What did it mean? I'd done nothing to demonstrate I was professional or capable in an employable way. Obviously, I wasn't experienced, not like he was. He certainly knew his way around my body, showing he'd had plenty of practice.

Without thinking, my hand was between my legs, following his command. The orgasm he'd drawn from my body this afternoon had sent me into the stratosphere. The word intense didn't cover it, and my best climaxes when I was alone couldn't touch it. I wanted his mouth where I grew damp and my fingers stirred now. I craved his dirty words and even dirtier touch.

My pulse picked up as I started to enjoy what I was doing. The bedroom was already dark, but I closed my eyes to picture him better. How hot had it been when he looked up at me, his mouth on my pussy? His demanding eyes had locked onto mine and there'd been a desire to give in to anything he asked for. Hadn't I?

I wanted him to possess me.

My fingers fumbled over the nub of flesh that eventually sent me over the edge, and I came quickly, Joseph's name on my lips. Whatever his job offer was, I'd take it, as long as I got to see him again.

chapter NINE

JOSEPH

Noemi must have been waiting for me just inside, because the revolving glass door spat her out into the cold before I'd finished pulling up to the curb. She climbed into the passenger seat and shut the door, then flashed a shy smile at me.

"Hi," she said.

"You didn't do as told," I said as I eased away from the curb and into traffic. "Where the fuck was my picture?"

There was a moment of stunned silence. She'd expected some sort of greeting, but this was so much more fun. I wanted to start right away. Didn't want her to revert to the timid version of herself.

The words came out tight. "You were serious?"

"Yes. Did you think about me when you rubbed one out?"

"I did." Her voice was uneven but I could tell she was trying hard to sound casual. "And you?"

"And me, what?"

"Did you think about me while you touched yourself?"

"That's a fairly personal question, Noemi." I scowled for effect. "A good girl wouldn't ask something like that."

A faint smile teased her lips. "So, did you?"

"You better fucking believe it."

She brushed a lock of hair behind her ear, trying to play it off as if she didn't care, but she did. This magnetic thing between us had just as strong a hold on her as it did me.

Fucking had only intensified it.

Her voice was hurried, another attempt to be brave. "What did you think about?"

"Specifically? You want me tell you all the dirty details?"

"Yes."

I laughed. "I will, but we've got business to attend to first." Not to mention, I didn't want to walk into the restaurant sporting a hard-on, like my cock seemed intent on doing anytime she was around.

"The job interview," she said.

"Yeah. Tell me about the boy who couldn't do what I did."

Her expression went skeptical. "You want me to talk about Ross? That's important for this job that you've told me nothing about?"

"Yes, if Ross is your ex, tell me about him."

Noemi fidgeted with her purse. "We grew up together. We started dating our senior year of college, but we called it off about a month ago."

"Why?"

Tension seemed to coil in her. "I'm pretty sure I mentioned that I've lived a bit of a sheltered life. I . . ."

"Tell me."

"I feel like I'm changing and he's staying the same." She shrugged her shoulders. "He's still the self-absorbed, elitist asshole I lost my virginity to." Her hand crept up to cover her mouth, like she wanted to stop anything else from coming out. "I can't believe I just said that."

"Why? Is it true?"

"Maybe," she whispered.

I shot a sideways glance at her. "Then why the hell do you feel bad about saying it?"

"Because he's my friend."

An alarm buzzed in my head. *Baggage.* "I'm sorry, friend?"

She shifted as if uncomfortable. "No. I don't know. He's only interested in being friends when he needs something."

"Like a quick fuck?"

Her head shook quickly. "God, no. That's over." Her hands pressed in her lap. "And now that I . . . because we . . ."

"Since I can fuck you to an orgasm?"

She cut off her gasp. "Yeah."

"I want to ask you some questions, and I need you to think about them, and then answer them honestly."

She seemed to understand the seriousness in my tone. "Interview questions."

"Yes. How old where you when you lost your virginity?"

"Twenty-one."

We pulled up to a stoplight and the only sound was my turn signal chiming quietly. "That's an unusual age. Why'd you wait so long?"

"I didn't want to have sex with someone I couldn't see myself marrying. I wanted to be in love."

I cocked an eyebrow. "Then, why did you let me fuck you?" We weren't in love and I wasn't marriage material, I'd made that perfectly clear. Hadn't I?

She took her time assembling an answer. "I've always done the right thing. I wanted to be wrong, and you said you could show me."

Oh, yes. My heartbeat kicked at her perfect answer. "Do you like when I tell you what to do?" She nodded, her lips pressed tight together. "Do you want me to show you all the dirty, bad things you don't know?" The hands on her thighs slid inward, her body clenching. That was enough of an answer for me to keep talking. "I want to teach you, Noemi."

The first night I saw her, I'd thought about auditioning her for the blindfold club, but being the only man to show her pleasure had created a desire too powerful to ignore. I wanted to show her everything. Push her boundaries and unleash the sexual creature inside that was desperate to come out. She'd be magnificent.

"How would you teach me?"

My hand left the wheel and settled over hers, and my fingertips traced her long, delicate fingers. "You'd be my submissive."

"What?"

"You'd give me control over you."

She'd gone as rigid as a statue. "I have enough people telling me what to do."

"But my control would set you free, Noemi."

"This . . . is the job you're offering?"

I curled my fingers around hers. "You're in a hard spot. You want things, but you're too shy to ask, or too scared of what will happen. I'm offering you pleasure like you wouldn't fucking believe, and you'll be safe from regret or judgement. If you say yes, your desires become my responsibility."

Her breath caught. "Have you done this before?"

"I have." My arrangement a long time ago with Tara had been pleasurable for both of us. She'd discovered a side of herself during that month that had changed her life forever. I had enormous pride as her former partner, watching her shed the shackles of conformity. But since then, I hadn't found anyone else who captured my interest.

Noemi stared down at my hand encasing hers. As the

silence grew, I wanted to know what she was thinking, but now was not the time to push. This decision needed to be hers, no matter how much I wanted it.

And it was scary how badly I wanted her to say yes. I'd planned out the evening with a best-case scenario in mind, and those thoughts were the ones that got me hard. They left me with a fist full of cum this morning.

"I don't really understand what that means," she said finally. "You'd be my . . . ?"

"Dominant. I control the scene, you control the limits."

She took a breath. "And we'd be exclusive?"

I nodded. "During the time of our arrangement."

Alarm flashed through her expression. "Arrangement? How long?"

"I was thinking a month. We can change that whenever, if it doesn't work, or if we both want to keep going." We neared the trio of restaurants that made up the Italian Village, and I drove up to the valet stand. "You don't have to answer tonight, we'll talk about it—"

"No need," she blurted out. "Yes."

Her abrupt answer surprised me, but I didn't get a chance to respond, because the valet opened her door and cold flooded the car. I grabbed my ticket and ignored the possessive feeling I usually had when handing my beauty of a car over to a stranger, focusing instead on the beauty of my brand-spanking new submissive. Yeah, there was definitely going to be spanking in our future. But as much as I wanted her to say yes, I didn't like how quickly she'd agreed. Something for us to work on.

We were seated in a quiet two-top in the upper level of the high-end restaurant, probably a far cry from her grad school dinners of ramen noodles. Although her apartment building was nice. She probably had roommates. Fuck, I'd let my cock do all the thinking. I still didn't even know her last name. I'd Googled her that first night after I'd driven her home, but my search had yielded nothing. Did her name end with two E's? Or a Y?

Her hazel eyes stared at me like I was a new person. "I have more questions," she said. "I probably should have asked them before saying yes, but I don't think your answers are going to change my mind." She pushed back the sleeves of her deep-red sweater dress and set her elbows on the table. "Questions about the details of the arrangement."

"So professional," I said.

I ordered a bottle of wine, and shot a smirk when she got carded. But the smirk drained from my face at the thought the waiter now knew her name and I didn't.

"I have questions, too," I said. "And I get to go first. Tell me about yourself, really. Who are you?"

"Is this because of my sister?" Her face fell. "She's having a hard time with my stepmom moving out. That's why she was in the papers."

Her sister was in the news? "You said the other day your mother moved out, not your stepmom."

"My real mom and I don't talk. She never had the mothering gene." Her expression changed to one of indifference. "My stepmom's always done the mothering things for me. For a while my parents had shared custody, but things . . . got complicated, and it was easier for everyone when I chose to stay with my father full-time."

"You had to choose?"

She blinked, and her face hardened. "It wasn't much

of a choice. I was a pawn to my real mom, just another way for her to get money out of my dad. I didn't lose a lot of sleep over it."

"But you said your parents are controlling."

She made a face. "Maybe that's too strong of a word. They have high expectations."

Already my dominant side kicked into gear. "I don't like backtracking. Be confident enough to say what you mean."

Her eyes were sharp and intense. Noemi didn't like critique. "Fine. They have the money and the power, so they usually get their way. Some people would say that's controlling." My girl took a sip of her wine and seemed to shrug off the tension the comment had given her. "But my dad's very smart, and I know it sounds cheesy, but he's a great man. He loves me. He only wants the best for me."

The loyalty in her words was disarming. She was a daddy's girl, and I found it charming. "And your stepmom?"

She smiled pleasantly, but it was empty. "He loves her very much, too." There was so much weight in what she wasn't saying, it nearly crushed the table.

"Why was your sister in the papers?"

Her expression turned serious. "It was a misunderstanding. She's young, and her mother spoils her, and like I said, she's taking the separation hard. She was a mess when she came over to my apartment in a cab, and got into an argument with the driver when he recognized her. He thought she hadn't tipped him enough." She glanced down at the menu, then her eyes flicked back to mine. "That happens a lot. People think money means nothing to us, just because we have some. Everybody wants something. That's part of why I didn't tell you my name, or . . . where I live."

I studied her critically. "I don't know where you live?"

She shook her head, looking guilty. "Becca was arrested for being combative and intoxicated while underage, right outside my building. My dad kept it out of his papers, but the picture was in the Trib. You didn't recognize me the night we met. But Becca and I look alike and I thought if you saw my building, you might put it together."

I didn't have a clue what she was talking about. "Put what together?"

"That I'm Becca Rosso's sister."

My dad kept it out of his papers. Her last name was Rosso.

Holy, fucking, shit.

chapter TEN

My body turned to stone. "You're Anthony Rosso's daughter?"

Noemi Rosso, my newly-minted sub, nodded back. She stared at me with concern. "Is that a problem?"

Yeah, it was a problem. It was huge fucking problem, so enormous I couldn't get my stupid head around it. I'd fucked Mr. Red's daughter. I'd asked to be her Dom. The Payton issue I'd recovered from and been able to salvage my relationship with Mr. Red, but this? My empire would be gone in a blink of an eye. He could destroy me. He *would*, if he found out.

How had I not seen it? I couldn't find any words, and Noemi's worried expression grew.

"Joseph, are you okay?"

"Yeah," I lied, but it wasn't convincing. "I'll be right back." I rose from my chair, needing to find some air. All of it had evaporated from the room.

"Should I order for you?"

"That's fine," I mumbled, hurrying from the table and down the staircase to the main floor. My heart raced, and I didn't notice a damn thing as I blindly stumbled to the restroom. I had myself locked in the stall before I felt the panic begin to ebb.

What the fuck was I going to do?

My hands balled into fists. Less than ten minutes ago she'd accepted my offer, and I'd been thrilled. Fucking *excited*. I'd wanted to race through the meal and get her back to my place so I could start executing my plans. There was so much I wanted to explore with her.

That couldn't happen now.

It wasn't like I could explain. Maybe down the road, I'd let Noemi know about all of my clubs, once I knew how she'd react, but now? I couldn't tell her that I knew her father because he bought pussy once a week from my brothel. I could be cold and ruthless in business, but I wasn't about to destroy a family.

Perhaps I could fake being sick and drive her home right now. Erase her number from my phone and just be done with it. It wouldn't be a lie, I did feel sick to my stomach, but the thought of erasing her number intensified the feeling.

You can't have her, the logical part of my brain warned.

What if she was worth the risk?

No, forget it. I made up my mind. Get through the dinner, drive her home and tell her that it isn't going to work. I'd fought too hard to have everything taken away from me a second time. It fucking sucked, but I'd have to get over it. Nothing lasted forever.

I washed my hands at the sink and pulled in a calming breath. By the time I'd returned to the table, I'd told myself a dozen times I could do this and act as if nothing was wrong.

"Sorry about that," I said, slipping back into my seat.

Her pretty eyes focused on me, and she looked relieved. Fuck. This was going to be difficult.

"I ordered you the special," she said. "Crab alfredo. Please tell me you're not allergic to seafood."

"No."

Her relieved look expanded into a smile. "I'm realizing we don't know that much about each other."

"That's the fucking truth."

She seemed displeased. "If you use that word all the time, it loses its power."

Her attempt to lecture me made it slightly easier to want distance. I snatched up my wine and drank, then set the glass down, watching the liquid roll side to side. I'd look anywhere but at her. "You said you had questions for me."

"Why do you want this?" she asked. "What do you get out of it?"

Looking at her was unavoidable, and when I did, I began to ache. It was so cruel to give me a taste and then take it away.

"Do you want an honest answer?"

She took her napkin and dropped it in her lap, and then set her gaze on me. "I looked some stuff up on my phone while you were gone. Honesty seems to be an important aspect of this arrangement."

This sensible, restrained version of her. Christ, it echoed *him*.

"I like the power. I like to be in control."

"Since the time in your life where you didn't have any," she said. "I want to know about that."

"No." It was sharp and aggressive.

"Why not?"

"I don't like talking about it, so we won't. What other questions do you have?"

My short tone had set her aback, and she scrambled to adjust. "Uh . . . you mentioned you'd control the scene, and I'd control the limits."

"You'd tell me what was and wasn't allowed. I take you to your limit, and decide when you're ready to push further."

Her eyes heated a degree. "How do I set the limits? I haven't done much."

"You won't know your limits until you reach them. We would find them together." Shit, no we wouldn't, I thought bitterly.

Subtle pink colored her cheeks. It would be so much better if she wasn't getting turned on, because it turned me on. I had to start shutting this down.

"Do you have limits?" she asked. "Other than talking about yourself?"

"You better watch that smart mouth, little girl."

"Or what?" she challenged back.

I couldn't stay on task. "I'll discipline you."

"How?" This single word from her wasn't condescending, it was curious. Intrigued.

"I'll think of something," I grumbled. "I don't mind talking about myself. What do you want to know, beside what I said I didn't want to discuss?"

She rattled off a list of questions, and I gave her curt answers. Where I lived, if I'd gone to college, which I hadn't, and how many businesses I owned. I told her about the front for the blindfold club, my membership-only wine bar.

"Does your family live around here?" she asked.

"No. My parents live in Florida. My older brother is a naval officer, stationed in Hawaii."

"Are you guys close?"

"Not really."

"You make me feel like I'm interrogating you," she said, "with your short answers."

I gave her no rebuttal, which seemed to only make her more displeased. It was interrupted when our food arrived.

My gaze fell away from hers and I stared down at the plate of pasta before me. My brother Conner and I had been close growing up, but when all the attention turned to me, he'd enlisted, and now the distance added to our divide.

Noemi twirled the noodles on her fork and took a bite. "Wow, it's good." The conversation fell in a lull, and she scanned the dining room. "You didn't answer my question," she said softly, "about whether you have limits."

"Everyone has limits. A person who says they don't is naïve, or insane."

"So, what are they?"

I took another sip of my wine, finishing it. "We can also find those together." *Again, no you can't*, the voice in my head reminded.

I watched her eat, fighting the urge to test her as I would if I was really her Dom. The long, white tablecloth hung over her lap. The command for her to touch herself beneath the table stuck in my throat.

She set her fork down and it clattered on the plate. "Are you mad at me?"

"No, of course not. Why are you asking?"

"You look upset."

I was pissed with the situation, and doing a terrible job of hiding it. I leaned toward her. "I've got a lot on my mind, I'm sorry for the shitty conversation." I struggled to ease the tension she'd picked up on. "How'd your case study go last night?"

She blinked at my question like it was the most bizarre thing she'd heard. "Fine. Uh, good, actually. We've still got a lot of work to do, but we should be ready to present soon."

"What's it about?"

"Contact lenses," she said, her lips pulling back into a slow smile, "for chickens."

I froze. "Come again?"

She laughed, and I didn't *want* to like the sound of it. Her soft, warm laugh was infectious.

"It's not a real case, but a farmer has the option of getting contact lenses for chickens that distort their eyesight. Apparently, chickens are picky about their feed, so they'll eat all the good pieces and leave the rest. The lenses make it so when they peck at a good piece, they come up with the one on the side of it."

"It cuts down on food costs."

"Exactly. We're supposed to figure out if the cost of the lenses and labor of administering them balances with the saved cost in feed."

"So, does the farmer invest in the lenses?"

Her eyes sparkled. "It's actually looking right now like he should, but we've got other factors to consider, such as some of the chickens figure it out, and you have to redo the lenses."

"Do you like your classes?"

She nodded. "I do. It's not really a surprise that I like finance and accounting."

"Because of who your father is," I said. Hopefully she didn't notice me gritting my teeth.

She spun her fork in her pasta, but didn't lift it to take a bite, almost as if stalling. "Making my choice to stay with my dad, it kind of forced this career path on me, but luckily I happen to like being in the boardroom."

"You've sat in on board meetings?"

She smiled knowingly. "My father hopes one day I'll

run the business he worked so hard to build, and I want that, too." The confidence I'd seen flashes of in my office returned, pouring through her. "You should know, Rossos are used to getting their way."

"I'll keep that in mind." But her statement felt like a challenge and I couldn't let it go. "Put your hand in your lap and touch yourself."

"What?" Her mouth fell open.

"I'm not going to repeat myself when we both know you heard me."

The air heated and crackled with intensity, swirling around us. Would she do it? Obey my first command as my submissive?

Her shoulder shifted hesitantly, and I felt hot on the back of my neck. She was doing as told.

"No," I snapped, when her gaze darted away, checking to see if anyone was watching. "Eyes stay on me. It's my responsibility that you don't get caught."

The outer rim of her irises were a soft, celery green, giving way to tan just before her dark pupils, that dilated now. I pictured her fingertips below her dress, rubbing herself over her panties.

The corner of my mouth tugged upward. "Do you like being a bad girl for me?"

Her chest rose and fell with her rapid breathing, her gaze fixed on mine. She nodded.

"Are you getting wet? Is your tight, little cunt aching for my mouth?"

She jolted. "I don't like that word."

"Are you telling me that's a limit? Pull your underwear to the side and get your fingers in there."

She swallowed a breath and blinked rapidly. The war inside her head was visible in her beautiful eyes. The want to give in, versus the desire to stay appropriate. If things were different, I'd train her so her *want* to submit would become *need*.

Her bicep flexed subtly. Power flared and burned in my veins. Now I pictured her finger sliding inside her body.

"It's not a limit," she said, her voice tight. "I just don't care for it. It's vulgar."

"Says the girl fingering herself in a crowded restaurant." I finished the last bite of my dinner. "Go faster."

Air was sucked in through her parted lips. She wouldn't come like this. Not sitting up, with other people around, and from penetration alone. But, goddamn, it was hot as sin watching her.

"I want that to be my cock that's fucking you right now." I wanted it with every cell in my miserable body. "Do you want that?"

"Yes." Her dinner had been abandoned. Her other hand clutched the edge of the table.

"Yes, *Sir*," I corrected.

Her eyes hooded. "Yes, Sir."

And . . . I was hard as steel. Fuck.

"Stop," I commanded. "Keep your hand exactly where it is."

Puzzlement flooded her eyes, and quickly turned to anxiety when the waiter appeared tableside.

"How is everything?" he asked, his attention on Noemi as he cleared my plate.

She had no choice but to answer. "It's great." Her strained voice was enjoyable.

"Are you all finished?" He gestured to her plate, and she nodded quickly. "Any dessert this evening?"

"No, just the check, please," I answered. He was gone a moment later and her tight shoulders relaxed, but I wasn't ready to release her just yet. "Put your fingers in your mouth and clean them off."

"Oh, God," she whispered, both nervous and excited.

Her hand came up quickly, darting to her mouth, but not fast enough. I'd seen the moisture there. She sank them in her mouth, closed her lips around the first knuckles, and drew them out slowly. Like her meal had been so good, she wanted to lick every last trace from her hand.

"Have you tasted yourself before?"

She flushed, broke the gaze, and looked guilty. "Yes."

"Look at me." The edge in my voice was dark, and it came out just louder than I wanted it to. If we'd been alone, I would have delivered a physical, negative reinforcement, but I couldn't do anything from across the table. "Yes, *Sir*, my filthy girl."

Her gaze snapped back to me. "Yes, Sir."

"Are you ashamed? You shouldn't be. That's hot, Noemi. So, fucking, hot."

We had to get out of this restaurant, but closing us in together in my Porsche was a bad idea. How the fuck was I going to drive her home while keeping my hands off of her? Without running my stupid mouth?

She argued to pay her half of the bill, but I shook my head. "Not a chance." As I tossed down my credit card, I realized grimly it didn't matter in the end. Rosso was footing the bill one way or the other, as most of my money came from him.

The wind chill was dangerously cold, and we waited inside the atrium for the valet to pull the Porsche up. She slipped an arm behind my back and lifted up on her toes so her mouth was beside my ear.

"Thank you for dinner, Sir."

Something inside me snapped, but I should have been prepared. I was aware I had no control around her. *One more time.* I'd already fucked her, the damage was done. I turned my mouth into hers and felt her body melt beneath me. Every layer of her kiss rationalized the concept more. Persuaded and seduced.

What difference would one more time make?

chapter ELEVEN

NOEMI

Last night the thought of Joseph possessing me had sent me over the edge, and tonight he'd asked for exactly that. Making that choice hadn't been difficult in the slightest, but as I stood in his luxurious living room, I started to have doubts.

Throwing yourself headfirst into an unusual sexual arrangement with a virtual stranger had side effects, the biggest being that he still felt like a stranger. Yet, I wanted to trust him. He'd never done anything to make me feel threatened or unsafe. Joseph often had demanding eyes, but he also had soft, warm ones, too. He was straightforward, but didn't treat me like I was inferior just because I was inexperienced. I somehow felt equal with him.

His living room was that of a man, not a college-aged boy, which is what I was used to. A black leather sectional sat beneath an oversized black and white print. The room was open to the kitchen, which had a butcher block island. Everything was tasteful and exacting. Every space was distinctly masculine. From what I knew so far, this place was one hundred percent Joseph.

"Do you want some more wine?" he asked, helping me out of my coat and hanging it in the front closet.

"Sure."

He shrugged out of his own coat, and my gaze lingered over his black V-neck sweater and charcoal gray dress pants.

"Red or white?"

"White would be great."

I continued to scan the room, searching for clues to the enigmatic man who was now my Sir. God, it still sounded so foreign. He strolled to the side-by-side fridge and pulled out a bottle, checking the label.

I was vaguely aware that he was opening the wine with one of those electric cork removers, but my focus went to the hallway, where a picture hung. I stepped out of my heels and padded silently across the hardwood toward it.

"That's me and my brother Conner," he said, passing me a glass of chilled wine. "Our parents took us whitewater rafting in North Carolina one summer."

Joseph looked to be about fourteen or fifteen. He sat at the front of a large inflatable raft, a white helmet on his head, an orange vest buckled on, and a paddle in one hand. Beside him, his big brother was a few years older, and he had a hand on Joseph's shoulder. Easy, excited smiles were captured on their faces.

"You look like a stick!" I said, grinning.

Joseph didn't seem to think it was all that cute. "Yeah, I was always a skinny kid. You want the tour?"

"Sure." I turned back to face the room and took my first sip from my glass.

"Is the wine sweet enough? I know how you college girls like your sugary wine-coolers," he teased.

I gave him a plain look. "My family has a villa in Tuscany. I've been drinking table wine since I was sixteen."

"Right." His gaze moved away from me. Why did he shut down whenever I mentioned family, mine or his? "Anyway," he said, "this is the living room and kitchen area. Follow me."

We went down the tall hallway and he gestured to the open door on the left. "Guest bathroom." He motioned to the dark doorway on the right. "Spare bedroom."

Business had to be good. He lived in a two-bedroom in downtown Chicago, by *himself*. He continued straight ahead, and when we entered the room, he turned on a light switch.

"*Master* bedroom," he said. It felt like he'd put intentional weight on this, as if implying that he was my master simply because he occupied this room. A huge beveled mirror hung over the sleigh-style bed with wrought iron railings. The silvery-blue silk comforter was refined and elegant. This room . . . it was seductive.

I smiled, but it froze when Joseph gave me that look he was becoming famous for, the one that was untamed lust. He took the wine from me and set both of our drinks on the dresser.

"Are you ready to play, little girl?" My throat closed up, but I must have given him some sort of confirmation. "Good. Take off your dress."

I set my palms flat on my thighs and began to drag upward, my heartbeat rising with every inch of my skirt. My sensible side was quiet, but perhaps I'd obliterated her when I'd accepted Joseph's offer.

When the skirt cleared my hips and revealed my black lace boyshort panties, our arrangement started to feel real. I'd followed his naughty commands at the restaurant, but this was different. We hadn't consummated the agreement, and standing naked before Joseph would be like signing a dotted line. My dress continued its journey up over my head and I tossed it aside.

His gaze swept over me slowly, invisible fingers

caressing every curve of my body.

"You look like a fucking wet dream. Did you wear that for me?"

I let out a pleased sigh and nodded. I'd bought it for him, hoping I'd get to show it off after the "job interview."

"I want to see it all, though," he said. He set his hands on his hips, and for a split second I had the weird thought he'd done this to prevent his hands from reaching for me. "Show me what's mine."

Oh, holy hell.

My hands twisted behind my back and undid the clasp on the demi-cup bra I'd worn. My breasts spilled free as the bra straps slipped down my arms and dropped to the carpet.

"Fucking perfect."

Goosebumps pebbled on my skin and I shivered, but I wasn't the least bit cold. My nipples hardened to points, aching to be in his hands and under his command. But he wanted to see everything, and I could tell he wouldn't touch me until I'd done as instructed. My thumbs slid under the waistband and pulled my panties down until I could step out of them.

I'd done it. I was naked, and shedding my clothes was shedding the last trace of sensible Noemi. I felt like I was vibrating with life.

"Are you nervous?" he asked.

I wasn't just vibrating on the inside. My core was trembling. Joseph's face softened and he closed the space between us, both of his hands cradling my face.

"Don't be. It's going to be amazing."

"You'll set me free," I said, talking more to myself than him. Yet, he sort of had already. I was wild and reckless, but

THREE *little* MISTAKES

I felt like I was my own person, making my own decisions without consulting anyone else.

His lips pressed down on mine, soft at first and then shifting to a more dominating kiss. His tongue shot past my lips, possessing my mouth without permission. He didn't need permission. I'd given him control. An arm wrapped around my back and a hand gripped my breast roughly.

I moaned against his mouth. This felt wrong, but not because of what we were doing. It felt wrong because we weren't doing *enough*. His urgent kiss matched his aggressive hands, until he was pawing at my body, as if desperate to touch me where he hadn't before.

My hands caressed down his shoulders, over his chest, until they landed on his belt. I hadn't touched him the last time we'd been together, and I was shy the first time in his Porsche. Now I was eager.

But he stepped back so abruptly I almost fell over. "Soon," he said. "But not just yet."

I swayed, woozy from his effect. Joseph pulled open the top drawer to his nightstand and something metal clinked together. My heart leapt into my throat.

"Handcuffs?" Not the furry play kind, but cold-looking steel.

"Trust me." He said it like it was just that easy. "Lie down."

I glanced at the open doorway, and that action was not lost on Joseph. He drew in a deep breath.

"You can leave at any time." His words were cold and professional. "But if you do, the arrangement ends. An easier solution would be to communicate that you're scared, and I can back off."

I understood his frustration, but didn't he know I was

fighting years of training to keep my mouth shut? "I'm not scared," I said.

His hand shot out and fingers twisted my nipple. I gasped and jolted backward, falling to sit on the bed. The pain was sharp but gone a second later.

"It's perfectly fine to feel scared, but you can't lie while we're doing this. If a sub doesn't communicate, the Dom can push too hard, and that's when people get hurt."

I stared up at Joseph, one finger hooked around the cuffs dangling from his hold. Even with a serious expression, he was still undeniably hot.

"You need handcuffs to set me free?" I whispered.

He smiled softly. "I do."

"If you tell me why you need them," I tried to regain my composure, "maybe I'd feel more comfortable."

My attempt to communicate seemed to please him. His hand slipped behind my head into the hair at the nape of my neck, tilting my head back to look at him better. "I have a theory this will get you to orgasm faster. Do you want to try it?"

Oh. The idea of bondage had always interested me, but I couldn't admit it to anyone. I thought there was something wrong with me. Why would a woman want to be restrained? It was in direct conflict with my desire to be strong and independent. Yet, I craved it. I was desperate to know what it would feel like, and if it would be as good as it was in my fantasies.

"Yes," I said. The hand in my hair tightened and I realized my mistake. "Yes, Sir." How was it addressing him like that turned me on? I lay down on the bed, the satiny comforter cool against my skin.

"Reach up and grab the railings."

I wrapped my fingers around the square-shaped spindles of the headboard. They were thin, but seemed strong. Joseph took a knee on the bed and snapped the first cuff around my wrist, tightening it closed with a ratcheting noise. My grip on the spindle clenched in response. He threaded the handcuff chain behind the rail, and clasped the other cuff shut with a click.

"Tell me if they're too tight, or if your arms start to go to sleep. Okay?"

"Okay." My voice was breathy.

His fingertips trailed from my wrists, tracing a line down my arm. I shuddered, clamping my legs together. It was disorienting how quickly I was overwhelmed with desire. The path of his fingertips continued, sliding over my breast, circling my nipple once, before journeying further south. The handcuffs rattled against the iron railings when I shifted on the bed, trying to hurry his fingers along.

"You want my fingers inside you?"

"Yes, Sir." The fingers drew a lazy, wide circle around my bellybutton, making the muscles of my stomach contract.

"Say please." His low voice was hypnotic.

"Please."

Joseph's index finger traced down until he hit the landing strip I'd groomed on myself. "I want you to go bare here for me."

I'd never done that, but nodded. "If you want me to, sure, I can try it."

Again, it looked like I'd pleased him, and I enjoyed the sensation. His finger crept lower, until finally he brushed over the spot where my need was acute. The handcuffs clanged as steel hit iron.

He stroked me once. "So wet for me." And then he was gone, off the bed and staring down with his dark, animalistic eyes. "You have no idea how much I've wanted you naked and bound to my bed, begging for my cock." His hand went to his crotch, pushing down his erection. "You're gonna beg, baby girl, and I'm going to love listening to it."

I swallowed hard, feeling that same mixture of nervousness and excitement he always caused. His hand disappeared into the open top drawer, and drew out a white . . . was it a microphone? No, wait, I'd seen one of these before in a porn clip. A large wand vibrator.

"Have you used one of these before?"

"No, Sir."

The wand had a long power cord and Joseph dropped out of view for a moment as he plugged it in. He turned it on, and it hummed quietly.

"I picked this up for you today. Let's see how you like it."

He set the vibrating head against my nipple and I jumped. It felt kind of good, but it also tickled. The bed shifted when Joseph climbed up on his knees, moving toward my legs.

"Open up for me."

He'd been right. Following his commands kept me free from shame or regret. I parted my knees and he crawled to kneel between them. God, I was totally exposed to him.

"Shit," I cried when he pressed the vibrator directly on my sensitive, damp skin.

"Can you have multiple orgasms?" His tone was light and casual, and the disconnect between it and his words left me scattered, not to mention the heat the vibration was sending through me. "Can you get more than one in when you're alone?"

It was hard to think. "Yeah. Um, yes." The sensation was gone as he pulled the wand away, and immediately I felt cold. "Yes, Sir."

I groaned and squeezed tighter on the rails as the vibrations resumed on my skin.

"Good. We'll try for two tonight."

Two? Talk about unrealistic expectations. Getting one was a major achievement. I'd have thrown him a ticker-tape parade for what he'd done yesterday if that wouldn't have been buckets of crazy.

"You think I'm being greedy?" he teased. The wand rotated on my clit, his gaze watching me intently. I bit down on my lip. If he kept at it with the wand, which felt amazing, he'd certainly get to one. "Trust me, Noemi."

Pressure increased on the wand against my flesh and I moaned. Joseph was kneeling between my parted legs, using a vibrator on me while he was fully clothed and I was naked, handcuffed to his bed. Oh, God. It was insane and incredible.

His hand not holding the vibrator skimmed along my waist and up, fondling my breasts. It took the sensation to another level and I began to pant. His warm skin on mine felt so good, and the vibration was sending waves of pleasure rolling through me.

"Tell me what you thought about last night," he said.

"I thought about . . . your filthy mouth."

"Filthy because of the things I say?" He leaned over me and put his mouth on my erect nipple, skimming it with his teeth. "Or filthy because of the things I use it to do?"

"Both."

Joseph chuckled. His tongue licked, and it drew a soft sigh from me.

Was I supposed to tell him? "I'm . . . getting close."

His head raised up and his gaze connected with mine. "Good girl."

The vibrator shook loose my tongue. "What did you think about?"

"Besides this? I thought about fucking you from behind and spanking you until your skin was a perfect shade of red, and then you'd ask for my cock in your ass."

"Oh my God." I don't know which was more shocking, his words or how my body responded to them.

"How would you feel if I spanked you? Do you want the sharp crack of my hand against you when you need discipline?"

I'd watched quite a bit of porn, and I was convinced it was much more than the average woman my age. An unhealthy fascination, bordering on obsession. Along with being tied up, this was something else I wanted, but lord knew Ross would never try it. I thought of Joseph taking me over his knee sometime, yanking the back of my panties down, and slapping me, leaving my ass stinging and hot. Bad girls got spankings, and that's what I wanted to be, right?

"Yes," I whispered.

The wicked smile that spread across Joseph's face brought me right to the edge. My moans grew loud and my feet dug into the mattress so I could shift to a better angle on the head of the vibrator.

"And if I wanted to take your virgin ass at some point, would you let me, or would that be a limit?"

I closed my eyes and turned my head to the side, burying it in my arm. I couldn't think with my orgasm so close and him watching me in this state of chaos. The concept was so dirty and wrong, not to mention, "It'll hurt."

"No, not if it's done right," he said.

I didn't know how to answer, so I gave him no response. I couldn't bring myself to say no and rule it out entirely, but it was too impossible to just agree to. Besides, the need inside me shoved every thought from my mind. My knees trembled as I closed in on ecstasy.

"So, that's a soft limit." He sat back on his heels, working the wand against me. Up and down. Left, then right. It'd pass over the exact spot I needed it, giving me a hit of pleasure and then moved off, just to the side. Toying with me.

"No," I whined, when he pulled the vibrator away.

"Tell me where you want it." Joseph swiped his fingers down through my valley and I jolted at his touch. My heartbeat was pulsing between my legs, hardest right inside my clit. "You want it here, little girl? Right on this pretty, wet *cunt*?"

I considered it the most obscene word in the English language. I hated it, and couldn't stop my face from twisting into a scowl. "Don't."

"Oh, baby girl, this is what I do. I'm going to push. Now say it."

"Please..." Already I could feel the orgasm slipping away.

"Please, what? You want this on your cunt, or you don't want me to make you say it?"

"Yes," I said.

Oh, no. The hum on the vibrator cut off and it thumped onto the mattress beside me. He moved so quickly, I gasped.

In a blink he was kneeling beside my hip and shoved me over onto my stomach. Above me, the handcuff chain twisted around the rail.

I heard the smack of skin against skin before it registered in my brain. The biting pain shot from my backside up my spine, and dissipated, but it had been intense and stole my breath.

"Why did I do that?" he demanded.

I swallowed. "Because I didn't say Sir."

His hand rubbed my hot skin tenderly. "How was that? If I hit you harder next time, could you handle more?"

I tried to evaluate the pain, but his touch now felt like pleasure and left me confused. I'd . . . holy shit. "Yes. I liked it."

Shame flooded through me and I pressed my face against the pillow.

"No." His voice was commanding. "You're not allowed to feel guilty about that. As long as you're mine, you never feel shame about what we do." His hands slipped under my body and he turned me in his arms so I was face-up again. He brushed hair out of my eyes, and I'd never craved anything like his touch. Soft or hard, rough or gentle, it didn't matter.

"Kiss me, please," I said, my voice breaking on the final word. "Oh, God, please fucking kiss me, Sir."

He gave me a stunned smile. "That wasn't the begging I was looking for, but it definitely works." He lowered his mouth to mine and I felt the electricity snapping around us, seeping in through our skin. My hands tried to reach for him, and were met with the restraint of hard metal. His kiss made me crazy and weak, and I tried to chase him when he pulled away.

"You're going to say it, Noemi." He picked the vibrator back up, and moved to kneel between my legs again, ignoring my frustrated sigh. "*Submit.*"

Holy hell, why not just douse me in hot oil? I felt every inch of my body burst into flames at his command.

It was just a word that I'd given too much emphasis to anyway. I raised my head and peered at him over my bare breasts to spy him positioned between my bent knees. "I want it on my *cunt*."

Unexpected power surged and swept me away. Demanding what I wanted, using such language . . . I felt strong and alive.

This smile wasn't like his others. Whatever power I'd felt, it was only a fraction of what he seemed to. Joseph's dark gaze emptied my mind. Pleasing him was shockingly sexy. The hum that resumed was mere noise.

"Oh . . ." Now I was aware the frequency of the buzzing was a higher pitch. The change in speed brought new ripples of bliss with it, building me right back up to the precipice.

"Are you ready to come?"

"Yes, Sir. Yes."

The wand pushed down hard, grinding against me when Joseph pushed my knees together, trapping it tight between my thighs. What—

"Oh, shit. Shit!" I cried.

His arms hugged my thighs, holding them closed, while I went on sensory overload from the vibrating mass between my legs. I wanted to escape, but his hold was too strong. It felt so good. Too good. And orgasming like this, with him holding me and trapped under his demanding eyes was like be thrown into the sun.

"Yes," he urged. "Show me what it's like when you come."

My hands ached from their hold on the rails and the sharp corners were unforgiving in my grip. I gasped for air and my whole body trembled as the pleasure became too much. I gave in. *Submitted* to it.

"God. Oh my God!" My eyelids slammed shut and sound faded from my ears. The orgasm was piercing and I fell apart in his arms, feeling broken yet free. I cried out so loud, maybe it was a scream. Heat and bliss poured from everywhere, flooding me until there was nowhere to turn to or escape. I convulsed and moaned. *Fuck*. Fuck, it felt so much better when he did it.

He released my legs and they fell, quaking and boneless to the comforter. The hum stopped. I blinked slowly, struggling to emerge from my fog. My heartbeat continued to pulse in my clit even after the last tendrils of the orgasm slipped away.

"Mmm . . ." I moaned. Feeling hadn't completely returned, but he was doing something. His head was flanked by my legs, and when I strained my neck, I watched his pink tongue slide between my folds. His indecent kiss was gentle and slow, but I couldn't watch. I was too turned on. In fact, I could feel that I was dripping.

I stared up at his plain white ceiling while he lapped at me. I needed to know everything about this man and all the filthy things he had planned for us.

"Joseph," I whispered, making him pause. "That felt so fucking good."

"Such language." His mocking voice teased me. Then his mouth returned to teasing me in other ways. Warmth crept up in my cheeks when his fingers spread me further open. The tongue slid all over, changing pace, darting inside . . . and then his mouth closed around the nerves at my center, sucking.

I was sweating under his command and the air in the room was thin. It was so much worse when he sat back from me, grabbed the hem of his sweater, and lifted, stretching it up and over his head.

"Whoa," I said.

Dark blue ink adorned his shoulder, intricate scrolls extending down his toned bicep to his elbow. Most tattoos seemed flat to me, but this one had depth. I could study it for a while and not grasp all of the beauty of the artist's work. Of course my bad boy came with a tattoo.

A voice in my head reminded me that there were other parts of his body to look at besides the magnificent art. It didn't disappoint either. Joseph had a narrow, lean build, where oversized muscles would look odd on him. Holy hell, his proportions were just right. He was hard and cut, and my gaze soaked in the abs that flowed down, disappearing beneath the waistline of his pants.

His long, skilled fingers worked the buckle of his belt, then tugged the zipper. He backed off the bed and dropped both his pants and boxer briefs to the floor, his massive erection reaching toward me. A chuckle rumbled from his chest.

"You look terrified," he said. A condom was plucked from the drawer, and he tore the wrapper open with his teeth. "Don't worry, we know it's going to fit."

I watched as he rolled the latex down on himself, and deep inside, I wanted those to be my hands. "You said I was going to get my turn to touch you." I moved my wrists so the handcuffs clanged for effect.

He slid onto the bed beside me, his mouth hovering over my breast closest to him. "Well, I had other things planned tonight, baby girl, but I can't wait any longer. I want to feel that pussy coming on me." He nipped at my skin, making me flinch. "You do this. Make me lose control."

His body was on top of me then, our naked flesh pressed together, and my throat closed up. No more talking.

All I wanted was what he wanted.

chapter TWELVE

JOSEPH

When Noemi's dress hit the floor, I began to doubt my stupid idea that one more time would be enough. It was destroyed when she admitted she enjoyed my rough hand cracking against her ass. This girl could bring men to their knees, and seemed completely unaware. I wanted to coax that out and set her on fire.

But now I was worried I'd be the one she'd put on his knees.

Her innocence was intoxicating, and her willingness fucked with my head. I was high off of my desire. My body moved to her, independent of my mind. Her face was in my hands as I settled over her. I rained kisses over her cheeks, her jawline, down her neck. I wanted the taste of her skin always in my mouth.

Her legs wrapped around my hips, urging me to take her.

If I had any goddamn control, I'd make her wait. I'd tease, or instruct her to beg. Anticipation played a huge role in heightening sensation and giving a better experience. But I could not wait one fucking moment more.

She whimpered as I began to intrude, but her legs strengthened their hold on me, driving me forward. Pulling me deeper. I buried my face in her neck, sucking softly as I sank inch by slow inch into her.

"You like this cock inside you?" I thought I remembered

how good she felt, but I'd been wrong. "Feels so fucking good."

A groan rolled from my lips as I was buried all the way to my balls. Her pussy was an inferno. It made sense; Noemi was insanely hot. The twisted part of me loved that she was dangerous. Fucking her put everything at risk, and it turned me on more, although I didn't need help there.

A soft moan escaped her as I began to thrust. Slow. Steady. Deep. This was prepping her for launch, not going for orgasm right away. I'd have more groundwork to lay before I'd bring her to the edge. As long as I could show a little restraint, I'd get her off. I had the Hitachi nearby to help with the final push.

Her moans swelled in intensity as I did, and suddenly I went off the rails. My mouth found hers, and my hands wrapped around her wrists, just below the handcuffs. I lost my goddamn mind when her lips were pressed to mine. Kissing her was a mistake, and I needed to stop doing it. I used my teeth to nip at her bottom lip.

Focus on her tits, I ordered myself. They were perfect. Tight, pink nipples that were hard knots, brushed against my chest. I snatched one up, rubbing my face over her flesh. My scruff bristled against her skin and Noemi exhaled loudly.

"Oh," she said, her back arching and shoving herself against me. Her knuckles squeezing the railings were almost white and her muscles strained. I began to fuck hard then. Our bodies slapped together and the force drove her into the mattress. The headboard knocked against the wall. Thump, thump, thump... perfectly in time with my rhythm.

Under me, she was desperate, writhing for something, and she probably didn't even know what. But I did. "You want more?" I asked it with a devilish voice. "Does my good girl need to be fucked harder?"

Her gaze found me through the cloud of lust that filled her eyes. "Yes," she said between two huge breaths, "Sir."

Part of me had wished the answer was no. I was already aching and wanted to come. All of my self-pleasure since I'd had her on that table hadn't taken the edge off; it seemed only Noemi could give me satisfaction. I slammed into her, shoving my cock in her tight pussy over and over, while my hand searched for the Hitachi on the comforter. Her eyes closed and she bit her trembling bottom lip. We were both slick with sweat, our skin gliding over one another as she moved beneath me.

I rose up to sit, pushing her knees back and wide open, all while staying deep. Her eyelids blinked when the vibrator sprang to life, and she cried out when I placed it directly on her clit.

The powerful vibrations reverberated through her body onto mine, but it was her tiny, internal clenches that made me moan. I had a hand still on her knee and squeezed, needing something to help me endure what felt so good it should be a felony.

"Shit. Shit, shit . . ." she whined. "Please. Right there."

I grinned. Sooner or later she'd figure out how sexy it was when she knew what she wanted and asked for it. I did as she said, kept the vibrator firm against her. I watched the slippery stroke of my cock inside and its slide out of her, before I plunged back in to repeat, endlessly.

She gasped for air, right on the edge of orgasm.

"Yes. Come on me, Noemi. Fuck that cock."

She brought her elbows together over her face, as if to quiet the scream that welled up. And there it was, the sensation I'd wanted. Her toes bent into points, and inside I felt the pulses signaling what was happening.

I made it one lousy thrust before I joined her. My balls tightened and heat shot up my spine, exploding out in a rush of pleasure. "Fuck," I groaned, dropping the vibrator. Her body milked me, and her scream rang in my head, catapulting me further. The goddamn orgasm kept going. Wave after wave of it, each spurt a new burst of pleasure while she shuddered around me.

I collapsed forward, my head falling on her heaving chest while the rush faded with each shallow breath I took.

Fucking hell. Thank God she'd been bound to the bed. How long would I have made it with those hands on me, scratching at my shoulders or wrapped behind my neck? I lay there, my head riding the gentle gallop of her breathing that slowed to almost normal.

"Joseph." Her voice was shaky. "I've got pins and needles in my arms."

Fuck, of course she did. I slid off the bed, grabbed the key from the drawer, and undid the cuffs as fast as I could. When she gingerly brought her arms down by her side, I yanked the condom off and tossed it in the garbage.

"Lie on your stomach." I said. There was a bottle of oil in the drawer, and I unsnapped the cap, pouring some in my palm.

"Is that drawer completely devoted to sex stuff?" she joked, but her voice was tight. She tried to hide the grimace from her face as she moved on her stiff arms.

"Pretty much." There was a lot more in the bottom drawer of my dresser, but she wasn't ready for any of that. I rubbed my hands together, then set them on her smooth shoulders, kneading the muscles of her neck, her back, down her arms.

"I'm on board with the handcuffs if this happens every time after."

"You don't need handcuffs if you want me to touch you. Just ask," I said. "Or, take off your clothes." She laughed softly, and it struck me again how much I liked the sound. I glanced at the glasses we'd left on the dresser. "Want your wine?"

"Yes, please."

This wasn't something I was used to. I didn't bring women home with me. I didn't climb into bed with them afterward, while drinking wine and fighting the urge to have a conversation that didn't revolve around sex. Yet it came naturally tonight.

I was curious about this heiress who'd given herself to me, even though I shouldn't allow this to continue. But silence was also nice, and not at all uncomfortable. When she finished her wine, she rolled onto her side, her gaze on my chest. Ah, no. My tattoo.

"It's beautiful."

"Thanks." I followed her gaze, which seemed to trace every delicate line. "It's my friend Silas' work. He has a gallery in Wicker Park." *Too much information.* I needed to keep my distance if I was going to maintain control.

"Are you a pessimist?" she asked.

"No, why?"

Her fingertips skated over the quote buried within the art. "*Nothing lasts forever.* That's not exactly what I'd call a hopeful statement."

"It can be," I said quickly, stretching my hand up and

tucking it back behind my head, obscuring most of the ink from her view.

A puzzled look flashed on her pretty face. "How can that be hopeful?"

"If nothing lasts forever, that includes weakness. Pain. Nausea, and doctors—" I snapped my mouth shut, but it was too late. I could see the thoughts in her head, reflected in the windows of her eyes.

I sat up. "Forget I said anything. We should get dressed."

"Oh. Okay."

The hurt in her voice stabbed into me. I didn't want to throw her out of my bed, in fact, I wanted her to get under the covers. To curl up beside me so we could go again in the morning. But I didn't know how else to get her away from the questions I knew were coming. The last thing I wanted was her to look at me differently, like I was breakable. I didn't bend or break. I was the one who did the pushing now. Others bent at my command.

She slipped off the bed and began tugging on her clothes, not looking at me. It was awful. Every tense movement of her body displayed how uncomfortable she felt, and I had to do something.

"Wait." My voice was unsteady, and I hated the sound of it, but I'd made the mistake. Might as well finish it.

Her hazel eyes were going to destroy me.

"I'm sorry, come back here." My hand patted the bed beside me. "I don't like talking about it, but I can try."

She crept to the edge of the bed and sat, her cautious gaze focused. "When were you sick?"

"I found a lump here when I was sixteen." I pressed two fingers in the spot where the ink started, the chest area just to the front of my armpit. "Hodgkin's lymphoma."

Her back straightened and the word came out tainted with horror. "Cancer?"

"Yeah. Cancer." The illness had defined my life for years and nearly taken everything.

Her expression was heartbreaking. "But you're better?"

"I've been cancer free for twenty years. Well, technically in a week." Noemi didn't look like she had a clue what to say, which I understood. I didn't either. The silence that stretched was awkward.

"Oh," she said, her voice uneven. "You should do something to celebrate. Like a party or . . ."

"Not too many of my friends know about it." Her gaze examined mine, urging me to elaborate. "I haven't found a good way to say, 'Hey, cancer and chemo almost killed me when I was seventeen.' It derails the conversation fast."

Her eyes were sobering. "But that had to be a major part of your life. I mean, you beat cancer."

"Yeah. Wasn't easy." There was a colossal understatement.

She shook her head, like she was shaking away a weird thought. She climbed over the mattress top and straddled my lap in a surprising move. Her warm hands bristled on my five o'clock shadow as she took my jaw in her grip.

"I'm sorry you went through that." Her soft lips pressed to mine in a gentle kiss. "I'm glad you're here."

I could have made a joke, something about how she was just saying that because I was the only man who brought her to orgasm, but her words carried way too much sincerity. They tore me apart and yet made me feel warm. I was glad to be here, too.

With Noemi Rosso.

In my bed, in my arms, and working her way into my head. A strong case could be made that she was already there. I wrapped my arms tighter around her slender body, pressing her to me, and deepened the kiss.

When my fingers curled around her bra strap and inched it down, she sat back. "You said we should get dressed."

"I changed my mind."

She smiled, but pulled her strap up on her shoulder. "Um, I have class at eight tomorrow morning."

"Shit, I can't remember the last time I was up that early." I'd always been a night owl, so I didn't have a problem getting used to the club schedule.

"So, unless you're interested in doing that, I'm going to need you to take me home."

"I will. Eventually." I pulled the strap down and let my tongue trace the faint impression left by the elastic.

Her hands wove through my hair. "Can I ask you something?"

"Mm-hmm." I was too busy to use words. My mouth drifted lower, tracing the seams of her flimsy bra.

"What happened at the restaurant?"

I flinched. I'd told her that she wasn't supposed to lie during our arrangement, but what about me? I was such a selfish, fucking hypocrite.

"You looked nervous," she continued, "when you found out who my dad is."

I folded and took the cowardly route. "One of the biggest customers at my private wine club is Henry Katzenberg. He wants to invest in my businesses."

I didn't know how the bad blood between the Rossos

and the Katzenbergs started. A failed merger, or maybe it was employee poaching, but their feud was no secret in Chicago. Rumor was Katzenberg had walked out on a deal simply because he caught the opposing VP reading a Rosso-owned newspaper beforehand.

And telling her this wasn't technically a lie. Katzenberg was a sometimes client at the blindfold club. It was a huge reason why I only allowed one client in the hallway at any time. If either of the men saw each other it would be beyond disaster.

"Oh," she said, stiffening.

"So perhaps we could keep our arrangement between us."

She nodded. "That kind of goes without saying. I don't think my dad would be thrilled with the concept."

No shit. "Is that why you said yes to me?" I teased, although there was a little truth buried underneath. "You like fucking a man your daddy wouldn't approve of?"

I'd expected shock, but instead a seductive smile widened on her lips.

"Yes, I do like *fucking* you. Was that not clear . . . Sir?"

I dug my fingers into her flesh and yanked her into my kiss. I wanted her on her knees and my cock buried down her throat. Didn't matter that I wasn't hard yet. Chances were she'd rectify that situation instantly.

But she had class, and I had my own shit to take care of, and I didn't want to overwhelm her with too much, too soon. *Get control of yourself.*

Eventually I forced myself from the bed and stepped into my pants. I begrudgingly dressed and watched her do the same. I fought my dominant side, who was adamant that she stay naked and under my power.

"There," she said, when I'd pulled the Porsche up the block from where I'd picked her up from. "That's my building."

The upscale apartments had a beautifully lit awning and large glass doors where I could see the security desk just beyond. If she had told me this was her place that first night, I would have known in a second that something wasn't right. Middle-class couldn't afford to live here, and certainly not grad students.

Unless their father was the corporate king of Chicago.

chapter THIRTEEN

NOEMI

It was two in the morning, and I had to be up in a few hours. I lay in my bed, unable to sleep. My body was still wired from his touch, and my mind raced with thoughts. Sex with Joseph had once again been amazing, and I was sure this was only the beginning.

So instead of sleeping, I sat up, yanked my iPad off the nightstand, and unsnapped the cover. I knew next to nothing about being in a Dom/sub relationship, only what I'd read in a few steamy books. Google could help.

There was a new message in my Gmail account from Joseph.

> **I bet you like doing homework, good girl, so here's a Tumblr account I've set up for us. You'll go through the feed and reblog at least five posts every day that you like. What turns you on. Stuff you want to try. Things you want me to do to you. I'll watch your posts and we'll discuss nightly.**
> **Joseph**

Holy hell. I'd thought his request for my email was strange, but he explained that as his submissive, I was supposed to give him access to all parts of my life. I'd never been on Tumblr before, but it's not like I lived under a rock.

I knew what it was about. I clicked on the link, installed the app on my iPad, and let the feed load—

Holy shit.

The stepmom had caught me touching myself once when I was watching the hottest porn I had on my laptop, and it was one of those 'we'll never speak of this' moments. Just remembering it made me flush warm and filled me with shame.

That video wasn't anywhere near as hot as this. The screen filled with short clips, looping over and over. Men and women having sex, going down on each other, or touching everywhere. As I scrolled, some clips were more hardcore, featuring bondage, spankings, or riding crops. Occasionally there'd be a gorgeous, erotic black and white still shot.

Good God. It was overwhelming, and I wasn't going to get any sleep tonight.

My father's meeting was running long. I sat in one of the oversized leather chairs opposite his desk and surveyed his office. Little touches of his life were scattered amongst the workspace, more reminders of me than anyone else from our family. Part of that was probably an impending divorce; the picture of Grace was missing. But the other part was my father had let me redecorate his office last year, and deep down, Becca and I had each gravitated toward one parent. Grace had never been rude to me, but her lack of effort or concern about my feelings left me cold.

I was my father's daughter, all the way.

The afternoon sunlight warmed the office that was

done in glass and dark wood. My gaze floated over the bookshelf on the side, which was cluttered. I set about rearranging the books and knickknacks while I waited. If I sat too long, I might nod off, and who knew how long his meeting might go?

I'd tackled two shelves when he rushed in and squeezed me in a quick hug. "Sorry you had to wait."

"No problem. Who were you meeting with?"

"Programming department head."

"Oh. Yeah, those always seem to run over."

My father smiled and sat at his desk, moving his mouse to wake the computer up. "It's because that man can't ever stay on topic." His expression was amused. "Redecorating?"

"Just rearranging." I continued to shift the accent pieces around to find a better display.

"Before I forget," he said, "I've set your summer internship up. You'll assist Evans' group."

My hand paused on the glass award my father had won years ago for his newspaper. "Do I know Mr. Evans?" I asked.

"Maybe. He oversees customer service. He's a good manager you can learn a lot from."

I turned to face my father, who scanned his email, indifferent. Customer service wasn't where I wanted to be, and it wasn't what we'd discussed. "What happened to accounting?"

"This is a better position for both of us. You'll get experience you can't get elsewhere, and people are less likely to cry nepotism if I put you in a department that's desperate for help."

It was desperate for help because the department was a revolving door. Handling customer complaints was hard and thankless. I was staring at a long, unpaid summer.

"Is that okay?" he asked casually.

It wasn't, but what good would saying so? My mouth filled with the taste of disappointment. My father thought this was best, and it would be hard to convince him otherwise. Maybe I could go somewhere else and search for a paid internship in a department I was happy to work, but it wouldn't be for the company I wanted to run.

"Okay," I sighed.

"Great." He shut down his computer and stood. "Did you decide where we're going for lunch?"

If I had, would I have been overruled on that, too?

I sat at the empty table, my eyes burning with exhaustion and a headache from the musty books of the university library. I'd met with my study group in one of the quiet corners earlier this evening, and chose to stay after they'd gone to finish my assignments. The temptation to go to bed would have been too great if I tried to study at home, and I'd gotten my work done now, but I wasn't looking forward to the commute home.

There'd been immense pressure on selecting the five clips to repost on Joseph's Tumblr account. What if I picked something he didn't like? How would he judge my choices?

There'd been a clip I'd watched over and over last night, mesmerized. It was shocking, but in my sick fascination, I couldn't look away. The pretty girl, maybe my age, stood with her back against a wall in the black and white video, her eyes turned up to someone out of frame. She had perfectly-shaped breasts and metal clips fastened to each nipple, a thin silver chain draped between them. As the camera moved left, a man stepped into view and wrapped a fist on the chain, lifting and tugging. Her face twisted like it walked a line of pleasure and pain. Her jaw clenched, stifling back her cry or plea.

She ached, but her expression said she ached for him more.

I wanted to be the girl and wanted Joseph to be that man. I'd look up at him with the same longing and need she had. I felt it now. But I didn't dare repost the clip. How on earth could I? He'd think I was a freak.

I slipped my laptop into my backpack just as my phone began to ring. My stomach did a flip-flop at the caller ID.

"Hi," I said.

"Hey." Joseph's voice made me feel warm, yet nervous. "How was your day?"

"Good," I whispered. "And you?"

"Fine. Why are you whispering?"

It was silly, really. It was eleven at night and the place was a graveyard back here in the stacks. "I'm in a library."

He chuckled. "Studying hard, little girl?"

"I'm done now, actually, but yeah." I raised the volume of my voice to a hush. "There are less distraction here than at my place."

"What were you working on? Cost analysis on hearing aids for cows?"

I zipped up my bag and felt myself smiling. "International economics."

"Sounds riveting." He paused. "I see you got my email."

My throat constricted and I eked the word out. "Yeah."

"I'm not sure you understood the goal of the assignment."

I felt off-balance. How could that be possible? The good girl in me *never* underperformed. "I did exactly what you said." I'd spent forever selecting the perfect clips.

"Yes. I asked you to post five and you did that, but I'm guessing they weren't what you wanted to post." His voice was soft and somehow still authoritative. "Either you were playing it safe, or they were what you thought I wanted to see."

Holy shit, how did he know? I sat in the hard, wooden chair and stared at the shelves of books, unable to come up with a response or excuse.

"Tonight you'll drink a glass of wine or two, and try again. This time you post for yourself."

I honestly didn't know if I could. After what we'd done, this felt surprisingly intimate, like giving Joseph an all-access pass to my fantasies, even the dark ones I shouldn't have. I drew in a deep breath, struggling to communicate as I knew he wanted me to. "I'm nervous about that."

"Why? Are you worried I'm going to judge you?"

"Yes."

His voice grew heavy, like the phone was pressed closer to his face. "No, never. I chose which accounts to follow, so I have a good idea what's showing up in the feed. Noemi, there's nothing on there that I'm not into. Fuck, there's hardly anything on there I haven't *already done*."

I pressed my knees together as the clip flashed in my mind, only it was Joseph's hand tugging on the silver chain between my breasts.

"If you're only into the tame stuff, that's fine, but I don't see that girl when we're together. You're holding back."

"Maybe," I whispered, although it had nothing to do with the environment, and everything to do with him.

"Let the alcohol help you take the edge off, and try again. I can give you anything you want, all you have to do is ask. Understood?"

It was a million degrees in this library. "Yes."

"Good. Did you shave your pussy for me today?"

I gripped the edge of the table, even though I was seated. His filthy, crass words knocked me sideways. "I . . . yeah."

"How do you like being bare for me? Does it turn you on?" His voice felt like it was inside my head. "Did you walk around all day with your panties clinging to your wet cunt?"

Oh. My. God. "Yes," I said quickly. My face was on fire.

"Yes, *Sir*," he corrected. "Turn on FaceTime."

My pulse jumped to a thousand beats a minute. His command had a strict tone, hinting whatever was going to happen next would most likely be punishment for not addressing him properly. I tapped the icon on my screen, and he came into view a moment later. He was seated on his leather couch in his living room, his face unshaven.

He looked rough until his sexy mouth tugged into a half-smile. "Look at you, college girl. Makes me feel like an old man."

My hair was pulled up into a messy bun. I wasn't wearing my contacts, instead I had on my rectangular black frames. True to the stereotype, I had on a baggy Loyola sweatshirt, leggings, and no makeup. "Yeah, I know I look gross—"

"Shut your smart mouth. You'll wear those glasses next time we fuck." My insides turned to liquid. "Flip the camera around and show me where you are."

The chair creaked as I stood. I tapped the reverse icon

and panned my phone slowly. What was he doing? A thought flitted through my head and anxiety ratcheted tighter. He was checking to see if anyone was around.

"Take your stuff and go down one of those rows. All the way to the back."

The tremble in my belly increases when I did as asked, sensing what he was going to command me to do next. I set my backpack on the floor in the corner beside rows of case law books that looked like they hadn't been touched in years.

When I reversed the camera back to me, he didn't make me wait another second. "Show me your naked pussy."

I glanced around, checking for the hundredth time there wasn't anyone nearby. My face was burning. "This is a public place."

"Didn't stop you before," he reminded. "You agreed to this. You're mine, Noemi. To have and look at any time I want. Now."

The lighting was dim with the tall racks of books, but it felt like spotlights on me. I lifted up the bulky hem of the sweatshirt and pinned it against my body with my elbow, then slipped my fingers under waistband of my pants and panties, extending the phone down to my lower body. I pushed the fabric over a hip, then the other side, working the leggings down until they cut across mid-thigh. Cool air washed over my exposed, bare skin.

He could see every pale inch of my flesh, and he made a noise of approval. "Those pants go all the way down to your ankles, naughty girl."

"What?" I almost shrieked it. A quick flash was one thing, but getting caught with my pants down around my boots was another.

"You pull those goddamn pants down now or next time I'll spank you so hard you won't sit right for a week."

Heat burst through me and I got drunk off being under his control. I set the phone down on top of the books, yanked my pants down my legs until they were bunched around my suede boots, and fumbled to pick the phone back up, showing him I'd done it.

"Put your coat on the floor, sit on it, and get those knees open. I want to see how wet you are."

My shallow breathing made me lightheaded, so I was grateful not to have to stand any longer, but holy shit. What I was doing was dangerous. The wool of my coat was scratchy against my bare ass, but I didn't give it much attention. I spread my legs open as wide as the leggings would allow, and balanced the hand holding the phone on my bent knee, angling the camera to show him.

"You're so fucking hot, I can't stand it. Touch yourself."

Sensible Noemi who'd been shut down, screamed back to life. "If I get caught, they'll kick me out of school."

"Be quiet and hurry, and no one will catch you."

Crippling anxiety coursed through my veins. "I've never . . . done that with someone watching."

Joseph's face disappeared from screen as his phone panned down. His pants were undone, a fist wrapped around his dick, stroking himself. The slow glide of his hand up and down was hypnotic. I moaned, unable to contain my desire at the image.

"You like watching this, don't you?" he asked.

"Yes, Sir."

"Join me. *Show me.*"

My upper body was pressed against the painted

cinderblock wall, and I let my head tip back to rest there when my left hand moved off of my coat, and went between my legs.

I touched my damp, aching body, rubbing a circle on my clit. It felt like an electrical jolt, shocking me incredibly close to orgasm.

"You're so fucking naughty. Play with yourself for me." Joseph's voice was strained. "Yes. Fuck, yes, baby girl. Those are my fingers touching you. Faster."

"Oh my God." I trembled at the edge, watching his dick pump faster and faster through his tight fist. "I want that to be my hand."

"It is. It feels almost as good as your pussy. So tight."

I couldn't believe what I was doing. Wild and risky, and letting him see something I'd never shown anyone. I shuddered and lifted my hand to stifle a moan.

"Did I say you could stop?"

His angry words forced my hand back. Two fingers pressed tight to my clit, rubbing back and forth in a furious motion.

"You're gonna make me come, dirty girl. Is that what you fucking want?"

I stopped trying to analyze everything. "Yes, Sir."

"What about you? Are you going to come on those fingers or do you need a hard cock now, too?" His harsh words made me burn, the heat consuming. "I bet you could find some guy there to help you. Would you like that? Would anyone's cock do it for you, Noemi, or just mine?"

"Oh God, just yours. Only yours, Sir."

The view on my screen tilted abruptly, coming to rest angled up at his ceiling. "Fucking shit," he groaned. "Fuck!"

His strangled breathing while he came was erotic.

Heat built from my own touch, and I was breathing so hard my vision grew blurry. The phone slipped from my grasp and clattered to the floor. The tingling sensation descended on me, and then exploded like glass shattering on concrete. Fast and destructive.

That was us. Delicate, breakable me against strong, unmovable him. I melted into the wall, gradually recovering from his effect.

"Noemi? I can't see anything."

I shifted on my coat and grabbed the phone, thankful its case had saved it from damage. "Yeah, I'm here, hold on." I scrambled to pull my pants back up.

"You made me make a mess. If you were here, I'd tell you to clean it up."

I shuddered again and pressed one of my cool hands to my heated face before picking the phone back up. "I'd do it."

He grinned. "I bet you would. What's your schedule like tomorrow? Can you meet me for a late lunch, three o'clock?"

I fought to calm myself. What the hell had I just done? My racing heartrate reminded me I was alive, and I fucking loved it.

I nodded. "I don't have any classes after one."

"Okay, I'll pick you up at three, then. We can discuss whatever you've posted tomorrow in detail."

His voice was teasing, and yet we both knew he was serious.

chapter FOURTEEN

JOSEPH

Noemi wore purple-gray nail polish. It was noticeable when she used a finger to push those black frames up to sit higher on the bridge of her nose. She sat across the table from me at the restaurant as we waited for our lunches, her gaze never staying with mine too long. My sub was nervous.

"I can't decide," I said. "The glasses are hot, but I can't see your eyes when they're hiding behind them."

She gave me a tight smile. "Can you stop torturing me and just get on with it? I want to know how I did."

Her desire to do a good job made me laugh. Such an overachiever. She'd been fidgeting on the car ride over, so I'd set a hand on her leg and ordered her to relax. I'd been waiting for her to give me the signal that she was ready to have the conversation.

"You're not being graded, but since you asked..." I gave her a smile that I hoped conveyed how I felt. "I was very, very pleased."

More like I was fucking ecstatic. Her first series of posts were full of tasteful, vanilla sex. I'd woken up to a different tone today. A woman having her nipple clamps tugged on by her partner, a man fucking a woman in handcuffs and a blindfold. And her last clip... All the blood in my body had rushed straight to my cock.

A naked woman tied down to a bench, her ass being

flogged while men and women wearing black tie sat in a semi-circle watching the display. That on its own was pretty hot, but there was so much more. The submissive being flogged? She had her face buried in the pussy of another woman, whose cocktail dress was pushed up to her waist. A hand was on the back of the sub's head, holding her still while the flogger struck.

I understood why Noemi was nervous. It was a huge leap forward for her. For *us*.

"I want to know," I said while she took a sip, "which woman you would like to be in that last clip."

Noemi coughed softly as if choking on her drink. "Uh, which clip?"

"Don't stall, you know exactly what I'm talking about. The one where everyone was watching." None of the other clips had sex acts on display. Subtle color lit Noemi's face and she stared at the drink in her hand as if the ice cubes were made of diamonds.

"I don't know." Her voice was unsteady, but fell to whisper-quiet. "I thought it was really hot."

Fucking hell. She exceeded my hopes every time. "Do you think you could really do it? Would you obey if I told you to go down on another woman?"

Her lips pressed together and her chest rose as she took in a breath. "Maybe."

We were going to find out soon enough. I'd already put the wheels in motion. "How many glasses of wine did you have to medicate with last night?"

"Just the one." Her fingers drummed on the tabletop. "Are you going to post back?"

I paused. "On the account? I hadn't planned on it."

Her fingers stopped their tapping and her eyebrow rose upward. "How is that fair?"

"Not everything in life is fair." I shot her a pointed look.

"You sound like my father," she muttered.

My jaw clenched in annoyance. I didn't need the reminder of who her father was, or the comparison. "Well, I'm certainly not your *daddy*."

She glared at me through those sexy glasses. "If you want me to keep posting stuff, you're going to have to, too."

I could feel my blood pressure rising. "You misunderstand how this works—"

"I'm not going to put my secret desires out there for you to just scrutinize and enjoy. Not unless you're going to give me access to some of yours, too."

People didn't tell me what to do, certainly not my submissive. "No, Noemi."

There was fire in her eyes. "Why the hell not?"

"Because it'd frighten you." It would scare her away and I wasn't ready for this thing between us to be over.

Her posture straightened and her expression went narrow. "You're worried I'll judge you?"

"Yes." Absolutely yes. My kink was too much for her.

"Joseph, I'm trusting you not to judge me, why can't you trust me to do the same? Isn't this arrangement supposed to be built on trust?"

Fucking shit. I was already hiding so much from her. "Maybe you have a point."

What she was asking for wasn't physically hard. And in the long run, this could be another tool to use to push her boundaries. To encourage her to expand her limits. I could find clips that only hinted at the worst and give her a taste.

"Fine," I said. "I'll do it, but remember you asked for this. Also, I don't care for the way you just talked back to me. You treat me with respect, little girl, or you get disciplined." I let my expression go hard. "I can punish you right now, or we can wait until we're in private." I glanced around. "We do seem to have a thing for restaurants, but it's your choice."

Her hand curled into a fist and she drew in a harsh breath. Last night she'd driven me mad with her obedience. If she chose here, what would she let me do? A blowjob in the women's bathroom? My cock hadn't been inside her hot mouth yet.

She shook her head subtly. "Later."

Later would work just as well, but my cock ached with dissatisfaction. I needed to stop thinking about her on her knees, sucking me off. "Were you always a good girl before you met me?"

"You'd probably say so . . . *Sir*."

She didn't have to address me like that when we were out in public. Noemi wasn't my slave. That kind of arrangement didn't interest me, and I'm sure it didn't interest her. Having 24/7 control over someone else was too demanding, and I already had enough fulltime jobs.

No, she was mocking me. "You're only making it worse on yourself," I said in a low voice. "Who were you, good girl? Straight A's and home by curfew every night?"

She shrugged. "I didn't drink, or smoke, or do drugs. I didn't have sex."

Yeah, she gave that honor to some asshole named Ross. A week with me and hopefully she'd forget his name.

"I never skipped school," she said, "or got in trouble. I never lived a life outside of the rules. I never lived at all."

"Until now." I smirked.

"Yeah, well," her eyes gleamed, "nothing lasts forever." We were interrupted briefly when the server delivered our food and then flitted off. "What about you? Were you always this . . . bossy?"

"No." I stared down at my plate as a foreign emotion seized me. A need I couldn't understand, or stop. "You can thank the cancer for that."

Her eyes widened. Why the fuck was I bringing this up?

"I spent the better part of a year doing exactly what everyone else told me to do. Doctors, nurses, my parents. All of them saying what drugs to take, when I could eat, or sleep, or piss . . . It got really fucking old."

"The time in your life when you didn't have control."

"Yes. I wound up with pneumonia when my immune system had been obliterated. The doctor told my parents only one out of three survive something like that. Right in front of me, he's telling them to start preparing themselves."

It didn't look like Noemi was breathing. She'd turned into a living statue. *Stop talking, Joseph.*

"I'd been out of school for months by this point. It was already a fact that I wouldn't graduate on time. My friends stopped coming by the hospital when my hair was gone and my weight went below a hundred. High school kids can be shallow and self-centered, and I couldn't blame them. I looked dead already."

Her hand drifted up to cover her mouth. I sat back in my chair, my appetite starting to wane.

"So I had a, I don't know, a moment of fucking clarity. I'd make it through the pneumonia, because nothing lasted forever, and afterward, I'd be the one in charge of my life.

Just me." I tore my gaze from hers, staring out the large window where people hurried past, living their lives.

The tension between us was suffocating.

My gaze finally returned to her. She was staring at her hands in her lap. Why did I let the conversation get so fucking heavy?

"Having everything taken away from you teaches you who you really are." The thought stormed into my mind. "You want that from me? To take away your control so you can find yourself?"

She took an enormous breath and blinked her clear eyes. "Maybe."

"I think you already know who you are, you're just afraid to let her out of the cage."

She gave me a half-smile that said she didn't believe me.

Conversation moved to lighter topics after that. Her lack of plans for spring break. Her terrible taste in music, and yet excellent taste in movies. My overpriced car was still a sore spot for her.

"You realize you live in Chicago, right?" she asked. "When the roads aren't under construction or clogged with traffic, they're covered in potholes and snow. Let me guess—you bought it for the spacious interior so you could make out with random girls you met at your club."

"Making out with you wasn't what I had in mind that night."

She gave me a knowing smile. "There's even less room for that."

"We would have been fine." I could have us try it sometime just to prove my point, but containing sex with Noemi in that small of a space would frustrate me. I didn't want any restrictions. "My brother had sex in the backseat of a Mini-Cooper once, or so he said, so it's possible."

"Your brother," she asked. "What's he like?"

"A normal big brother. A pain in the ass when he wants to be, but he's mostly grown out of it. He actually called me the other day and invited me out to visit." I took my napkin out of my lap and set it on the table. "He's receiving an award from the Navy. His squadron had twelve hundred hours of flight time without incident."

"Are you going to go?"

I ran a hand over my jaw. I hadn't seen Conner in a while. "It's a long flight to Hawaii."

"I'm sure he knows that. If he invited you, it'd probably mean a lot to him if you went. I was raised to believe family is important. You make time for them."

Once again, she had a point. "My schedule's a bitch to work around."

Her expression shifted to amusement. "You have time for me."

Before something cheesy came out of my mouth, my phone rang, a number I didn't recognize. It was the property manager of a building I was interested in by the lake. The owner had been giving me the runaround about scheduling a showing, and the manager said he could fit me in, but only if it was right now.

Noemi mentioned she didn't have any more classes for the day.

"Fine," I told the manager. "I can be there in twenty minutes."

She watched as I pocketed the phone, an expectant look on her face. "I guess you'll save my punishment for another time?"

I scribbled my signature on the bill and rose to my feet. "Delayed. We have to make a stop first."

On the car ride over, Noemi pulled her blonde hair back into a ponytail.

"Now instead of looking twelve, I look fourteen," she muttered.

I chuckled. "Come on, you at least look legal."

"Great, thanks. Maybe don't call me little girl while we're in there." She closed the visor and turned to me. "Can you tell me about the property?"

I explained how the space was set up. A large parcel on the main floor for leasing as retail space, and currently offices above.

"The plan is to renovate the office space into luxury apartments."

"Condos?" Her voice had a hint of disdain.

"It's a great location."

"There's no money in property management."

I glanced at her, surprised. "That's a blanket statement." And unreasonable coming from her. "What about what your father is doing? I heard he bought a place in the loop. Don't tell me he's moving closer to the city."

"He's not." Her voice was flat. "That's for Grace and Becca."

Shit, of course. Her stepmother and half-sister. "Your sister went with her?"

"Yeah." Noemi's voice was soft and sad. "My dad's on his own now. It's hard."

I didn't want to think about Mr. Red as a heartbroken husband. I tried to pretend there wasn't a connection between him and Noemi, but this was her father. He played such a major role in her life; it seemed shitty not to make an effort. "Can I ask what happened?"

"I'm not sure. Grace's always been a puzzle. I don't know what he sees in her, or what he saw in my mother. Grace hasn't cared about him for years, but once my dad falls in love, he can't see anything." She played with the clasp on her purse, mindless. Always fidgeting. "He's totally oblivious to her faults."

Noemi would never know just how right she was. It didn't matter how many times Payton had told Mr. Red she didn't do love, he'd fallen for her anyway.

"Don't worry, Joseph." She gave me a sweet smile. "I didn't inherit that trait."

"I'm not worried. We both know you're much too smart to fall in love with me."

chapter FIFTEEN

NOEMI

The showing was a joke, and Joseph was pissed. He'd been used in a negotiations battle between the property owner and the tenant currently in the space. We'd stormed out of the office building, and I'd climbed into the front seat of the Porsche, grateful to be away from the Realtor before anything unprofessional came out of my mouth. Always think before acting, my father lectured me. Think about the brand.

"We're not going to your place?" I asked, breaking the tense silence when Joseph exited the expressway.

"No, I'll drop you at yours."

His gruff voice wasn't my fault, but it set me on edge. "Drop me off? What about—"

"That's not a good idea. I'm not in the right mindset, thanks to those fuckers."

He'd unleashed a craving in me that I couldn't ignore. The sexual tension from lunch twisted like rope around my body, and I needed him to cut me free, to release me. I still struggled at being bold, but I'd done it before. I angled my shoulders toward him, reached my hand out, and set my palm flat against his zipper, running down the length of him.

He didn't fight me, but it sounded as if he were gritting it out. "What are you doing?"

"What do you think I'm doing, Sir?"

"I think you're trying to push me, and I don't fucking

like it. Knock it off."

Beneath my slow moving hand, the bulge grew and thickened. His mouth said no, but below his belt it was all yes.

"If I don't do as I'm told," I whispered, "what happens?"

He glanced my direction for the briefest of moments, but it was long enough for my heart to skip. At the showing, he'd turned his ruthless glare on the property manager and the man had gone ashen. Now the glare was fixated on me, only it swirled with desire. Similar to the devouring look he'd given me in this car our first night, only now the look was amplified by a thousand.

"By all means," his hand covered mine, "keep pushing and find out."

I teetered at the edge, unsure which was the right decision. What he wanted was unclear, whether I should be bad and disobey so he could discipline, or if he was actually pissed and I should leave him alone. The good girl would retreat and put her hands folded neatly in her lap. She wouldn't keep rubbing his dick through his jeans, and she most definitely wouldn't say what I was about to.

"I want you to fuck me. Do I have to be bad for that to happen?"

His eyes hooded and the hand on mine clenched so hard it was almost painful. "You want this cock inside you, you filthy slut?"

I mentally stumbled over his words. Once again, his mouth put me off and turned me on. No one talked to me like that, and I liked it. I steadied my breathing, but my voice wavered. "Yes, I want you inside me."

"Unzip and get it out."

What the hell was he talking about? "You want me to..."

He took a hand off of the wheel so he could unbutton and unzip his jeans. "Since you don't know how to control your mouth, I'll do it for you."

My body tensed when his thick, erect dick was freed through the open fly of his boxers. I didn't get time to react. Joseph wrapped a fist around my ponytail and yanked my head down, putting my face in his lap.

It was after five and the sun was setting, but it was still bright outside. His straight, hard dick was an inch from my face, and he'd made it very obvious what I was supposed to do. "Someone might see," I whispered.

"Great. I'm sure they'll enjoy watching you suck me off, but not as much as I will."

Why did the idea of a stranger watching me do this turn me on so badly? There was something wrong with me, but at least Joseph seemed to feel the same way about getting caught. We could be wrong together.

The center console dug into my stomach, but I wrapped my fingers around him and licked my lips to wet them. God, he was so big, how was this going to work? How would it be pleasurable for him with so little of it fitting inside my mouth? *It's because he gets off on the power.*

The tip of his flesh was soft as silk against my tongue, and a quiet groan came from above. Heat flashed down to my toes, encouraging me to take him.

When I did, this groan was louder and so much sexier.

His warm flesh slid against my tongue, until he filled my mouth, all the way to the back of my throat. I pulled back, using suction as I retreated.

"Shit. Use your tongue."

I began to bob on him, swirling my tongue over the fat

head of his dick. Up and down, I let him possess my mouth. His hand covered mine that gripped him at the base, and he squeezed, showing me he wanted more pressure. His commands, verbal and non-verbal, were all over me. It was like Joseph owned every inch.

His breathing picked up and his words grew hurried. "You can take me deeper."

I relaxed as much as possible, forcing my way further down, and . . . I pulled back abruptly, all the way off of him, and struggled to catch my breath. I'd gotten embarrassingly close to gagging audibly, and my eyes flicked up to his.

His smile was diabolical. "We'll work on that."

His hand, which had been resting on the back of my neck, moved so he could pluck the glasses off of my face and gently toss them on the flat spot of the dashboard. I didn't mind. I was already a strung-out mess inside, aching and desperate like a hopeless addict. Not being able to see every detail was a good thing, and I closed my eyes anyway when I skimmed my tongue over the slit of his dick. I opened my mouth and wrapped my lips around his hard flesh.

My purse was on the floorboard, and my phone began to ring. It didn't slow me down. There was no way I was going to answer it. My head bumped against the steering wheel as I tried to move at a faster pace, reminding me where we were. This time when I looked up at him, I had him lodged as deep as possible in my mouth. Without my glasses, I could only see a blurry version of him, one hand on the wheel, his gaze forward. His expression was intense. Pausing on him must have drawn his attention. His gaze shifted to mine.

"You look so perfect with my cock in your mouth. I don't know if I ever want to take it out."

The moan slipped out from me and filled the quiet interior. It was like a starting pistol on him. His hand tugged my ponytail, forcing me to go faster. And faster. Control began to swing away from me when his hips moved in a rhythm, pumping against me.

He fucked my mouth. Hard, and fast, sometimes skating dangerously close to my reflex.

"Goddamnit. Fuck." His hand left the wheel and went to his forehead—the car had stopped moving. When had that happened? I rose up to peer out the window and wiped the saliva from my lips. We were parked on the street a block down from my apartment building.

His dick was still clenched in my hand, and I looked at him. Was I supposed to finish him here? There were parking cops that patrolled the street all the time. If we got caught, it'd be public indecency.

Think about the brand, Noemi.

I could be bad, but the last thing my family needed was another PR nightmare, especially so soon after Becca's. My father was strong, but he could only take so much. I stared at Joseph's dark eyes, silently pleading he wouldn't put me in a position where I'd have to say no.

"We'll continue this upstairs." He threw open his door and buttoned his long coat, hiding the effects of my blowjob.

Thank God we're going upstairs. I grabbed my glasses, scrambled out onto the sidewalk, and hurried alongside him to the front door.

"Afternoon, Ms. Rosso," the front desk clerk said. He scanned Joseph with interest, but said nothing.

I nodded a hello and ushered Joseph into the elevator, anxious to get him inside my place. The dull, chrome doors shut, sealing us in together, and I stared at his reflection. There were a lot of things I wanted from Joseph, and right now it was to see his clothes on my floor and his tattoo clenched under my hand, his chest slick with sweat.

I dug my phone out and checked the missed call. Ross. He hadn't left a message.

Joseph said nothing, and every floor the elevator climbed, I felt my pulse rising with it. Tension thickened like liquid and filled my lungs. What waited for me on the other side of my apartment door, when I was alone with my Dom?

I swallowed a breath when the doors peeled back, and he followed me down the narrow hall to my apartment door on the end. There was no biting comment about how I had a corner unit on the top floor, one of the most expensive apartments in the building. Joseph's silence and stiff posture were a warning. There'd been hints that something dark lingered below the surface, and it seemed ready to appear.

My hand shook as I put the key in the lock, and he shoved me out of the way, doing it himself to speed us along. I stepped inside, flipped on the light, and the door banged shut behind us. He scanned the room quickly as if looking for something specific, while taking off his coat and tossing it on the back of the couch that jutted out into the room.

The apartment was spacious and boho-chic, and like his, I hoped every inch of it announced it was mine. I enjoyed picking out the little details which made the place my home. Ross had laughed at me when I'd bought mismatched furniture, but I loved the eclectic look. "Do you want the tour?" I asked, my voice faltering as I tried to echo back his confidence when I'd first been in his place.

"No. Strip."

I exhaled loudly. His intense expression fed into my excitement, and my hands began tugging at my clothes, never mind that we were standing in my living room. The coat came off first. Then the top, followed by the jeans, one leg at a time, and I tossed the clothes beside his coat on my oversized couch. I was already out of breath as I reached for my bra clasp. It sprang free, but his hand came up in a gesture that said for me to stop when I reached for my panties.

"That's enough. I'll take those off."

Yes. I trembled, beyond ready for his touch. Soft lighting glowed from my kitchen, and it made Joseph look darker. Rougher. His hard edge grew in the shadows of his gorgeous face. It was fascinating.

Cool hands locked onto my waist, slipped to the back, and traveled down. I gasped when one of those hands grabbed the back of my underwear and yanked up. *Hard.* It forced the lace deep in my cleft and between my cheeks, an uncomfortable feeling like he was going to split me in two.

"You seem to have forgotten your place, little girl," he said. "Who's in charge here?"

My hands fell on his chest, balling his shirt into my fists. "You, Sir. You're in charge."

"Who do you belong to, Noemi? Who owns this pretty, little ass?"

He yanked so hard on the underwear I heard stitches ripping, and I rose up onto the balls of my feet to get relief. It catapulted me into his arms.

"You, Sir," I cried.

His mouth slammed against mine. Oh my God, it was so hot. He kissed me like he both hated and loved me, and I clung to him, unable to stand on my own. His untamed kiss was paralyzing yet freeing, a contradiction I was beginning to love. Sinking into him relieved me of choices and decisions. All I had to do was submit and feel.

His rough hands released and shoved me so I stumbled backward.

"I'm going to make sure you don't forget." His angry, aggressive tone paled in comparison to his actions. He undid his belt and pulled the leather strap free from the loops in one swift motion.

Oh my God. Oh, shit.

I was sure when I was little I'd been spanked when I was bad, but never anything serious. My father's approach had been subtle. Telling me he was disappointed was far more effective that corporal punishment. An invisible hand squeezed me and made my lungs useless as Joseph folded the belt in half.

"Are you going to hit me with that?" I asked, barely a whisper.

"It depends," he folded the strap in half again, "entirely on you. Open your mouth."

It was easy enough. It was hanging open anyway. He took the folded belt and shoved it between my lips. The smell of leather invaded my nose and the taste was bitter.

"Bite down," he ordered. My teeth closed on the soft leather. "Good." Fingers burrowed under the lace and pulled my panties down. Once again I was stark naked and he was fully clothed . . . except for the belt he'd shoved in my mouth.

He walked me around so I was facing the front of the couch and guided me forward. I had to put my knees on the couch cushions.

"Lean over the back of the couch." A hand pressed in

my back, urging me into position. "You keep that belt right where I put it. If you drop it or use your hands, Noemi, that's you giving me permission to use it however I want."

I shuddered with anticipation. How did he want it? I imagined it slapping against my pale skin. What would that feel like? Why did I want to know? Already my jaw ached from clenching, my lips were uncomfortable, and saliva pooled in my mouth.

His hands gripped my ass that was up, as if presented to him, since my elbows were on the back of the couch.

"We're going to find a limit today, baby girl. I'll take you right to the edge and nudge you over."

Fingers caressed down my slit, brushing over where I hurt for him, and I moaned against the leather. The finger intruded, just the tiniest bit inside, and stopped. I waited for him to do something, but he remained motionless. I pushed my hips back, taking it deeper.

"So eager," he said. "All right, go on. Fuck my fingers, slut."

Two fingers shoved inside me and I had to draw in my breath through my nose. The slut comment was shockingly thrilling. I wasn't a slut for anyone but him.

I worked my body on his fingers, riding them slow at first, but it did nothing to satisfy the heat inside. I wanted more. I *needed* more, yet I couldn't ask for it. If I tried to talk, the belt might fall from my teeth, and then . . . what? Did I want that to happen? *Yes*, a dark part of me answered.

The fingers abruptly retreated from my body, and I moaned at the broken connection. Joseph grabbed his coat and dug in one of the pockets, pulling out a black drawstring pouch.

"You'll wear this whenever I tell you to, but we'll see how it fits right now."

I blinked at the small bag, confused. What could I wear that would fit in something so small? He opened the bag and dumped a silver object into his hand. It was shaped sort of like an acorn, with a thin stem that grew to a wide, jeweled disk.

Last week I wouldn't have known what it was, but I did now. I'd seen plenty of them on Tumblr. My teeth dug harder into the leather strap as Joseph disappeared from view. I was going to leave marks on his belt, but he'd probably like that.

The oh-so-annoying tremble began in my legs when his hand touched the small of my back. His softly calloused hand trailed down.

"Always so fucking wet. Don't you like that bare pussy? You get any more turned on and it'll be running down your leg." He rubbed his hand over my pussy and then it was gone. Oh God. He was lubing the plug with my own moisture. The tremble graduated from my legs to a full body shudder when he pulled a cheek to the side and something foreign began to press down on my other entrance.

"Are you going to let me put this in your ass, you filthy girl? Or are you going to tell me to wait?"

I inhaled sharply and shook my head, and then made a nervous noise as the belt almost broke free of my hold, but thankfully stayed in my mouth. I locked my teeth tighter, and—

Oh!

Pressure and stretching as the plug advanced. Oh my God, I *was* filthy. So fucking dirty. I moaned against the belt.

The stretch got worse, but then, better. Discomfort passed to only a weird sensation.

"Shit, Noemi, you're amazing. You look so hot like this. How does it feel? You like it?"

I did, and I couldn't believe it. I was the girl who turned off a porn clip anytime the concept of anal was hinted at. To me, it was dirty and gross and wrong.

I didn't feel that way now. All I felt was pride at Joseph's words. Pleasing him gave me so much pleasure, and I craved more. I nodded my head to confirm I liked it, but I'd been foolish. In my excitement, I'd loosened my grip, and one side of the belt tumbled from my lips.

chapter SIXTEEN

Gravity took effect and caused the rest of the belt to fall. It hit the floor with a thump, even as I reached out to grab it. It slipped through my fingers.

"Shit!" I said.

I froze, unable to breathe.

"Pick it up," Joseph's voice was total authority, "and hand it to me."

Oh my God! The plug was still inside me, and I could feel it as I leaned over and snatched the belt from the floor. It was an odd sensation, not unpleasing, but I could hardly focus on anything but what was going to happen next. I'd wondered about this for so long, and now he was finally going to give it to me.

I extended the belt out behind my back, not able to look at him. I didn't want him to see that I was nervous, and stop. The fascination in me grew larger every second. He took the belt and I tucked my hair behind an ear, struggling to keep myself together. The anticipation was making me insane.

Joseph's steady breathing was all I could hear, and I flinched when the leather touched the bare skin of my ass, only he was gently caressing me.

"I get off on this, baby girl. Watching you tremble makes my cock so fucking hard." The belt smoothed over my skin. "You dropped it on purpose, didn't you? You want my marks on you. Yes?"

I clenched my hands on the couch back, squeezing until

my hands ached, and slammed my eyes shut.

The belt cracked against his hand, making me jump. "Answer me."

"I want to know what it feels like." I wanted him to *show* me. "Put your marks on me." An alarm sounded in my head. I hadn't said Sir, and I'd just given *him* an order. "Wait, wait—"

The leather slapped against my skin and air left me in a burst. It stung, but it wasn't any worse than when he'd spanked me. Warmth rushed to the skin, and as I'd hoped, the heat brought more desire with it.

"You have an issue with that word, and I'm moving past it. If you want me to stop, you say stop. That's a command I'll always respect, but otherwise you don't ever get to tell me what to do. That includes telling me to wait. Understood?"

"Yes, Sir."

His hand rubbed over the warm spot he'd created with his lash. "Are you telling me to stop?"

I couldn't keep up with the game he was playing, he was so much better than I was. He'd asked a seemingly simple question, but it was loaded as hell. Not telling him to stop was permission to continue, to strike me again. But I wanted it. Perhaps I even needed it.

My voice was shockingly strong. "I'm not telling you to stop."

I'd swear I could hear the whoosh of the belt cut through the air before it fell against my flesh, making tears spring into my eyes that I blinked back. Holy shit. That one hurt. The bite lingered on my skin and ached, telling me that I was his. The effect was powerfully intense, and while I loved it, it was overwhelming.

I pushed upright and turned to face him, the word *wait* on my lips, but it died as he kissed me. More like, he devoured me. He used everything he had to own me, his lips, his tongue, his teeth. I could kiss this man the rest of my life and never feel like I'd experienced all of it. It was a powerful distraction, and I didn't notice his hands still had the belt, or that they were moving upward until he slipped the strap behind my neck.

"Get on your knees."

I stepped down off the couch and fell to my knees. My mind didn't have to approve the action, I was under his spell. I stared up at his intense eyes as he threaded the end of the belt through the buckle and pulled, cinching the belt around my throat.

"Suck my dick."

Holy fucking God, who was I? A plug in my ass, a belt around my throat like a leash. I should have been horrified and shivering with fear, not shaking with excitement. My hurried hands worked his zipper, yanking the jeans down to his knees, then the black cotton I found beneath. His gorgeous dick bounced when I freed it, swinging toward me. I closed my mouth on the tip of his cock, sliding down as far as I could.

The strap around my neck constricted. He rolled his fist on the leather, his grip firm on the end of the belt.

"Where's that shy girl now?" he whispered. "Did my cock chase her away?"

Yes, in a way, but it wasn't just the sex. The confidence I was building with him bled over into other aspects of my life. The entire man made me feel alive and powerful. He was in charge when it happened, but I was the one who said what could and could not take place, and that meant deep down I was the one with the most control.

He groaned and thrust himself into my throat, the collar on my neck keeping me from running from him. I had to stay still as he sawed his dick in and out, shoving it past my lips with a driving tempo. He pulsed and throbbed on my tongue.

"Fuck, yes." He curled a hand on the back of my head, and pushed me forward.

Too far. Way, way, too far. I gagged loudly and he released his hold, letting me pull back off of him. I put a hand over my lips, needing a moment to regroup.

"Stop," I whispered. It had barely been a word, yet it changed everything. Joseph dropped down to kneel in front of me, bringing us level again, and it was as if he couldn't get his clothes off fast enough. He tore his shirt over his head and kicked off the jeans on his ankles.

He buried his face in my throat, kissing just above where the belt hung on my neck. "You belong to me." He mumbled it between kisses, his hands roaming over my curves. "Shit, Noemi, say it."

I felt hazy and weightless. "I belong to you," I rasped.

It was the first time I could really touch and explore a naked Joseph. His smooth skin belonged under my hands. If I belonged to him, he belonged to me as well. Did he know that? My hand coursed down the ink on his toned arm. *Mine. All mine.*

We were wild animals pawing at each other, until he broke the kiss. "Where's the bedroom?"

I gestured to the hall, and suddenly he tugged on the belt, pulling me forward. I put my hands out to stop myself, bent on all fours.

"Crawl."

My mind went blank. "What?"

Joseph stood and pulled on the belt. "Crawl."

No part of me found this sexy. It was demeaning. "No." When I tried to get off my knees, a hand locked on my shoulder and kept me down.

"No? Did I ask if you wanted to crawl or did I tell you to do it?"

"I'm not going to—" He spanked me, and with the plug still inside, I felt the impact both inside and out. This was the first moment I'd been overwhelmed by his domination.

"I gave you a command. Obey. You can't crawl twenty goddamn feet?"

The longer I was on my hands and knees, the more nervous I got. "I'm not a dog."

He yanked on the belt. "I never said you were. You're my submissive, Noemi. So *submit*."

"Why?"

"You don't get to ask why. You do it because it pleases me."

It was a power trip. I stared down the hall. It was the longest twenty feet of my life as I crawled on my hands and knees, my bare breasts swinging as I moved. He walked beside me, the leather strap in his hand. My leash.

But he'd asked for control and I'd consented, and I knew there would be things he wanted that I wasn't comfortable with. Joseph said he was going to push. This was degrading, but not hard to actually do, and I'd said I wasn't going to judge him. His job was my pleasure, and my job was pleasing him.

We'd barely made it through the doorway before he put

a hand under my arm, helping me to my feet, the belt dropping slack.

"No one has ever submitted to me like that," he said, pressing me against the wall, his breath hot beside my ear. "You're a fucking revelation."

His mouth descended on mine at the same moment he embraced me and made it all worth it. I'd crawl through hell for his kiss.

My unmade platform bed filled the room, but Joseph didn't lead me to it. There was an enormous full-length mirror I'd purchased at an estate sale last summer which I'd propped up against the wall, and he turned me to face it.

"Is it anchored?" he asked as he put his hands on mine, placing my palms on the cold glass. "I don't want it to kill us both, although I could think of worse ways to die."

"It's anchored."

I could not stop staring at the reflection of us. My blonde hair was disheveled and the end of the belt hung between my breasts. Behind me, his tattooed skin and lust-filled expression loomed. My hooded eyes searched for his in the mirror.

"Do you believe me when I tell you as your Dom, your safety is the most important thing?"

"Yes, Sir." His lips ghosted over the curve of my neck, causing shivers and goosebumps. Was he really that concerned about the mirror falling on us? One hand cupped my breast and the other traced down my body until it teased between my legs. Watching him touch me was hotter than molten lava.

"And you trust me?" he asked.

I nodded, distracted by both the visual and the sensation

of his movements.

"I'm clean, Noemi. I *always* use condoms unless I'm in an arrangement and know we're both all right. You'd be safe if you said it was okay for me not to wear one."

I tensed. "Now is when you ask if I'm on the pill?"

"No, we don't have to worry about that."

His hand stirred faster and I shuddered. How could we not worry about it? It was the whole reason my parents leaped into their ill-fated marriage. "Joseph—"

"They had to use aggressive radiation. I can't get you pregnant."

I died a little, hearing what had been taken away from him. Another thing beyond his control. "You can't have kids?"

His movements slowed to a stop and his gaze found mine, his expression uncomfortably blank. "I can, just not the old fashioned way. I don't want to talk about that right now." The fingers stirred and I twitched in response. "I want to talk about whether you want me to put on a condom, or if I can fuck this pussy with nothing between us."

Joseph's control was everything to him. He wouldn't put himself in a position to get sick and have more taken away. And even though I believed him absolutely, I *was* on birth control, too. His hard dick pressed against me, slipping in the hollow between my legs, so he could rub against my clit. The skin on skin contact caused my eyes to roll back in my head. *Think about how good it will feel* . . .

I took a hand from the mirror, reached between my legs, and tried to guide him inside. He nudged my hand out of the way and took over, positioning me better so he could bring us together. The head of his dick pushed past my entrance and I gasped. The sensation with the plug . . . it felt good and distracted from the initial discomfort whenever Joseph crept inside.

He was so much bigger than what I was used to. It's not like he was going to rip me in half, but my body needed time to adjust, and he always seemed aware.

"Jesus," he said, letting out a long, deep sigh. "You feel so, fucking, *good*."

Our breathing synchronized as he drew back and then gently pushed forward, all the way in.

"Fuck," I whispered, unable to control my mouth. His dirty words were rubbing off on me.

"I'm about to lose my damn mind and fuck you senseless. Get ready."

I lowered my face closer to the mirror, supporting myself better on my hands and putting my body in a more submissive position. Wordlessly asking for him to do what he'd said he was about to.

When he started, my heart pounded in my chest and thudded so loudly I wondered if he could hear it over the smack of our bodies together. My moans swelled as his steady, furious rhythm did. Every deep thrust touched the plug, reminding me of its filthy presence.

I throbbed and trembled, wanting the wave of pleasure he'd been able to coax out of me before. But he'd had battery-powered help last time. Would he touch me? Could his fingertips sliding on my clit while he pounded into me be enough to get me there?

"I want your hand between my legs, Sir," I said breathlessly. "Please."

Heat flashed in his eyes and a thrilled smile crossed his lips. "You asked so nicely."

I moaned when he touched me. His thrusts sent me further forward until I had my forearms against the glass, and I clenched my hands into fists. Oh, God, it felt so good. My eyes closed and I gave over to the sensations.

The leather strap was swinging with his thrusts, so I pushed it over my shoulder, wanting it out of the way. He groaned and my muscles clenched. The belt around my throat began to tighten. What? My eyes fluttered open and went wide, realizing . . . oh God, when I'd put the belt over my neck, did he think—?

Yes, he did. The leather constricted and dug into my skin. It was uncomfortable, and the pressure on my windpipe made it even harder to breathe, and yet, it was unbelievable how badly I wanted him to go tighter. I stared at him through the mirror, my face full of need, and he watched me right back, his expression intent. Focused. His deep eyes seemed to study every attempt I made for air.

"If you want to stop," he ordered, "open your hands."

The belt tightened, the buckle biting into the side of my throat. I couldn't breathe at all, and my mind began to turn, inching toward panic. My vision narrowed to a tunnel and blurred until we were nothing but blurry, faceless shapes. There was no way I could speak or tell him to stop, so I slapped an open hand against the mirror. I was going to pass out, any second now—

"Fuck, fuck . . . *oh fuck*!" I screamed as the belt released its choke. Only I wasn't screaming in pain or anger. I was coming. I shattered with ecstasy so powerful it made my legs buckle and my eyes slam shut. Behind my eyelids, stars exploded and everything went tingly numb. The numb alternated to heat as if standing in a blast furnace, then back to arctic cold, with bliss layered on top of it all.

My scream faded to moans, as I just kept coming. My body broke apart, and Joseph gripped me tightly. He held me together as my mind disconnected from the rest of me and floated off to someplace else where everything felt like warmth and pleasure.

While I drifted in the space, he slowed to almost a halt, buried deep. His hands freed the belt from my neck and it thudded to the carpet. Then, he caressed me, slow and leisurely with wicked hands.

"Did I make you come too hard, baby girl? Your filthy mouth makes me think so."

My body was still a shell while the rest of me remained floating above, so I couldn't respond. I felt him gently pull the plug free and drop it to the floor. This time when he began to move, it was for him. Each thrust he gave tugged me back to reality until I was completely present again.

I blinked my sluggish eyes at him and he gave me a smoldering look. His cock grew harder inside me and his hands, which had settled on my waist, gripped me fiercely. Fingers burrowed into my skin. Listening to his rapid, uneven breathing was so hot. I craved his orgasm, wanting him to reach the same peak he'd given me.

Joseph groaned as he drove into my body with a violent thrust, and it seemed to break the dam he'd built to hold himself back. Inside, I could feel the pulse of his release, mimicked by his moans as he came. Heat and satisfaction flooded down my spine and settled in my belly.

He stilled. We remained like that for a long moment, our hurried breathing the only communication between us, telling the other how deep the pleasure had been. He pulled out slowly, but didn't release his hold on me. Instead I found myself pulled up against his chest, his lips beside my ear.

"Are you okay?"

I was a hell of a lot better than okay, but words didn't come easy. "Yes, Sir."

"Are you dizzy?"

I didn't get a chance to answer. He scooped me up into his arms and walked to the bed, taking a knee so he could set me down on the sheets. What was the expression on his face? I put my palm on his cheek. "What's wrong?"

"That was too much. We should have talked about all of that beforehand. I put a lot on you."

His expression—this was guilt? It didn't fit him.

"Hey, I'm okay." I yanked him down into a kiss. "God, that orgasm. I'm still shaking."

He crawled onto the bed beside me and wrapped me in his arms. A powerful emotion swept through—I wanted to cry at how good it felt. His hand smoothed up and down my arm, a reassuring gesture. I tucked myself beside him, snuggling close. The beat of his heart was hypnotic and if I wasn't careful, it would lull me to sleep.

"Can I get you anything?" His quiet voice made my eyes flutter open.

"Anxious to get out of bed?"

The arms that were banded around me squeezed. "No. Not in a million years, baby girl."

chapter SEVENTEEN

JOSEPH

Fuck no, I didn't want to leave this bed. I was tired and Noemi might experience sub drop after the out of control scene I'd just put her through. But the biggest reason? I didn't fucking want to let go of her. It was unnerving how strong the desire to hold her was.

Part of my responsibility was taking care of her. Whatever she wanted, after what I'd done. I'd drive my Porsche through a blizzard to get her mint chocolate chip ice cream if that was what she asked for. My lack of control had crossed over from annoying to downright dangerous. We never discussed a safe word or boundaries. I never asked her hard limits. What if she had asthma or some other medical condition I didn't know about? I was fucking lucky I hadn't hurt her, and my stomach turned at the thought.

Her soft hair smelled like coconut, and her skin like vanilla. The combination made me weak. I ripped my gaze away from her and evaluated the room instead. Our smears were on the floor-length mirror from where she'd braced herself with her arms. Watching the belt choke her while I fucked her from behind was scorching hot. I'd remember it forever. How she'd looked when the orgasm took her.

The room wasn't overtly feminine, but had a woman's touch. Like the living room, it was a collection of mismatched furniture. Patterns worked with stripes, oversized paired with petite. The proportions were just right, and a common theme held the space together—in this room it was a pale yellow. A careful hand had put it together and although it wasn't what I'd pick, it was pleasing and comfortable.

"I like this room." My voice was quiet. "Your decorator's got talent."

"My—?" She looked confused. "I don't use a decorator. I did it myself." A shy smile broke on her face. "You like it? I've been told it's too busy."

"No, it's nice. It doesn't look... generic. It looks like you."

Her eyes blinked wide and turned warm. "Thanks. I could say the same of your place. All heavy pieces and sharp lines. Rigid." Her fingertips glided over the tattoo, following the curved lines. "It's very you."

"Should be. I did it." I took pride in my home, making the space my own.

She laughed as if something amused her.

"What?" I asked.

"*Nothing lasts forever*," she read. "Except, you know, a permanent tattoo." Her fingers continued to trace the contours.

"Do I need to give you and my tattoo a moment alone?"

She grinned. "Could you? That'd be great."

We lapsed into lazy silence, and again I was struck by how natural it felt. Normal, when it was anything but for me. She shivered subtly, so I sat up and yanked her fluffy comforter around us. Talking about decorating, snuggling under the covers... who the fuck was I around her? Why did I kind of like this?

"Okay," she whispered. "I'm sort of thirsty."

"Me, too. What do you want?"

THREE *little* MISTAKES

"There's a pitcher of some red . . . stuff in the fridge."

"Red stuff? What is it?"

She made a weird face. Embarrassment, and it was fucking cute. "I don't want to tell you."

"Why not?"

"Because it's not exactly a sophisticated drink and the little girl comment is going to come out of your mouth."

I laughed, figuring it out. "Oh, please tell me it's cherry Kool-Aid."

"It's not." She scowled. "It's fruit punch Kool-Aid. Don't judge me."

I swung my legs over the side of the bed and stood, giving her a smile. "I told you I wouldn't, little girl."

Her exasperated sigh chased after me as I went down the hallway. I yanked on my underwear when I got to the wad of clothes on the floor. Jesus, I'd been locked in a Dom space I'd never reached with anyone else when my clothes came off. More proof that whatever this was with her, it was something . . . unique.

The cupboard was where I expected it to be and I pulled down two glasses, filling them with the pitcher of *red stuff* from her fridge. I hadn't had Kool-Aid in at least a decade, and it was as sugary-sweet as I remembered, but nice. It was hard not to think about good times with Conner and my parents.

Thirty-eight goddamn years old, and I was drinking a kid's drink. Would the Kool-Aid Man break through the wall at any second and be horrified to find an adult standing there in his underwear?

No. The wall didn't burst open, instead the front door did. There'd been no knock. A key slid into the lock and that sound was what forced me to turn. As the man stepped inside, opposite emotions flared in me. Relief that it wasn't Noemi's father, and annoyance at the other man who seemed likely to have a key to her place. Her ex.

Ross looked like a boy who hadn't quite finished growing into a man. Probably Noemi's age or a year older. A wholesome, poster-boy Republican look, with dimples that the good girls went apeshit over. We were miles apart.

When his gaze zeroed in on me, he went as wooden as a tree. The thoughts in his head were loud on his face as he took in my lack of clothes and the tattoo she was fond of.

"Who the hell are you?" he asked.

I kept my gaze locked on his and took an unhurried sip from my glass, leaning casually against the counter. Even without clothes, I was the one in the position of power here. I had all of the information, including who he was.

My lack of urgency to respond only made him more anxious.

"Em?" he called out, glancing down the hall. "Seriously, dude, what the hell are you doing here?"

Just what you never could.

"Ross?" Noemi's hurried footsteps pounded down the hall, and she came into view a half second later, her hands cinching closed the belt on her silk robe. Her wild hair was loose around her shoulders, and makeup smudged under eyes. This girl looked like she'd been properly fucked, and Ross figured it out instantly.

The boy's face was fucking priceless.

"What are you doing here?" she demanded of him.

His focus left her and swung back my direction, horror in his eyes at what he'd been upgraded to. "I can't find my flash drive that has MacKenzie's practice test on it. Did I lend it to you? Or maybe I left it here?"

"I don't think so."

It was then that Ross noticed the pile of clothes on the floor that we'd shed earlier, and I didn't bother hiding the grin. It was petty, but I disliked everything about the guy, from his stupid, pretentious look, to the way he'd put his needs before hers. He moved to the desk in the living room where her laptop rested, and opened a drawer.

"I don't believe," my tone was threatening, "she gave you permission to look for it."

He straightened and turned. "So, you do speak English. Em, who is this guy?"

"Her boyfriend," I spat out.

I hated that word. The immaturity of it, because God knew I wasn't a boy, but there wasn't another word adequate or appropriate to use that Ross would understand.

"Her *what*?" Ross's voice cracked. He turned to Noemi with disbelief smeared on his face. There was disbelief on hers as well. We hadn't used that label, but our arrangement was a relationship. I dared her to deny it, but she wouldn't. If anything, she looked pleased.

"You could have just called," she said, her voice tight.

"I did, but you didn't answer and I need it for class tonight."

She shook her head. "I'm sorry, but it's not here. I save everything to my Dropbox, so I wouldn't borrow it." She motioned to the door. "You should go to the labs or the library and check the lost and found."

He nodded, looking deep in thought. "Can you call over there? I'm going to swing by John and Derrick's place next.

The flash drive is white with a Cubs logo on it."

The way Ross didn't wait for her answer and began to move toward the door made me realize he expected her to say yes.

"No," she said, her voice quiet. "No." This time was louder, confident. "I know you don't like doing that kind of stuff, but you have a phone, Ross. Be an adult and use it. I'm busy."

His mouth hung open, probably shocked she'd said no, but he snapped it shut. He gestured to me and the clothes on the floor. "Yeah, I guess so. Thanks for all your *help*."

"Aren't you forgetting something?" I asked as he yanked the door open.

He turned and glared at me. "What?"

"As much fun as it was having you interrupt Kool-Aid time, you've got something that doesn't belong to you." He didn't get it. "You didn't have to break in."

He still didn't understand, and looked at Noemi.

"Your key," she said.

Ross pulled his keychain out in a huff, extracted the key, and held it out to her.

"No," I said. "I'll take that."

The Kool-Aid had to be laced with something. It was the only excuse I could think of as to why I wanted a key to her place. Claiming her as my girlfriend felt somewhat necessary, but this was something . . . else. I could lie to myself and say it was just so I could have access to her whenever I wanted, but that was pointless. Coming here to her place was stupid and dangerous, and I already knew I was going to do it again.

I ignored her stunned expression as I took the key from

her ex's hand. Ross went quickly after that, and the door shut with a bang.

The key dug into my hand as I closed my fist around it. "I know I said I wasn't going to judge, but . . ."

Her shoulders pulled back as she braced for a comment.

". . . I actually like the Kool-Aid."

She exhaled and closed her eyes. "Did he even knock?"

"Sure didn't."

She shook her head. "He's, like, completely unaware of anyone else. He didn't used to be that way."

"It's too bad he didn't show up thirty minutes ago when you were choking on my cock. He might have noticed that."

Her eyes went completely white. "Oh my God."

"Or maybe when we were fucking in front of the mirror. Would you have liked that, filthy girl? If he'd seen how hard I got you to come?"

I strolled to her, putting the glass I poured for her in her hand. In my other, the key burned.

"Is that what you would have liked?" she whispered. "Does my *boyfriend* want to rub it in my ex's face?"

Instinct and logic wanted to push her away. She was Mr. Red's daughter, and the lie I was keeping from her ate at me. I'd told her to trust me. No, fuck, I'd demanded it, even as I lied about who I was on the inside, although she'd definitely gotten a peek behind the curtain today. But as much as I knew I should back away, I wanted her too strongly.

I held out my hand and peeled back my fingers, both of us staring at the key, as I offered it to her. Maybe she'd take it and save me from this choice I'd made, which was probably a mistake.

She put her fingers over mine, closing my hand on the

metal. "I thought I told you, Sir," her voice was shaky, "I belong to you."

Noemi had gotten her first taste of the wolf this afternoon, and it hadn't sent her running. Perhaps she was attracted to the darkness in me.

Maybe someday I could show her more of it.

Choosing five clips to post back to her was surprisingly difficult, only because I felt like a kid in a candy store after the scene we'd done in her apartment. There was so much I wanted to watch her experience. So much I wanted us to enjoy together.

I sat behind my desk at the blindfold club, scrolling through the feed on Tumblr, trying not to think about the fact that Mr. Red had called and scheduled an extra visit with Claudia tonight. His standing appointment was typically Saturday. Was this because he was lonely? Fuck, don't think about. I was already concerned about what to do when the actual event took place. It was her father. My *girlfriend's* father. I was contemplating how fucked up it was when Payton appeared in the doorway.

"Hey," she said, "Regan has a migraine, and asked me to fill in for her. Is that okay?"

Regan was one of my best sales assistants. Gorgeous, charming, yet slightly aloof, which proved to be a deadly combination for the johns' wallets. She'd never once gotten on the table as the other sales assistants had. She lived for the thrill of negotiating and taking home lots of cash. Payton was better than most of the sales assistants, but she was also out of practice.

"Yeah, honey, that's fine." Although inside I grumbled about the money I'd potentially lose. "Thanks for helping out."

She lingered in the doorway.

"And?" I asked.

"Dominic's back from his business trip on Tuesday," she said, then turned on her heel and marched away.

chapter EIGHTEEN

NOEMI

It was crazy how quickly things escalated with Joseph. I didn't know if there was a "honeymoon" phase of a Dom/sub relationship, but we were definitely experiencing some sort of high. Or maybe it would be like this all the time. Joseph would be quick to remind me that nothing lasted forever, good or bad.

His dirty texts filled my phone during the day, and his even dirtier words filled my head each night before I went to bed, the phone typically on FaceTime. Our Tumbler account was *filthy*, and I loved it.

I did not love how our schedules never seemed to align. He worked all the time, and whenever he had a few free hours, it was always when I had class. I'd never missed a class unless I was on death's door, even if I was trying to be a bad girl.

I hadn't seen him in person in five days, not since our late lunch that ended with a belt around my throat and the most intense experience of my life. I snuggled into bed with my iPad and fired up Tumblr. Posting clips no longer induced worry. I simply posted what I liked, and every now and again . . . we'd inadvertently post the same clip.

You have class at eight tomorrow, Sensible Noemi rumbled. She hardly made an appearance anymore. Joseph had run her off. I curled up under the covers and drifted to sleep, wondering what he was doing and if he was thinking about me as much as I was him.

I was awake.

I rolled over and peered at the alarm clock, having to get close since I didn't have my glasses or contacts. Holy hell, it was three in the morning. I flopped over on the bed.

"Hey," a male voice whispered in the darkness.

I screamed and bolted upright, wrapping the comforter tight around my body. Holy shit, I needed a weapon—

"Noemi, it's me, it's Joseph." In the moonlight, I could see the figure had his hands up.

"What the hell? I almost had a heart attack, are you trying to kill me?"

"No." His blurry figure moved, like he'd reached a hand behind his head to rub his neck. His voice was resigned. "I came to sleep with you."

My brain refused to function. "Excuse me?"

The bed shifted as he lowered, coming into view. His expression was . . . unsure. Part of me was excited to see him, but a much larger part was just plain exhausted. I felt anything but sexy right now. He was my Dom, though. He liked to keep me guessing and on my toes, and I'd given him a key to my place. Using his own hand could only stave off the need we both felt for so long.

"I came to sleep with you," he repeated. "I'm sorry, I know it's late and you've got class early, but . . ." His arms wrapped around my shoulders and pressed me back into the mattress. "I still haven't actually slept with you, and that . . .

bothers me."

He settled beside me on the bed, and as he got comfortable, my breathing grew short. Never would I have guessed he'd be into this. The distance he held himself from me seemed to be shorter each day.

"You still have your clothes on," I whispered.

"Precautionary measure."

I laughed softly. "What are you trying to prevent?"

"You know exactly what would happen if I took my clothes off."

Now that I was fully awake, I rose up onto my elbow. "Oh? What would happen?"

"I'd be the third wheel to you and the tattoo." He tucked my hair behind my ear and his fingers slipped down to cradle my face. "We can't sleep together without the sleeping part, little girl." He brushed his lips over mine, and warmth poured through me. "You need to get some rest. We've got plans tomorrow night."

"We do?"

"It'll be twenty years cancer-free, tomorrow. You said I should have a party."

I smiled. "Yeah?"

He made a face. "It's not going to be a big deal, just a few friends. Don't go ordering me a sheet cake or anything." Joseph urged me to lie back down, my head resting against his chest. "Your last class is at six, can you be ready by nine?"

It was stupid, but it always caught me off guard when he knew my schedule or remembered a detail I'd mentioned. With as busy as my father was, the way the professors treated me as another faceless student, and of course Ross's general attitude, I didn't realize how invisible I felt. Not until

Joseph noticed me.

"Yeah, nine, no problem. I'm sure I can have the balloon bouquet ready by then."

"Perfect. Now go to sleep before you say something that gets you in trouble." I imagined all the sexy discipline he'd give, but before I could open my mouth, he added, "I'll take away your pillow."

I smiled, closed my eyes, and enjoyed the quiet with him for a moment. "I'm glad you came. Good night, Joseph."

He let out a soft breath. "Night, baby girl."

I steadied my hand as I swiped another coat of mascara on my lashes. I needed to stop stalling with the makeup and make a decision about what I was going to put on. What did one wear while meeting their Dom's friends? *Boyfriend*, I corrected myself. He'd undoubtedly introduce me as his girlfriend. He'd kept cancer from them. His friends probably didn't know he was into the BDSM lifestyle.

I gave up, left the bathroom, and snatched my phone from the dresser to text.

> I don't know what to wear.

> I'll come up.

Which worked out better all around. I made my bed, laid out some options, and fifteen minutes later I opened the front door for him. My hand gripped the knob tightly. He looked amazing. Oh, God, he *smelled* amazing. I stood before him in stunned silence, wearing an old tank top and a pair of ratty pajama bottoms. I hadn't thought this through.

"Hi." He planted a quick kiss on my lips.

"Hey." I struggled to keep my voice unaffected. When I'd crawled out of bed this morning, he'd been fast asleep, disheveled in his clothes, and sexy. But this version of him, when he was refined and prepared, this was when I had difficulty keeping myself from sliding into the shy girl I'd been.

"I put some different options out," I said, leading him into my room.

"That." He gestured to the simple sleeveless black top with a high neckline that I'd paired with a mango-colored fitted skirt.

"It's not too summery?"

He gave me a look that made me think about sinking to my knees and undo his belt. "If you give me options that include a skirt, that's what I'm going to choose."

"Okay." I looked at the clothes, then back to him. It seemed weird to get dressed with him watching. "I, uh, got you something."

His gaze didn't waver from my hesitant hands as I pulled the shirt up over my head.

"It's in the fridge," I continued.

His lips quirked into a slight smile. "It can wait. I'd rather watch this."

Thank God I'd already put on my sexiest panties and bra, because getting naked in front of him would make us late. I had enough indecent thoughts in my mind and didn't need the temptation. I was thrilled he was taking me to meet his friends and see another part of his life.

I tugged on the top and shimmied into the skirt. Even

when I had my back turned to him, I could feel his hot gaze on my skin.

"I'm going to freeze in these shoes," I said as I followed him into the kitchen, carrying my strappy sandals by the heels. Joseph opened the fridge and I pointed to the main shelf. "It's in the white box."

A suspicious look washed on his expression as he withdrew the medium-sized cardboard box and set it on the counter, and as soon as he lifted the lid, he began to laugh. "I told you not to get me a cake."

I smiled and shrugged. "I thought you'd get a kick out of it."

He had. I could see the warmth and amusement in his eyes, even if he wouldn't say it out loud. And knowing I'd pleased him was worth the hassle I'd gone through trying to get the cake last minute.

He set his hands on his hips and gave me a smoldering look. "So, tell me, little girl. Did you write 'Fuck Cancer' on this cake yourself, or did you have to get the decorator to do it?"

"The woman at the store did it."

He grinned. "What'd she think about your language?"

"Her mother's a breast cancer survivor. She wrote it with pleasure."

He took another look at the white, round cake decorated with elegant roses and seashell piping. The decorator had done it exactly as I wanted, in classy, tasteful script to play against the inappropriate words. But were they really inappropriate? I'd scolded Joseph for overusing the profanity, but he'd been through so much and almost died. If ever there was a time to use strong language, surely it was then.

"What are we going to do about this?" he said, gesturing to the cake.

"Nothing, it was just a joke. We don't have to eat—"

"No, Noemi. I told you not to do something, and you disobeyed." The wicked gleam in his eye had my pulse racing. "You'll need to be disciplined. Should I do it now? Or later?"

"You said not to get you a sheet cake," I reminded. "That one's round."

His eyes narrowed, but his expression remained playful. "Are you talking back to me?"

I clenched tighter on the heels in my hands and bit my lip, considering my options. Oh, hell, I was tired of fighting my desire. "Okay. Now," I whispered.

He grabbed the box, strolled to the couch, and began to put on his coat. "Get your shoes and coat on."

"We're leaving?" Disappointment flashed through me. I'd expected him to take me over his knee, as I'd posted several clips of it on Tumblr already. "What about—?"

"If you're choosing now, it means you *want* it, and I can't use that as a form of negative reinforcement." He came to me until we were chest to chest, his dark eyes staring down into mine. "The frustration I'm seeing from you right now? I like it. This is part of your punishment. The rest comes later."

Victory burned in his gaze the half-second before he turned and moved to the door.

"You don't have to take the cake," I eked out.

He chuckled. "Maybe I want to. It's mine, after all."

I'd been in Joseph's presence less than fifteen minutes and I already felt like I was drowning. The frozen, nighttime air assaulted my lungs when we stepped out of my building and gave me strength. Joseph put out a hand to hail a cab.

"Where's the overpriced car?"

"At my place. I wanted to celebrate without having to worry about driving."

We huddled into the warm backseat of the cab, and when Joseph gave the driver the address, I blinked.

"Your comedy club?"

"It's not open tonight." He tapped on the top of the cake box. "Private party."

"Who's going to be there? Did you prep them that I kind of have babyface?"

He chuckled. "It'll be Payton and her fiancé Dominic, and I told her you were still in school." His expression went serious. "Payton sometimes helps me manage at the wine club, so I never used your full name. I don't think she'd recognize it, or you, but I'll stick with the nickname tonight. She might accidentally mention it around Katzenberg."

"Oh. Okay." Katzenberg was a mood-killer if ever there was one. A few years ago my father had backed out of a deal when it looked less solid than Katzenberg made it out to be, and Katzenberg took it very personally. He'd been a grade-A asshole, or so my father said, ever since. I tried not to think about Joseph associating himself with a man like that. Grudges were petty and immature.

The cab dropped us at the front of the darkened building. As Joseph passed me the cake box and drew his keys out of his pocket, a couple began to approach from down the sidewalk. My mouth dropped open as the woman smiled and nodded to Joseph.

These were his friends? The power couple looked like they belonged in a fancy perfume advertisement, all sex and allure. The brunette woman, Payton, was only a little older than me. Utterly gorgeous. She had her arm threaded through her fiancé's, and my gaze worked up to his. Short, sandy blond hair and strikingly blue eyes. Handsome barely covered it.

I wasn't in the same class as these people, Joseph included. I was a 'six' trying to fit in with a pack of 'tens.' He worked with this stunning woman? It was impossible not to feel a tinge of jealousy.

A hand pulled me through the door and into the lobby where it was warm, and Joseph slipped an arm casually behind my back, gesturing to the couple that followed us in.

"I'm Payton." Her voice was like a purr, and she scanned me with interest. "Em? This is Dominic."

"Hi," I forced out and smiled. *Don't be awkward, Noemi.*

Joseph held out a hand to the other man. "Thanks for meeting us."

Dominic shrugged his broad shoulders and flashed an easy smile as he shook Joseph's hand. "Payton gets whatever she wants."

"I've trained him well," she said, her gaze turning up to her fiancé.

His eyes filled with heat. "That's enough out of you, devil woman."

When Joseph had said "party," this wasn't what I pictured. We wandered past the ticket booth into the club, which was one large room. The long bar lined the back wall and the room sloped toward the stage on the other side, square tables and wooden chairs filling either side of the aisle. The unlit stage was only a step up from the main floor, and a brick wall served as the backdrop.

Joseph took the cake box, set it on top of the bar, and

moved behind it, taking off his coat. "What are we drinking?"

"Is she old enough to drink?" Payton asked, her voice teasing.

"She's only three years younger than you, honey." Joseph shot her a plain look. He pushed back the sleeves of his navy blue cashmere sweater and got to work mixing our drinks, looking right at home behind the bar. I needed to stop staring at him like a moon-eyed idiot before anyone noticed.

While she waited for Joseph to finish preparing her drink, Payton flipped open the lid on the cake box and froze.

"What is this?" she said, her concerned gaze darting from me to Joseph.

"We're celebrating." He plunked her cosmo down on the bar in front of her, the pink liquid threatening to spill but didn't. "I'm twenty years cancer free today."

"What?" Her concern grew ten-fold. "You never told me that."

He moved to the sink and washed his hands. "It was a long time ago."

Watching her struggle to process the information was oddly touching. It was clear she cared for Joseph. Not sexually, I didn't think. There was a frantic energy radiating between her and Dominic that was undeniable, like they only had eyes for each other. Payton took a deep breath and blew it out, rolling her shoulders back. "You should have fucking told me."

Joseph raised an eyebrow. No, I don't imagine he liked that.

"So, Dominic," I said abruptly, trying to ease the tension, "what do you do?"

"I'm the VP of international project development at Chase Sports."

Holy crap. Chase Sports wasn't a small company, and he was a VP? At his age? He looked younger than Joseph. "How'd you two meet?"

The room went silent and I'd swear their gazes turned to Joseph, like they weren't sure what to do.

"That's a story for another time," he answered for them.

Confusion tugged my eyebrows together. Was it embarrassing, and Joseph was protecting them? The expression on his face told me to leave it alone, and I chose not to disobey. He already had one punishment in the works, I didn't want to pile them on. Joseph slammed his glass of whiskey and thumped it down on the bar.

"Let me finish getting it set up, and you'll be ready?" he asked of Payton.

A diabolical smile slid across her lips, and her gaze sharpened on me. "Oh, yeah."

It sent my stomach twisting, although I wasn't sure why. What was Joseph up to? He went down the aisle and took a step up onto the stage, then disappeared into the wings.

"That's a nice purse," Payton said, nodding toward my bag on the bar.

"Thank you, my sister—"

"Can I be honest?" she interrupted, taking a step closer to me. "I find this shit fascinating. He's never had a girlfriend, at least, not in the four years I've known him."

"Oh?" I whispered.

"I couldn't fucking believe it when he told me. He's had a few subs before, but they were . . . not like you."

Oh my God. Well, I guess his friends knew he was into

the lifestyle.

"Payton," Dominic warned under his breath.

She reached out and wrapped a hand on my wrist, and the sudden contact made me jolt. "I'm gonna give you some unsolicited advice, because Joseph and I are a lot alike. Don't let him push you too far, but don't give up on him too easily, either. He's a good guy."

I glanced down at the hand on my arm, and her enormous engagement ring glinted back at me. She thought she had to convince me? Somewhere along the way, I'd already made this shift unconsciously. My bad boy was so very good.

Her pretty blue eyes watched me closely, and . . . where they hopeful? "I'm glad he's decided to let someone in."

Lights jumped to life and flooded the stage, and I blinked at brightness.

Dominic helped Payton out of her coat and hung it on one of the barstools. Beneath it, she wore a black strapless corset, her large breasts barely contained inside.

"Is that new?" her fiancé asked.

She nodded, her cherry red highlights in her hair glowing in the light. "Yuriko gave it to me as a going away gift."

Dominic's lustful gaze lingered a long time on her flesh. I couldn't blame him for it. The boning in the corset emphasized her figure beautifully, and I was envious. Payton wasn't classically beautiful, she was *hot*. I couldn't find a better word for her, she was like a version of an extremely high-end porn star.

Joseph appeared on the stage and motioned for us to come to him. We brought our drinks to the table closest, and without words, the men grabbed another table and carried it up on stage.

"What's going on?" I asked.

The table was set up on the stage, and Joseph turned his attention to me. His dark, sexual gaze forced my heart into my throat.

"Payton and Dominic are going to fuck on this stage, and we're going to watch."

chapter NINETEEN

I had a moment of hysterical deafness. "W-What?"

Joseph jumped down off the stage as Dominic stepped up, leading Payton with him. She set her large purse on the floor beside the table and then every pair of eyes in the room seemed to fall onto me.

Joseph's hands trapped my waist and he pressed his forehead against mine, our warm skin touching and his breath on my face. "I want to see you squirm in your seat, little girl, while you're watching her come all over his cock." A chair squealed as Joseph turned it to face the stage. "Sit down, now."

Holy fuck. I looked at the innocuous chair as if it might be on fire. Could I really do this, watch two strangers have sex just ten feet in front of me? I didn't remember making the decision. Yet I found myself in the chair, and Joseph seated right beside me.

On stage, Payton pulled her long, glossy hair up into a ponytail seated high on the crown of her head, then busied herself with undoing the snap of her pants. My breathing went shallow when I caught the first sign of lace. She took off her black heels, sat back on the table, and let Dominic pull the pants slowly down her long legs, one at a time.

Her gaze never left his, and Dominic's never wavered from hers. They were beautiful people, but seeing the real emotion behind it was what made it swelteringly hot.

"Put those fucking heels back on," Dominic said.

"Yes, Sir," she quipped back, although it was sarcastic and not respectful. That tone would have gotten me into trouble, for sure. Payton slipped her feet into the heels and stood, showing off her shape. My gaze flowed down her ample breasts to her tiny waist, on to the band of skin where the corset ended, all the way to the flare of her hips.

Joseph had said I looked like a wet dream that night I'd become his, but how could I compare to her? She looked so amazing even *I* wanted to sleep with her. The black mesh and lace panties didn't leave much to the imagination, and they were cut low enough that the small, black symbol tattooed by her hip was visible. No, not a symbol. It was a character in Japanese.

"Watch your tone," Dominic said, "or I'll put something in your mouth to shut it up."

"This cock?" Her hand went to the fly of his jeans, rubbing.

He pushed her hand away. "I'll have your boss give us his girlfriend's underwear and I'll stuff that in your mouth." He spun her around, revealing she was wearing a thong. He put a hand on her back and shoved her to bend over the table. "Would you like that, you little slut? I'm sure you're dying to know what her pussy tastes like. Am I right?"

I bit back the startled cry that grew inside me, which was both shock and excitement. Payton didn't answer, and Dominic's hand came crashing down on her ass, the tight cheek barely jiggling, but the skin flushed red.

"Yes," Payton moaned. "One, thank you."

What did that *yes* mean? Was this in pleasure, or a response to his question? Joseph moved and knelt before me, his hands sliding over my knees. Up my thighs. Disappearing beneath my skirt.

"Holy shit," I gasped.

His gaze was inescapable, and even though I wasn't up there, I felt a million stage lights shining on me.

"There's going to be some audience participation tonight." Joseph's voice was authoritative and hot. "Lift up." His fingers curled under the sides and began to peel the fabric down. I put my hands on the sides of the seat and it creaked as I lifted up so he could pull the underwear toward my knees. "Fuck, you've got them nice and wet for her."

A whimper fell from my lips, and I covered my mouth with my palm, embarrassed. Joseph grinned, his eyes full of wickedness, and the panties continued their descent, all the way past my sandals. I stopped breathing as he rose deliberately, went to the edge of the stage, and handed them to Dominic.

A stranger was holding my panties, wet with my desire. I pressed my knees together, uncomfortably turned on. It became unbearable when Dominic turned to his soon-to-be-wife. "Open up."

She moaned when he shoved my wadded underwear into her mouth. She locked eyes with me and she *fucking* moaned, like she was enjoying my taste. The scene alone was enough to send me in a frenzy, I didn't need the audio to go with it. I flattened my hands on my thighs, and glanced at Joseph.

Who was watching me, not them.

"Aren't you going to watch?" I whispered.

"I'd rather watch you right now. Besides," he added loudly, "it's nothing I haven't seen before."

"Ha," Dominic said, his face twisting into an evil smile. "Challenge accepted." His focus went back to Payton. "Stay just like that."

While he dug through Payton's purse, I couldn't help but remember my first time with Joseph, being in that same position. Were her hip bones uncomfortable against the edge of the table as mine had been, or was she too lost in the scene to care by this point?

Dominic pulled a large coil of red rope out, his hands moving quickly to bind her wrists together, and when it was done, he smacked her ass again. She flinched, and her eyes slammed shut, her words unintelligible because of the underwear still in her mouth. His large hand rubbed the red spot he'd struck and she let out a moan.

Then, a foreign language spilled from his mouth, spoken softly. Lovingly.

"What language is that?" I asked in a hushed voice.

"Japanese," Joseph answered. "They lived in Tokyo for a while."

Dominic pulled the panties from her mouth and left them on the table, hooking his hands under her elbows and lifting her to stand. After she turned on her heels, the kiss she gave him was raw and intense, and it made me ache. I'd had that same kiss from Joseph, and I wanted it now.

Joseph leaned in and brushed the hair away from my ear. "Always fidgeting," he whispered. His hot breath made me shiver. "You don't look like you know what to do with your hands."

"I'm fine." It would have been better if my voice hadn't wavered.

On stage, Dominic was worshipping her body. His palms smoothed down over her corset, fingers trailing, and he took a knee before her. The black lace was peeled down painstakingly slow, all the while her gaze burned into me.

I only got a flash of her bare skin before Dominic's head was in the way, and her eyes hooded. "God, Dominic, I love your fucking tongue."

He paused. "Just my tongue?"

"Right now? I love it more than any other part of you."

He chuckled, grasping her hips to hold her steady. "Yeah? We'll see what you have to say when my pants come off."

She drew in a shuddering breath when he stopped talking, his mouth preoccupied with other things. Watching him go down on her like this was so sensual. I knew what was happening only from her reaction, not by sight. Not until he shifted on his knees to the side, using his fingers to spread her wide. The sliver of his tongue darting between her bare slit set me on fire.

"Holy shit." I clamped my hand over my mouth.

"No." Joseph grasped my wrist and pulled it away, a faint scowl darkening his expression. "I want to hear every sexy sound you make. Let's put your busy hands to use. Uncross your legs and touch yourself."

I felt the blood drain from my face. "What? They'll see me."

He glanced at the couple, then back to me. "I don't believe this is a limit, since you let me fuck you out in the open. You're just nervous."

"Yes," I admitted.

His warm mouth latched onto the side of my neck at the same moment his hand was on my knee, pushing me to uncross my legs. "This is the other part of your punishment, bad girl. Put those fingers on your pussy. Let them see how much you like their show."

I exhaled a long, torturous breath. My eyes pleaded with him both to make me do it, and not to. The wrong, bad part of me was eager and I was pulsing, aching between my legs for relief.

My fingers gripped the hem of my skirt and lifted, drawing the material toward my hips. I'd made it halfway up my thighs when Joseph scooted his chair closer and set a hand on my knee. The hand traveled up the inside of my leg, brushing the sensitive skin, all the way until he stroked me where I was soaking.

I sighed, but he probably couldn't hear it. On stage, Payton was moaning loudly. Her shoulders shook and her back arched.

"Fuck, I don't want to come like this," she cried.

One of Dominic's hands abandoned its hold on her hip and he buried it between her legs. "That's too damn bad."

Joseph's fingers rubbed one tiny circle on my clit, before he plunged his finger deep inside, pulling a groan of pleasure from me. The slow thrust of his finger was mirrored by Dominic's on stage.

"I told you to touch your pussy," Joseph said. "Why am I repeating myself?"

But... he was already touching me. I'd thought—Forget it, it didn't matter. Fire spread from the building pace, and concern over modesty was consumed in the flames. I pulled my skirt up so it banded high across the tops of my thighs, and put my fingers just above where he was fucking me.

"You don't know where to look." His voice was velvety soft. "Do you watch my finger as it slides inside your tight, wet pussy? Or do you watch him while he makes her come all over his tongue?"

Joseph was absolutely right, I didn't know which one was hotter. My gaze reeled from one to the other, desperate.

"Oh, fuck," Payton gasped. She attempted to step back from Dominic, but he wasn't having any of it. His other hand clenched on her waist, his fingers digging into her flesh until the skin dented around them. She began to pant. "Dominic... I'll fall over..."

"No, I've got you."

His mouth and hand worked with precision to get exactly what he wanted from her. Her legs shook and her eyes went wide.

"Shit, I'm coming. Oh... fuck. *Fuck!*" Her knees buckled and she sagged into his arms, unable to do anything but collapse since her hands were bound behind her. Dominic held her tightly as she convulsed, bucking against the orgasm.

Watching the pleasure seize her was crazy powerful, and my frantic gaze searched for Joseph. Bliss crept up my legs, and tremors built in my belly. The idea of coming with another person still felt new and foreign, but with two other people in the room?

"Faster," Joseph commanded. "Don't stop. I can tell you're getting close."

I swallowed hard. I was unbelievably close. Shockingly close. My hips moved, meeting the thrust of the finger pumping in and out of me, and my hand rubbed, stimulating where the ache was greatest.

"Yes, baby girl. Just like that. I'm going to do that to you sometime. Tie you up and fuck you with my mouth until you can't stand."

My mouth hung open as my lungs demanded air. Oh,

God. Oh my God. It'd been impossible to peak for so long, but being with Joseph made it practically easy. Something snapped inside me, a calm focus amid the storm of pleasure. I reached out, wrapped my hand around the back of his neck, and pulled him so his face was an inch away. "Kiss me with that filthy mouth when you make me come."

I'd never seen him shocked from my words before, but it lasted only a single heartbeat. A dark, aggressive look overtook him, like a predator. He launched forward the last inch and took my mouth with his, consuming me as the orgasm did.

I moaned into his kiss while shards of ecstasy burst from deep inside, destroying me. Oh, shit. Shit, it felt so amazing. His tongue stroked mine, fucking my mouth, and it only added to the overwhelming sensation of it all. The pleasure rolled through quickly, but it was intense.

"You," he said, tearing his lips from mine finally, "don't get to give the orders." He took in a rapid breath. "But I'll let that one slide." For a long moment he lingered, giving me time to pull myself together. He withdrew from my shuddering body and turned his focus to the stage. "What else have you got in that purse, Payton?"

She was on her feet again, her face flushed. "Lots of things. What are you looking for?"

"More rope, or handcuffs."

"You could use her bra," Dominic offered. My heart stopped beating. I'd lost myself in the orgasm and my legs were spread wide in the chair, my pussy on clear display. Dominic's gaze dropped down to take a curious look, and I bolted upright, hurrying to push my skirt down.

"Handcuffs," she said, nudging her fiancé with her

shoulder. "Then, get back here and untie me."

"Not a chance." Dominic pulled out the metal cuffs and slid them noisily across the stage floor toward us. "You love it."

"I'd love it if I had use of my hands when I'm sucking your cock. I think you would, too." Her face was pure seductress.

"Goddamn, you're persuasive."

She smiled triumphantly, but it died when he set her on her knees with a loud thud. She'd expected him to untie her, and her mouth dropped open.

"Perfect," Dominic said, undoing his buckle. "Keep your mouth just like that, devil woman. You're such a whore for my cock."

Joseph had grabbed the handcuffs off the stage and was headed my direction, but he spun abruptly at this. His voice was coated in dread. "*No.*"

"It's okay," Dominic said quickly. "I know what I'm doing."

Joseph glanced at Payton, and she smiled back. "It's true, I am a *whore* for his cock."

I didn't understand what exactly had happened, but something had set Joseph on high alert. His tightened shoulders slowly melted to relax when Payton looked up at Dominic, a bright smile on her lips.

Dominic shed his shirt, exposing the hardened frame of a man who worked out, often and with weights. He wasn't too bulky, but he was a slab of defined muscle. Payton had a body to kill for, but so did her future husband. His pants made little noise as he lowered his zipper.

"Look at me," Joseph commanded, and my gaze swung

to him. He opened the handcuffs. "If you want to stop, you say *stop*. I'll treat any *waits* that come from you as check-ins. Understood?"

Did he suspect there'd be things that were going to happen that would have me uttering my famous word? I swallowed a breath and nodded. He moved behind, looming over me, silently waiting for me to offer him my wrists. Having the handcuffs on seemed just as scary as last time, but for a whole different reason. This time I didn't worry about what he might do, but what *I* might. The more control I gave him, the more wild I became.

My back straightened as I slipped my wrists behind the chair.

chapter TWENTY

I fought to hold the tremble at bay. My body was a cage, I told myself. Joseph will set you free.

"Good girl," he said. The metal snapped on and the jarring noise made me flinch.

On stage, Payton licked her lips. Dominic's underwear had been pushed down and he clenched his massive, hard dick in one hand, stroking. "You want it?"

"Yes," she murmured.

"Yeah? Say it."

"I want your fucking cock in my mouth."

"All right." He seized her head in his hands and drove himself between her lips. She moaned, and greedily took it.

Joseph grabbed the back of his chair and pulled it behind me, so he could sit right up against my back. My handcuffed hands reached out and brushed the soft fabric of his pants and the thigh beneath, but he moved away. "I didn't give you permission to touch me."

It was the same thing he'd said the night we'd met, when I'd tried so hard to be brave and forward. Just like it did then, his authoritative tone chilled me and made me burn. "May I touch you, Sir?"

"Not yet. I want you to focus on the show."

I watched the slide of Dominic's thick cock between her petal-pink lips, his skin glossed with her saliva. Once again, I pressed my knees together, squeezing. Was it normal to be this turned on?

"Jesus," Dominic groaned. "I love you. So fucking real."

She moaned and her gaze drifted up to stare at him. The passion reflected in both their expressions stole my breath. Love and desire flooded every inch of the room until there was no escape.

"I want to go down on you, Sir," I whispered. "Please."

"I want that too, but we'd miss the main show, and Payton made it sound like this was a one-time deal." His fingers moved the hair off of my neck so he could set his lips there. Every deep breath he took or brush of his mouth against the delicate skin gave me a fresh wave of goosebumps.

So I sat in the chair with my hands handcuffed behind my back, my head tilted to the side so Joseph could kiss, lick, and bite my neck, all while I watched Payton suck on Dominic's enormous dick.

I had so much need, there wasn't any room for shame.

"Okay," Dominic said abruptly, "that's enough of that. Are you trying to make me come in your mouth?" He stepped back and . . . was he blushing?

Payton held an evil smile. "You should have let me have my hands."

He took off his shoes, and pants, tugging off his socks, until he was completely naked. His body was flawless, but at the same time, not perfect to me. Both Dominic and Payton were polished and maintained, her with perfectly sculpted eyebrows and manicured nails, and him with his ridged muscles. I preferred the realness of Joseph.

But I was still a woman with eyeballs. Dominic looked pretty damn good, and on his hip . . . the same black tattoo in Japanese. This couple matched in almost every way possible. He leaned down and undid the knots, rubbing the marks left on her wrists.

"Dominic," she said, climbing to her feet, her hand instantly on him, stroking and twisting her grip. "I want this inside me. Make the ache go away."

Dominic's head swung to us, his eyes narrow. "Joseph thinks he's seen it all." He turned back to his fiancé. "Wanna show him what I taught you?"

She frowned. "That's not how I want it, but . . ." The frown melted away into a smirk. "Yeah. You have my permission."

The lips on my neck paused, as if Joseph was watching them. Dominic wrapped his strong arms around Payton, threading a hand through her hair, holding her head steady while he stared down at her. "Come for me. Right now."

She gasped. Visible tremors traveled up her legs, and her body went limp. The gasp built into a moan, then crescendoed into a cry as she shuddered in his embrace. *Coming.* Only from his command.

Dominic's focus turned from the woman moaning in his arms to us, but I knew he wasn't seeing me. His expression was challenging toward Joseph and . . . territorial?

"Shit." Joseph's voice was loud by my ear. "Not bad." His mouth came back to my skin at the spot where my neck met my shoulder. "If I trained you to come on my command," his lips feathered over my skin, "I wouldn't ask permission. I'd just do it over and over again until you passed out."

Could that happen? Could Joseph make the orgasms come so easily he could just demand them? Heat poured through my veins. Joseph's fingers walked across my waist, slipping both hands beneath the bottom of my shirt. Cool air crept in.

The word was unstoppable, and I spoke it on barely a breath. "Wait."

"No. You want this. You're arching your back and making it easier for me."

Oh my God, I was. The shirt was carried up with his hands, exposing my midriff. Further until it was bunched up around my chest, my bra-covered breasts visible. He was right. A fever burned in me, craving for his hands to tug on my nipples through the flimsy fabric. Holy hell, I wanted him to pull my bra down and twist my breasts until they ached. And I wanted Dominic and Paton to see.

But the couple was busy. She kissed him aggressively, set her hands flat on his chest, and shoved him down to sit on the table. He slid further onto the tabletop so his bent knees hung at the edge, and leaned back, bracing himself on his arms. Without words and using a single look to communicate, Payton climbed up on him, straddling his lap, her hands on his shoulders.

Her hand glided down his chest, curling her fingers around him, and held him steady as her hips began to lower down.

Holy fucking God.

My chest was so tight, I couldn't breathe. Joseph's fingers rubbed my nipples and brought them to painfully hard points. I gave a noise that was like a soft whine. His touch was overpowering, and although I wanted to close my eyes to enjoy it better, I didn't dare. He'd order me to open them, and deep down, I couldn't miss a second of what I was seeing.

Dominic's moan was deep when she was fully seated on him. "Take it off. I need to see all of you."

Payton's hands went to the center of the corset, her

fingers quickly undoing the slide clasps that held it closed. Her breasts burst free, and she tossed the garment aside, instantly filling her hands with the large, round globes. Pushing them together, she leaned forward so Dominic could bury his face between them.

That was when she began to move up and down. Riding him with her knee only an inch from the edge of the small tabletop they filled. I clenched my jaw. I had to stop panting because it sounded embarrassing, and I shifted in the seat, unbearably uncomfortable.

"What do you want?" The dark voice whispered in my ear. "Tell me, little girl. What do you need?"

I was half out of my mind. "I need you to fuck me."

He exhaled and the breath rolled over my skin in a wave, caressing down my chest. There was no response. Joseph had definitely heard me. Dominic and Payton would have too, but they were in their own world right now. She shifted forward and back in his lap, hammering down on him so hard her breasts bounced with each repeated impact. Her head was cast back, and his mouth on her neck.

As her pace grew in intensity, Dominic used only one hand to support himself, and put the other on her waist, helping her keep the furious tempo.

"Look at how deep he's fucking her. Imagine how good that feels. You want my cock that deep inside you?"

"Yes." I was sure I had never wanting anything more.

But once again, Joseph fell silent. What was he waiting for? I was smart enough to know we were playing a game, but didn't know the rules.

I turned my head toward his. "Please." My plea was soft and filled with desperation. "Joseph, please. I need you inside me. I want them to watch as you fuck me."

The hands left my body and I shivered when their warmth was gone, but sighed in relief as his chair slid quietly away. He came into view, and the lust that painted Joseph's expression made each nerve in my body tingle. Every inch of me was at his attention.

"Listen to you beg. You're a dirty girl," he said, although in his tone it sounded like a compliment. "You'd let my friends watch?"

My sex-drunk mind had my thoughts sluggish. Could I do it? "Yes." Oh yes, I could, especially with the way Joseph stared at me. The smile that I'd pleased him intensified the emptiness I felt, which only he could fill.

I was marginally aware that he undid the side zipper on my skirt and pulled it down. I'd been bashful at first, but now I embraced it all. Naïve, inexperienced Noemi was about to go down in a blaze of sin so hot it'd melt metal.

But... wait. I was sitting in a chair, how was this going to happen and not be uncomfortable for both of us? When I moved my arms, the handcuffs answered back. He hadn't just handcuffed them together, he'd put them through one of the slats in the chairback, which meant I couldn't stand up.

"Joseph—"

On stage, Payton took in huge gulps of breath, her gorgeous face sheened with sweat. Beneath her, Dominic wasn't fairing much better. He was slick with sweat and his supporting arm shook with exertion.

They disappeared when Joseph blocked them. My Dom, with dark eyes and an obscene mouth which turned my insides into liquid, leaned over and undid my bra clasp. The bra and shirt were pushed up above my chest. I stared at him, filled with a mixture of anxiety and excitement. There was trust, too. Oh, he had some sort of plan, it was clear in his eyes.

He stepped to the side so he wasn't blocking my view of the bodies connected on the stage, where the table rocked gently with the force of passion happening there. Doing this, meant they now could see me. All of me.

"Show them," Joseph ordered. "Let them see how badly you want this, baby girl."

I exhaled a stuttering breath, and parted my legs. Payton's head turned first, her mouth dropping open.

"Fuck," she said, getting Dominic to follow her gaze.

My face burst into flames, but I didn't look away. My nerves made me oddly strong. Payton's rhythm slowed to a halt, and her gaze seemed to trace every inch of my bare skin. Breath stuck in my throat when her expression changed into . . . my brain scrambled to come up with the right word. Its first attempt had been *want*, but that couldn't be right. Oh, shit, was it? Did this beautiful woman currently having sex with a gorgeous man somehow desire me?

"Holy fuck," she gasped. "She has perfect tits. I want them in my mouth."

Everything moved too fast. Dominic threw a look to Joseph and grinned back at Payton.

"Come over here," Joseph said to them.

chapter
TWENTY-ONE

I jolted upright in the chair and snapped my legs closed. My nervous eyes turned to Joseph. "Wait."

The table groaned in protest when Payton climbed off of Dominic and walked on her high heels toward me. The sway of her hips and bounce of her breasts were mesmerizing. Hypnotic.

Joseph strolled to stand behind my chair, curled a hand under my chin, and tugged my head back to look up at him. "Wait? Or do you mean stop? Because you're perfectly safe. Payton can see how fucking sexy you are, and I'm not going to deny her if she wants to make you feel good. Watching that would please me, and you want that, don't you?"

I couldn't get my brain to function. I blinked, held immobile not just by the steel on my wrists, but by his eyes. His head dipped down, sealing his lips over mine when a new pair of hands touched me. Her soft palms were on my shoulders, sliding inward and down.

My moan was swallowed by Joseph when she found my nipples with her fingers, tugging.

"Joseph," Payton sighed softly. "She's so fucking perfect." The out-of-control feeling her words gave me sent me spinning. Something wet brushed over my nipple. Her tongue. It was gone abruptly, so she could speak. "*Yes.*"

"Watch," Joseph commanded quietly, releasing his grip so I could. "Watch him fuck her while she sucks on your tits."

I don't know how she could, my chest was heaving hard.

One of her hands gripped my shoulder firmly, the other held my breast up to her lips. Behind her, Dominic's hands circled her waist, gently thrusting into her.

"Oh my God," I said. Her response was to nip at me.

"Open your legs, Em," she urged. "Scoot to the edge of your seat." So it would be more comfortable for her.

"Do it," Joseph said.

My eyes drifted closed for a moment as I complied, only to feel the sharp sting of Joseph's pinch. Payton's cheek was warm and damp against my breast as Dominic's thrusts became more urgent.

"You look so good like that, Payton. Your face in between her tits. Suck on them for me."

I bit down on my bottom lip and strangled back a cry of pleasure. My pussy was shamefully wet. The taboo of the experience turned me on more than anything else, although the suction of her mouth was hot, too. My arms ached and I couldn't help but want the handcuffs gone.

"What would you do," Joseph said, still looming over me, "if you had your hands? Would you touch yourself, or her? Would you push her head down until she was licking your sweet pussy?"

"Fuck," Dominic groaned. His hand was on her shoulder, and the fingers clenched as if the visual had brought him much closer to coming than he expected. And Dominic's hand was only a few inches from my breast. What would happen if he slipped and brushed me accidentally? What if he touched me purposefully? It was all so dangerous.

"Wait." I immediately wanted the word back. Payton's startled expression turned to mine, her hands hesitating.

"Keep going," Joseph said to her, then his gaze swept

back to me. In the low light he was frighteningly beautiful. "We're getting close to something new and exciting whenever that word comes out. When you say *wait*, all I hear is *push*. Now tell us, because I know Dominic's dying to hear if Payton can slide her tongue inside your pussy. Yes, or no."

My hands had balled into fist and my nails dug into my palms. The mouth working my breast was nice, but my body demanded satisfaction lower. I'd silenced the conservative side of myself, and a new woman rose up in her place. Wild, free, and sexual. I wanted someday to be a shark in the boardroom, but a shark in the bedroom now? Even better.

"Yes," I whispered, too quickly to change my mind or think about repercussions. What had I just agreed to? I wasn't bisexual. Was I? Women were attractive, and I'd felt weirdly turned on watching the occasional threesome that was two girls and a guy, but this was such a huge leap. Would I be filled with regret and shame tomorrow?

No. Joseph had told me I wasn't allowed to. I gave over and submitted.

Payton's mouth was locked on a nipple, drawing it between her teeth right on the edge of pain, as Dominic's pace suddenly sped to the mind-erasing one Joseph had given me in front of the mirror.

"Shit," he said breathlessly. "Fuck, Payton, I'm getting close."

Her head tilted up to Joseph. "Can he come on her?"

He must have given her a signal because she stood abruptly and stepped out of Dominic's way so he could stand between my legs. What was . . . oh, holy shit. Dominic's hand clenched his dick along with Payton's, both of them pumping their grip on him.

"Wait," I said, my annoying reflex I couldn't get control of. "Wait, wait, wait—"

All the other people heard was push, push, push. Then Dominic gave an enormous gasp, followed by a slew of profanity as his hot cum shot onto my naked flesh. Ribbon after ribbon of white struck my skin, painted on my belly and . . . lower. I moaned as he coated my pussy, so needy for any kind of contact that even this felt good.

I didn't blink and my chin rested on the shirt wadded around my neck, my mouth wide open so I could choke in air. Payton's hand slowed on Dominic's dick as his soft moans did, his body recovering from the explosion.

What was I supposed to think about what had just happened? It was so far out of my comfort zone I wasn't sure. But what about Joseph? My head lolled toward him, and he watched me back with interest, as if gauging my reaction. His lips pulled back into a pleased smile, which heated me all the way to my core.

"Clean that up." Dominic's deep voice cut through my fog. This was an order he'd given to Payton. Clean it . . . ?

"Oh, shit," I said. "Wait." *Dammit, stop doing that.*

There was a flurry of activity when Payton sank to her knees between my thighs. Both men grabbed chairs and sat on either side of me.

"Is that a 'stop'?" Joseph asked lightly. His fingertips touched my knee, gently pulling it back so Payton had more room. The warm, thick liquid was creeping down my stomach, slowly making its way to my aching clit. *No, it wasn't a stop.* I pressed my lips together and shook my head.

"I'll try not to say it again." I was tired of being a scared little lamb.

Joseph's other hand rested on the back of my neck and he kissed me so softly it made me woozy. "It's more than fine, baby girl. You're nervous and I'm asking a lot of you, but I know you're going to like this. And me? I'm going to fucking love it." He glanced across the way. "Dominic, you mind?"

He gestured to my legs, and Dominic understood. His hand slipped onto my knee, so the men held me open for her. Payton's hands rested just on the inside of the men's, warm hands on my legs.

She made a noise of appreciation. "Look at how she fucking trembles. God, feel it in her legs. It's so sexy." She leaned forward and licked just below my bellybutton, getting me to flinch, and both men tightened their grip in response. She licked again, this one lower and dangerously close to my pussy. "She makes me feel," her tongue swiped lower, "powerful."

"Yes," Joseph said. I couldn't tell if it was in agreement to Payton's words, or encouragement for what she was doing. I moaned when her tongue lapped at me, then slid up. Apparently following Dominic's command was the first order of business. I grew lightheaded from how hard I was breathing.

"Do you like it, you filthy slut?" Joseph whispered, his hand shifting to wrap around my throat, his thumb pressing gently across my windpipe, asserting his control. "You've got another man's cum on you."

I stared back at him, unable to find words. I could feel his power at all times, but now it was like a blanket, covering me completely. Her tongue danced on my wet skin, slicking over it, taking her time as she removed all traces of Dominic from me. The tremble continued, making me vibrate in the seat. My arms had gone numb behind my back while the rest of me was on fire.

As Payton's head moved steadily toward my center, her long ponytail fell against my skin, tickling me, and a nervous half-laugh came from my throat. Oh my God, another woman was about to go down on me while two men watched.

"Mmm," I moaned and arched my back when she made contact, unintentionally shoving my breasts toward the men. Joseph dipped his head and captured the one closest in his lips.

Dominic's hand squeezed my knee. "Payton, I love watching you eat pussy."

Her tongue swirled just as Joseph's did and I bucked in the chair. Payton's hand covered Dominic's and pushed it up my thigh, but he turned to stone.

"No, devil woman. She's Joseph's—"

Payton issued an exasperated sound. "Sharing isn't one of his limits."

The thought stopped me cold and I kicked myself for not realizing it sooner. Joseph and Payton . . . had they slept together? Oh, shit. Had she been one of his subs? She seemed to know a lot about him, but then again, he hadn't told her about his past.

Joseph gave a wicked laugh. "I don't mind. She certainly won't."

Because I'd posted a clip last night of a woman blowing one guy while another did her from behind. I held the fantasy that most other women did, but performance anxiety filled me now. One man took so much focus, how on earth would I handle two? Or two and a woman?

My brain went quiet when Payton's hand guided

Dominic's onto my other breast and her tongue continued its wicked stroke. His large, rough hand gripped me firmly.

"Fuck," I moaned. Having three people focused on me at once sent me into meltdown. Overload. Joseph's mouth carved a path up my throat until his lips were on mine, delivering a dominating kiss that leveled me.

Hands were everywhere. On my knees. My breasts. Payton's fingers spread me open so she could suck in a pulsating rhythm right on my clit. Blood roared in my ears. My heart raced and I struggled for each breath as my eyes fell closed. It felt so impossibly good. Everyone caressing, licking, and working together to get me there.

When my kiss with Joseph ended, his forehead pressed against mine, his hand still gripping my throat and his face filled with power. "Use your fingers, Payton. I want to watch this bad girl come apart." Even as he spoke to her, his intense stare never wavered from mine.

I gazed back and my eyes hooded when a finger teased my entrance, then pushed inside.

"Oh," I said on a broken breath, no louder than a whisper.

"This is what I wanted," Joseph said. "Watching you right on the edge." The finger thrust over and over, coupled with her tongue working back and forth on my sensitive clit. "Are you ready to go over?"

I swallowed hard, which he had to feel with his grip on my throat. His fingers tightened, his head dropped down, and he licked my erect nipple.

"Make the anal virgin squirm," he commanded.

Oh, shit. What did that mean?

"Yeah?" Her voice was pleasantly surprised, and one of her fingers nudged down.

"Wait." I mashed my teeth together. "Oh, fuck." The new finger was pushing deeper, pressing against me.

"Dominic, distract," Payton said, her lips pausing against my quaking center long enough to get the words out, and then there were two men with their mouths on my breasts.

I was holding back a tidal wave and fighting a losing battle. Each tiny inch further her finger intruded, the harder it was to keep myself from bursting. Looking down at the men with their tongues on my flesh, hers between my folds while she peered up at me with big eyes, was the image that sent me over.

"Joseph, I'm gonna come . . ." I quivered right at the precipice, as if I needed his permission.

"Good girl. Do it all over her dirty fingers."

The bliss detonated from my center and I cried out, my leg muscles tensing painfully. But everywhere else—pleasure. Pure and total ecstasy. My limbs went numb and boneless as the sensation rocked my foundation.

Maybe there was something wrong with me. Vanilla, old-fashioned sex wasn't enough to get me off, but I no longer gave a fuck. If this was what I needed, and this was who I was, I was fine with it. Even a little happy. I rode the surge of my orgasm all the way down on Payton's fingers, finally unclenching my body's grip as the amazing tingling began to wash away.

Joseph held my gaze, his dark eyes shining. He was still fully dressed, while everyone else was essentially naked. Tonight had been about my pleasure, but watching me receive it seemed to have given him plenty of satisfaction.

Reality strengthened with each heartbeat, and now I was aware everyone was staring at me. I didn't know what to say, so I blurted out, "Wow. That was a . . . long one."

Payton grinned, wiping her mouth with the back of her hand. "Sounded like it. I'm a little fucking jealous." She glanced at Dominic. "Can you get the keys out of my purse? Her arms probably feel awesome right now."

Oh, no. As soon as she said that, it made me aware of the shooting pains. I grimaced as I slipped back in the chair to sit straight. I silently encouraged Dominic to move faster as he went to her purse and dug out the keys, tossing them to Joseph.

As he unlocked my first cuff, I stared down at my legs, unable to look at anyone else. It made no sense to be shy now, and yet, cold pooled in my belly. What did they think of this trembling girl Joseph had brought along to play with?

The metal cuffs clunked to the floor and I pulled my shoulders forward, staying quiet even as my stiff muscles were in agony. His hands settled on my biceps, massaging.

"Better?" he asked.

"Yeah, thanks." His hands were heaven on my aching body.

Payton and Dominic went to the stage and I watched as Dominic yanked a leg into his pants. Payton slipped her panties back on, and set about refastening the corset. A signal that the show had ended.

Joseph seized my hands when I tugged my bra down back in place and attempted to hook the clasp. His voice was sharp. "What do you think you're doing?"

I exhaled a concerned breath. "I was going to get dressed."

"Did you ask if you could?"

Every second that ticked by made me more naked than anyone else. "No, but I thought since they were—"

"You don't want to be naked."

Wasn't that obvious? My arms hurt and I let it get the better of me. I threw Joseph a plain look. "No, of course I don't."

Huge mistake. His expression soured.

"I'm sorry," I said quickly. "May I get dressed, Sir?"

"No," he snapped. "Tell me why you don't want to be naked. Are you uncomfortable with your body?"

Not really, and yet, yes. I was raised Catholic, and learned early on that women's bodies needed to be covered appropriately. Being indecent was a sin. "I . . ."

His hand hooked under my arm and gently pulled me to my feet, and then he was lifting my shirt and bra up over my head. Stripping me of everything except for my sandals.

"Go to the bar and bring me the bottle of Jack Daniel's." His order was stern.

My mouth went completely dry. It was a million feet to the bar and back, and Payton and Dominic were already dressed, watching our exchange. I pivoted on my heel, held my head as high as I could muster, and went on my unsteady feet toward the bar. Going would be easy. Coming back would be much harder as I had to face them. Maybe I could pretend not to find the bottle and stall, but what good would it do? Joseph would treat it as disobedience and wouldn't let that stand.

The whiskey with the black label wasn't hard to locate. I gripped the neck of the bottle and turned around, steeling my expression into one that I hoped was blank. It felt like there were a billion pairs of eyes watching me and not just three as I paced forward.

"Look at them," Joseph demanded. "You think they're

judging your body? Fuck no. That's lust. Desire. You're gorgeous and sexy, and watching you come only made them want more."

My pulse jumped. "More?"

Joseph smiled, his eyes glittering in the dim light. "Yes. Unless you want to get dressed and I can take you home."

Dominic stood behind Payton, his hands splayed on her hips. What Joseph had said was true. They eyed me like I was delicious, and a new fire ignited low in my center. It was a powerful feeling.

"Which is it?" Joseph asked lightly, like he didn't care one way or the other, and perhaps he didn't. But he'd said he believed this was a one-time opportunity with them, and I wasn't going to waste it.

My tone was confident despite the lack of clothing. "More."

He thundered toward me, ensnared me in his arms, and crushed me tightly against him. His voice was so low, it was a growl. "You're so fucking amazing, Noemi."

chapter
TWENTY-TWO

JOSEPH

There were no words for how hot this girl was. The way she let me push, which really was the way she pushed herself. I would back down if she wanted me to, but she didn't. She wanted... more.

Me? I wanted it all.

This arrangement had been a joke the moment I'd declared her mine. Our relationship was far more serious than the arrangement I'd had with my other submissives. An undeniable need compelled us together.

"You can get dressed," I said to Noemi. "But don't expect the clothes to stay on long, and those panties stay where Payton left them." She pressed her lips together, nodded, and passed the bottle of Jack to me. When I released her, she hurried to the pile of clothes I'd discarded.

It was a fucking crime to hide that body. Why she wouldn't be proud of it, was beyond me. But perhaps it was good, too. She was still unaware of how much power she had when she was like that. Noemi was smart. It wouldn't be much longer before she figured it out and I'd have to step up my game.

The whiskey had a nice burn to it, and the heat lingered in the back of my throat. Hell, heat lingered everywhere in me, but it was the burn for her. Did she have a clue how crazy she made me? I'd crawled into her fucking bed last night, wanting her near.

It's not like we had all that much in common. A handful of similar interests, not including her father. Noemi Rosso was so much better than me. In an entirely different class, but like a selfish prick, I'd keep her as long as she'd let me. I couldn't get enough.

When she was dressed, her nervous expression had the Dom inside me salivating. "You want something else to drink?" I asked. "Rum and Coke?"

She shook her head. "Something stronger."

I laughed, knowing her reasons. "Like a shot of Everclear?"

She strode close and leaned in to me, her voice hushed. "I just want something to take the tremble away."

Her waist was small in my hands, where it fit so perfectly.

"But I fucking love your tremble."

"I don't." Her expression was pained.

I set my hand on her cheek and brushed my thumb over her lush lips. "The things I'm going to do to you, they're going to make you tremble no matter what."

She inhaled. "Then some liquid courage won't hurt."

I gave a short laugh and abandoned my hold on her, strolling to the bar. I made another round of drinks for everyone while Payton went to the restroom, and I watched as Noemi grasped the shot glass, determination in her eyes. She tilted it back and swallowed the clear liquid, and immediately gagged.

"Shit." She dropped the glass on the bar and it fell over, rolling until Dominic stopped it and set it upright. "Oh my God, did you give me rubbing alcohol?"

I grinned. "Watch your tone, and you did ask for it."

Noemi's lips rounded into an 'O' and she blew out a long breath, as if trying to cool the fire in her mouth. I handed her the glass of Sprite I'd had ready, and she gulped it down.

Once recovered, Noemi stood straight and turned toward the sound of Payton's heels clicking across the floor. "Can I ask you something?"

Payton gave her a friendly smile. "Only if I can ask you something back."

"Your tattoos." Noemi gestured to both Payton and Dominic. "What do they mean?"

I hadn't seen Payton's ink before tonight. In fact, the last time I'd seen Payton naked had been more than a year ago and the last time she'd seen a client—Dominic. Before him, she'd never do anything like that. The old Payton would have looked at her tattoo and instantly thought she'd been branded.

"It means 'real' in Japanese," Dominic answered.

Normally I would have said the sweet exchange of glances between them was sickening. But the way he fucking *looked* at her, like she was the whole world . . . If I tried to give either one of them shit about it, I would be a bigger asshole than I already was. And since Noemi, nothing for me was normal anymore.

Nothing lasts forever.

I took another long pull on the bottle of Jack, drowning the voice into silence.

"What's your question for me?" Noemi asked.

Payton's face was unreadable and filled me with worry. "How'd you two meet?"

"At his other club, Dune. I'd been too busy staring at him up on the balcony to get out of the way of a fistfight, and afterward Joseph wanted to make sure I was all right."

She'd been staring up at the balcony? Unexpected warmth spread over me from her words. Noemi turned the glass of Sprite absentmindedly on the bar, displaying her adorable fidget when she was anxious. She must have felt my gaze on her, for her shoulders straightened and she turned to face me head-on. Giving me her full attention, which I very much appreciated.

"Do you want another shot of courage?" I asked.

Her eyes widened. "No, thank you. One was . . . great. More than enough."

I smirked, then glanced at Dominic. "There are a pair of couches in the holding room backstage. I thought we could head there, unless you need anything from here first?"

Dominic ran a hand through his short, dirty blond hair. "Champagne?"

Payton laughed and a wide smile spread on her lips. "Oh my God, of course. I'll grab the cake." She lifted the box off the bartop and wrapped an arm around Noemi. "You bought him a fucking cake. I love it."

Noemi's hazel-eyed gaze captured mine and my chest tightened. Her silly white cake with the roses and its obscene message had gotten to me. How could I admit part of me didn't want anyone else to eat it? She'd gotten it for *me*.

There were two bottles of champagne in one of the fridge units beneath the bar, and they were cold in my hands as I escorted everyone backstage to the green room. It wasn't impressive. A narrow room with two couches opposite each other, the one on the right much bigger than the one on the left, and along the back wall, a table with a row of globe lights over a mirror.

Payton set the cake down on the table while Dominic and I got the champagne open.

"To twenty more cancer-free years," Payton said, taking a swig from the bottle and passing it back to Dominic.

"Hopefully a lot more," I said dryly.

I handed our bottle to Noemi and waited until she was mid-sip. I leaned over, shoved my hand under her skirt and ran my fingers up between her legs. All the way until I hit the soft, wet pussy I was going to claim very soon. I brushed my fingertips over her clit. One light stroke and then I dropped my hand, letting the skirt fall back in place. "Take off everything, little girl. You'll be naked as long as we're in this room."

She choked on the champagne, a little leaking out of her pursed lips and had to use a finger to wipe it away. I took the bottle from her, and set it on the floor beside the smaller couch as I sat down.

"Same rule for you," Dominic quipped to his fiancé.

Payton had no shame, and no reason for it. You'd be hard-pressed to find a man who wouldn't jump at the chance to fuck her. Long legs, perfect ass, big tits, and a gorgeous face. Hardly anyone suspected an intelligent mind lurked behind her sparkling blue eyes. A college-educated woman, who'd been the star of my brothel for more than a year. People assumed she worked for me because she had little options, but she'd come by choice. She'd love it just as much as I had.

But nothing lasts forever. I'd assumed she'd stay as I had. Single. Unattached. Shit, the same could be said of me.

Noemi's shaky hands lifted her shirt over her head. This girl was a thousand times more appealing to me than

Payton. Noemi's mixture of innocence and eagerness was fucking addicting. My cock throbbed when her bra was undone and her breasts revealed. Tight pink nipples surrounded by creamy, pale skin that begged to be touched, and licked, and fucked—No, fucking her between her perfect breasts would have to be some other time. More important things were on the agenda tonight.

My gaze followed the descent of her skirt. I wanted to own every inch of her skin, to command all of her. I needed to hear her moans of pleasure like I needed oxygen. Holy shit. Maybe the Jack Daniel's was exaggerating my thoughts. Hopefully.

"Come here," I said, taking her hand and tugging her down into my lap, straddling me. My hands cupped her breasts as I thrust up against her. "Feel that? My cock is so fucking hard for you."

She rocked her hips and I clamped my teeth around a nipple, firm enough until I heard a sharp hiss. But it made her rock against me faster.

"That's what you like, filthy girl. A little pain, just enough to show you you're alive."

I hadn't paid much attention to the other couple, my blinders were on when Noemi's clothes were off. Payton was already naked. She'd pulled out a short crop with a heart cutout on the black leather tip, and held it up for Dominic. It must have come from her purse. This was for soft play, not big enough for a serious scene.

I adjusted Noemi in my lap so she faced sideways and could watch the new show starting.

"Bend over the couch," Dominic said. It was the first time he'd used that tone, the distinct voice of a Dominant.

He'd thought showing Payton come by command alone was something new for me, and it was, but I was most excited to see this. No one at the club, myself included, had been able to get her to really submit. Everyone was too focused on their own needs. Trying to 'get' from Payton instead of 'give.' I was curious to see the man in action who had tamed her.

Payton crossed her arms and rested them on the back of the couch, shoving her ass out into the air, ready.

"You want this?" he asked.

"Fuck, yes."

"Where?" He teased the tip of the riding crop over the curve of her ass. "Here?"

It came out as a desperate sigh. "Yes."

He kicked her feet further apart, pushing on her back and positioning her lower. Noemi's gaze was fixated on Payton's glistening pussy, all bare and waiting. Anticipation seeped into the room.

"You want it?" Dominic's tone was aggressive and harsh. "Say please."

"Oh my God, Dominic, please."

His first lash struck her left ass cheek and blood rushed to the irritated skin, leaving a perfect heart of pale skin surrounded by red. The snap of the crop made Noemi jump and her stiff posture told me she was trying very hard not to do it again. Like she wanted to appear unaffected.

I had my arms around her, one hand rested on her bent knee and the other on her hip. So I tightened my arm around her back while the hand on her knee traveled deep between her thighs. Her breathing went shallow as I kneaded her swollen clit.

"Do you deserve another?" Dominic's rough voice pulled

my attention back to their scene. He had the tip of the crop tapping lightly right against her pussy, and Payton's back arched. Soft moans came from her.

"Yes, please," she said.

"I don't know. You were awfully bossy earlier."

She exhaled slowly. "I'll be good."

The crop sliced through the air suddenly, landing hard against her other ass cheek, and Payton let out a startled cry.

"I know you'll be good." His voice was patronizing. "You'll be fucking amazing like you always are, but you," he tapped her clit gently with the crop, "are *not* in charge." His free hand grabbed a handful of her ass, squeezing. He had to speak loud to be heard over her pants for air. "Tell me, Payton. Who owns this?"

"You. Oh, fuck, you do."

He slapped the crop once more on her flesh, watching the heart develop on her stinging skin. He snarled the word, "Mine."

My fingers had paused their wicked movements between Noemi's legs, distracted by the display of power. I was so hard it was painful. Every subtle shift of her body on mine was blissful agony.

I slapped my fingers on her clit, just a little too aggressive to be playful, and she jolted. Her shocked eyes blinked wide, but then hooded again when I rubbed her. Her quiet moan of pleasure shot straight to my dick, so I slapped her pussy again, this time harder. She let out a little yelp. Pain? Surprise? I couldn't tell, and her hand covered her mouth.

"I think you need one more," I whispered.

Her unblinking gaze focused sharply on my hand. Where was the *wait* from her lips? Or the *stop*? I reared my hand up and brought it down swiftly, halting suddenly an inch from her skin, but the effect worked. She flinched for the incoming blow, and as soon as she realized what I'd done, her shoulders relaxed. That was when I slapped her clit a final time.

"Fuck," she cried, shuddering in my embrace, and her hand fell away from her mouth to clench on my forearm.

"There's the tremble." I massaged her slick skin, teasing. "Doesn't it feel better now when I touch you?" Fuck, I could get lost in those big eyes of hers which seemed to see right into my soul. Her fingernails dug into my skin.

"Yes, Sir."

I kissed her, and for the first brief moment she tasted of the champagne, but then it was one hundred percent her. The flavor of Noemi Rosso, another hit of my new drug. I wanted my cock in her mouth. In her cunt. Deep in her ass.

"Get on your knees," I said.

She moved swiftly, kneeling between my legs, her hands on my belt. She rushed to get the leather end undone.

"My, we're enthusiastic." I pulled her silky hair up into a loose ponytail so it wouldn't be in her way, but also gave me a point of control. Noemi's fingers deftly extracted me from my pants and boxers, and I groaned at her touch. *Finally.* I'd chosen not to participate earlier, wanting to draw out the anticipation, but holy fuck, I'd almost broken a dozen times during it.

The half-smile on her lips was my clue something was up, but then her rosy lips opened and she welcomed my cock into her scorching mouth.

"Shit," I said quietly.

Overall I liked fucking better, where we were both

getting off, but there was nothing that matched the pure sensation of oral. Her tongue swirled over the sensitive spot on the tip, forcing my free hand to clench into a fist.

"That's right," I whispered. "Just like that."

Warmth slid down and then up, and she pulled me from her mouth. She ran her lips all the way down the length, skimming the edge of her teeth on the way back. I appreciated the visual, and my lust burned a thousand degrees hotter when her eyes fluttered open to catch me watching.

She took me once again in her mouth, her tongue spinning around the head of my cock, before pushed down to take me further. And further.

"Yes, baby girl. Oh, fuck, yes." Holy shit, she moved slowly but was inching along, taking me much deeper than before. I hit the back of her throat and she kept pushing, her mouth like a vise. Then, she made a gagging sound and backed off abruptly.

"What happened here?" I teased. "They're offering cocksucking classes at that Catholic school now?"

She looked like she found it both amusing and offensive at the same time, but brushed the comment away. Her expression was determination and she stared at my dick, wet with her saliva. "I can do this."

A short laugh tore from my lungs. "I love that you're such an overachiever. You don't have to immediately be the best at everything you try."

She ignored me and wrapped her hand around my cock, running her tongue over the tip, licking. My toes curled inside my shoes and my balls ached. Her mouth descended on me again, and it was more torturous pleasure. Why was I giving her a hard time about this? She *wanted* to practice deep-throating on me. I needed to shut my stupid fucking mouth and thank my lucky stars for this girl.

But the wolf inside me would not be quiet. "Maybe if you make it all the way to the base, I can get you a cake."

This time she didn't choke on my cock, it was my words. She retreated and tried again, her eyes squeezed shut in concentration as more and more of my dick disappeared in her mouth.

"Goddamnit." I fought back the urge to push on her head. She didn't need any help, and I had to stop being a fucking asshole. "Jesus, that feels so good."

She pulled off me, breathless, a scowl on her face. Disappointment, and it was fucking adorable. I clenched my grip tighter in her hair, forcing her gaze on me.

"Has someone been reading deep throating tips on the internet?"

Her bottom lip quivered. "Among other things."

"Yeah?" I leaned forward and brought my face closer to hers, gently wrapping my other hand around her neck. I liked this position. On her knees and both of my hands on her, controlling exactly where she looked. "What else?"

Her pulse quickened beneath my fingers, pounding in her neck. "I looked up . . . ideas on dirty talking."

I couldn't stop the grin that spread across my face. "You looked up *how* to talk dirty?"

"Yes, Sir." Her gaze began to slip in embarrassment. *Shit.* I corrected her with a soft tug on her hair.

"Hey. I'm sorry. You're already good at this stuff, sometimes I forget it's still new for you."

Her eyes softened. Then, the warmth there burned hotter. "I also looked up stuff about . . . um, anal."

I turned her head to the side and pressed my lips against the shell of her ear. "You've no idea how excited I am to hear that, little girl. I'm going to make all of you mine."

She shivered.

We'd ignored the other half of our party, and it was Payton's moans that got me to pay attention. Dominic's pants were bunched around his ankles, his knees spread wide. Payton was seated on him, facing us, her hands covering his on her tits. I watched her ride his fat cock, and was pleased Payton was in this position. Not just a great view, but it made giving my next command easier.

I released my hold on Noemi and let her turn to watch my friend slide up and down on her fiancé's dick, coated in her arousal. Noemi's shoulders rose as she took in a sharp breath. It was hot watching them fuck, but my girl's reaction was even better. I came to my feet and pulled a distracted Noemi to hers, guiding her closer to the couch where Payton bounced. Her tits undulated with the rhythm of the man thrusting beneath her.

Payton watched me, curious. She had to know what was coming. There were a million ways she could have fucked Dominic, but she'd chosen this one. Hesitation grew in Noemi as we came within reaching distance of the couple, and as I stood between the girls, I felt a rush of power. Ultimate control. I put a hand behind each of their heads and drove them together.

Payton's palms latched onto Noemi's jaw and yanked her into a brutal kiss. Noemi endured it, her body tight at first, and relaxing as the kiss deepened. Kissing was kissing, regardless of gender. They made a great picture. Noemi's wavy blonde hair and fresh face in contrast to Payton's deep brunette color and exotic look.

I could not wait any longer. My dick was throbbing too painfully and threatened mutiny. I went to the couch, grabbed two cushions, and dropped them at Noemi's feet. "Back on your knees, little girl. You need to show Payton some gratitude for earlier."

Noemi bolted upright, breaking her kiss, her cheeks flushed. "W-What?"

"You heard me just fine." I used a strict tone. "On your knees. I'm going to fuck you while you lick her pussy."

chapter
TWENTY-THREE

I tugged off my shirt and tossed it onto the far couch, ready to be sans clothes like everyone else. Noemi was frozen until her wide eyes blinked at my tattoo.

"Are you nervous about doing that?" I asked her, undoing my belt.

Her gaze went to Payton, who looked thrilled, then returned to me. "I've never . . ."

"What's there to be nervous about? You can't make a mistake. If you don't like it, just say stop, and we'll know it's a limit." My pants hit the floor and I yanked everything off. Shoes, socks, underwear. I wrapped my arms around her shuddering body, and kissed the hairline on her forehead. "The nerves will go away. Nothing lasts forever."

"They're having sex," she whispered.

I felt a dark laugh build in me, but I silenced it before it bubbled over. "If you're worried about him, I don't think either of them will mind if your tongue wanders."

"And you?"

"I want you to do whatever you want to. That's not a limit for me."

The smack of skin against skin was loud and Payton gasped. Dominic had spanked her, and from the sound, it had been hard.

"You're doing it again, woman," he said. "Let me fucking drive."

Payton grinned, sheepish.

THREE *little* MISTAKES

I didn't have to tell Noemi what to do. She sank to her knees on the couch cushion, positioning them so we could both kneel on them, and faced the writhing couple. A shaky hand was set down for support as she leaned over. So close. Noemi's mouth hung open as she gasped for breath.

"Not yet," I commanded. "Stay exactly like that."

Noemi's perfect body was on all fours in front of me. My gaze traveled the subtle ridges of her spine up to her delicate neck. My hands molded to her hips, skirting up.

"You're so beautiful." It came from me without hesitation. I'd have to keep telling her until she understood.

I stroked my cock and steadied it, and nudged her wet entrance with my tip. I couldn't tease anymore. My body wouldn't allow it, and even though I was the Dom, I was just a slave to my need. I took that first crucial inch of her body, filling her tight heat.

"Oh my God," she whispered, her voice encouraging.

"More?"

"Yes." Her head jerked as she realized her mistake. "Yes, Sir,"

Hearing the title from her lips was the same as the stroke of her tongue on me. "Fuck, take it." The glide of my cock disappearing as I pressed deeper was crazy hot. "Shit," I said on a long breath.

She sighed when I was fully inside and my balls pressed against her swollen, damp clit. I ground my hips into her, giving her another moment to adjust to my possession.

"Now," I drew back, and pressed slowly inside her again, "lick that pussy."

Noemi's body gripped me, squeezing involuntarily at the command. Her trembling hand tucked a lock of hair behind her ear and she reached out, setting a hand delicately on Payton's thigh. Noemi would need something to stabilize on when I started thrusting.

Payton stared down at Noemi with a welcoming, seductive smile. Noemi's hand crept up, stopping right at the juncture of Payton's legs. The head of blonde hair lowered a fraction of an inch.

Payton's voice was desperate. "Don't tease me, or I'll get him involved."

Him being me. Payton respected the rules and knew Noemi didn't have to follow anyone's orders but mine.

Abruptly Payton's back bowed and her head dipped back, disappearing from my view, blocked by her tits. "Go slow," she urged, but this seemed to be to Dominic. "Oh, fuck, just let me enjoy her tongue for a minute." She moaned, and a hand clenched on Noemi's head.

Fuck, it was filled me so much desire I couldn't see straight. "Good girl," I said, my voice tight. "My filthy girl. How does her pussy taste?"

"Oh, no, no, no." Payton's hand held Noemi firm when she tried to lift her head. "Fuck, don't stop." Payton's gaze traveled to connect with mine, pleasure rippling through her expression. "Joseph, don't let her—" Her eyes shut tightly and she bit down on her lip.

Noemi's head turned to rest against Payton's thigh, giving me an exact view of Noemi's tongue sliding around as if restless. She'd tease Payton's clit, then dart away, only to return after gasping for breath. I increased my pace, being careful not to thrust too hard and jolt Noemi out of her tenuous position.

"You dirty slut." I grasped her hip firmly and dug my

fingers into her flesh. I wasn't going to last long watching this, and judging from their moans, neither were the future Mr. and Mrs. Ward. I put my thumb in my mouth to wet it. I'd need to prep Noemi so she could enjoy what I had planned.

"You. Dirty. *Filthy*. Slut."

Noemi exhaled in a burst as my thumb pressed down on her tight asshole.

"Wait." I heard it in Noemi's voice, but all she meant was push, and so I did. Her back arched and she tensed.

"Deep breath and relax, baby girl." My thumb worked its way along. I'd come to a stop with my cock lodged deep inside so I could focus on going slow and gentle while I took her into unfamiliar territory.

The cautious first movement of my thumb made her hand clench on Payton's skin. I worked her looser with each push and pull, until Noemi's hand softened. Her eyes closed, but her expression, at least what I could see from the side, seemed to be enjoyment. *Good*.

"Who said you could stop eating pussy?"

There was a deep moan from Payton when Noemi's pink tongue resumed its fluttering path. Dominic's hands were on Payton's waist and helping her ride him slowly. His fingers splayed out over the black tattoo. The symbol of their connection. *Real*. And for the first time in my life, I wanted that. A bond to someone else that was meaningful.

God, the Jack and the anniversary had done a number on my emotions.

Focus. Control.

I gave a thrust to Noemi that was serious, both in her pussy and her ass, and she cried out with surprise, but it melted into a moan. Because I was so deep in her, I could feel the thumb on my cock, pressing between her walls. She was so tight, and it felt amazing.

"You're licking pussy while I've got my dick inside you, and a thumb in your ass, little girl. What would your father say?"

"Oh, God," she uttered. Only it was in pleasure. Her body rocked against mine, trying to fuck me right back.

"Such a bad girl, you can't stop now. Help Dominic make her come."

"Don't *need* help, Joseph," Dominic answered instantly, his voice harsh.

"My mistake." I grabbed a handful of Noemi's hair and tugged her head back toward me.

"No!" Payton whined. "Fuck, Joseph, don't be an asshole."

I laughed and released my hold, guiding Noemi back to her original position. "I want to hear you make her scream."

As she got back to work, I wondered how she felt about all this. Her total submission made me burn and ache. Made me want to stretch and reach. Maybe be a better person so I could give her more and stay with her longer.

Noemi's tongue withdrew back into her mouth for a moment with a saliva trail, and she swallowed to catch a breath. "I'm . . . getting close."

Payton's purse was nearby, as was their bottle of champagne. Noemi gave a noise of disappointment when I pulled away from her and climbed off of the couch cushion. "Keep going, I'll be right back."

I'd asked my friend to pack some items for the evening, and the small bottle of lube was right on top of her purse. I grabbed it and the bottle of champagne, taking a swig. The bubbles fizzed on my tongue as I took in the scene. I'd have taken my phone out and snapped a picture, but the last thing I wanted was for it to somehow wind up in the wrong hands. That kind of scandal would destroy not just Noemi, but her entire family.

I tried not to think about what would happen if the media found out Noemi Rosso was dating the owner of an illegal brothel. I was nothing more than a pimp. The shitty truth was it was worse for women. Her father would recover eventually if his activities at my club were discovered. He was going through a divorce and lonely. They could spin that however was needed to make people sympathetic.

But Noemi? Her reputation would be damaged beyond repair. Maybe it could play as I'd been manipulative and preyed on her innocence. Taken advantage, but still, it wouldn't matter.

Didn't you?

"Please, Joseph," Noemi pleaded. "Please. I need you inside me."

My brain stopped working. I was kneeling behind her, the lube uncapped in my hand, and I squeezed out a generous handful. The silky glide as I stroked it on my cock was satisfying, but not the satisfaction I hungered for. I spread the rest of the lube in my palm down between her cheeks.

Payton's cries of pleasure built in intensity and volume. Dominic's pace had increased to short, fast thrusts, his balls slapping against Payton as they fucked. It was much too fast for Noemi to use her mouth, and without prompting, her hand rested just below Payton's belly. Noemi's thumb dipped down and rolled circles on Payton's clit.

Because I'd given my sub a command, and she was

following it.

"Yes, Payton." Noemi's voice was unsteady but determined. "Scream for me."

So fucking hot. I slipped two fingers in her ass, widening her further when Payton let out a cry.

"Oh, fuck. *Fuck!*" Her thighs on either side of Dominic's lap were quaking as she screamed. Shoulders shook in her orgasm, and beneath her, the legs tensed while his movements were erratic.

Seeing these two people come at the same time was a violent, passionate explosion. Their shuddering, sweaty bodies clung to each other as they went to oblivion. Gasped breaths, heaving chests, and after the climax began to pass, their hands tangled. Fingers laces together, and she turned to kiss him.

I was still getting used to seeing that. Payton didn't kiss. Hell, we'd done a lot together, but never kissed. Neither of us was interested in it. But she kissed Dominic now with a raw, passionate intensity that made me jealous. No. I was fucking envious of them. Of what they had. My gaze worked its way along the curve of Noemi's trembling body, who waited on me to claim her.

"You're going to let me put my cock in this tight, little asshole, aren't you, baby girl?"

She shook harder than she ever had before, and it gave me pause. But she nodded, probably unable to find her voice.

I removed my fingers slowly, then prodded my cock against her. "Tell me if I hurt you."

Getting the head in was the worst part, or so I'd heard. I'd never had a cock in my ass. I wasn't open to that kind of domination. I pushed into her resistant body, letting the lube help, and . . .

Noemi gave a hiss of breath as I gained access. "Wait."

This time I listened. I caressed my palms over her skin, trying to distract from the discomfort. The couch shifted as Payton moved off of Dominic. She slithered down beneath us to lie on the cushion, putting her legs between ours. There was a flash of red when Payton's polished nails tunneled through Noemi's hair. The other feminine hand slid down Noemi's waist, disappearing under her body, but it was unmistakable what Payton was doing. Noemi arched from the touch.

"Does that feel better?" Payton whispered into Noemi's ear, her gaze locked onto mine.

I pushed further, just enough so I could move inside her channel that was so impossibly tight. And with that movement, things began to change. A soft moan came from her, which probably had more to do with the fingers on her clit than anything I was doing. I was only in a few inches, but flames of pleasure licked at me. Begged me to take her completely. Own her forever. No one had had her this way, and I'd always be the first.

Payton's lips skimmed Noemi's neck, and I used the opportunity to slip further inside. "Yes, fucking yes," I babbled on an endless loop. Sensations blurred and disoriented me as I pulsed my hips, urging my cock deeper on every advance.

"Oh my God," Noemi murmured.

I was all the way in, utterly connected. I leaned over so I could set my mouth on the opposite side of Noemi's neck from Payton. "You gave me all of your body, Noemi, and it's fucking amazing. You're amazing."

Her pulse raced beneath my lips.

I'd slipped and uttered her full name, but Payton didn't seem to notice. I hadn't planned for it to go like this, but I was pleased having the woman under us, focused on helping Noemi. I assumed her fingers were darting back and forth on the spot that would get Noemi where she was sending me.

"Do you like it?" Payton asked. "His big cock fucking your ass?"

Noemi took in a huge swallow of air, her fingers white-knuckled on the couch cushion. "Yes."

I throbbed inside, moving faster until I was thrusting with force, driving her body against Payton's. Did she like that? Payton's tits flattened against her own? Dominic watched the scene, his expression full of lust but his body looked spent.

Noemi's tremble was so severe it shook all of us. "Joseph, oh my . . . I'm, fuck, I'm—"

I was right there with her, heading to overload. "You're so filthy, and I love it. You want me to come inside your ass, filthy girl?"

"Yes," she cried. "Yes!"

I sawed my cock into her, desperate to send her over the edge before I went. Maybe I should tell Payton to put two fingers inside Noemi's pussy, but she—

A short scream burst from Noemi as her body seized. "I'm coming!"

The snug fit of her was already too much, so when her rhythmic pulses began, I was doomed. "Shit."

No thought was involved. My body went instinctively, driving into her until I crossed the threshold into pleasure that traveled in waves of numbness. I felt the hot torrent rush from my cock, each spurt carrying a new round of bliss with it.

"Holy shit," I moaned, rocking in the cradle of her body. "So good, baby. You make me feel so good." I stopped my words by planting my mouth on her sweat-damp skin, ghosting kisses. Her orgasm receded one breath at a time.

I extracted myself gently, giving her another minute to recover. She lay with her head on Payton's breasts and her arms outstretched, one hand gripping Dominic's ankle. I quirked my mouth into a smile. I'd thrown this little lamb into a pack of wolves, and she'd survived. Not just that, she'd flourished.

I'd underestimated her at every turn, and I needed to stop making that mistake.

chapter TWENTY-FOUR

After we finished the cake and champagne with Dominic and Payton, we finally dressed and parted ways with my friends. Our friends now, really. Wasn't that what couples did? Referred to things as ours? I'd cleaned and locked up the club, then hailed a cab to take us back to her place.

She'd snuggled tight against me in the backseat. I liked my arm around her shoulders, sitting quietly while the city whizzed past us. When we were in her apartment, I helped her out of her coat and she stepped out of her shoes. Without words, I urged her toward her master bathroom.

Once the shower was warm, I peeled off our clothes. We were both feeling the alcohol, and she laughed when her bra gave me trouble.

"I'll just tear it off."

She grinned. "Okay."

I followed her in under the rainfall showerhead, closing the glass door behind us. I couldn't keep my hands off of her and she sighed into my touch.

"This is nice." Her voice echoed off the tile.

"Yeah." And it was. So much so, I was annoyed when she stepped out of my embrace and grabbed a bottle of body wash. Her hands slicked the soap over our bodies and lingered on my ink. "Careful. It'll wash off."

She giggled, tipsy. "Nothing lasts forever."

I crushed my mouth to hers, letting the steam envelop us. Her fingers traced a line along my jaw, edging the stubble. The shower swayed, a side effect when my tongue slipped into her greedy mouth. Kissing didn't arouse me until her. Her hand curled, grabbing a fist of hair at the base of my neck.

She sipped air through parted lips as I walked her backward, leaning her against the tile so we could be out of the water falling from the ceiling. I rested my palms on either side of her head, flat against the cool tile, and it forced her to look up at me.

God, those hazel eyes. "You're so beautiful, Noemi."

She swallowed a breath. "Thank you." A shy smile crossed her lips, but her eyes gave nothing away. I needed to know how she felt. It was odd and interesting that I couldn't read her like other people.

"You have to tell me if I pushed you too much." Because once again I'd thrown her into the deep end and demanded she swim without asking if she could.

Her head thumped back to the tile and her eyes closed, not giving me a response. *Shit.* My blood pressure spiked, and I scrambled to fix the mistake I'd made. "Hey, it's okay," I said. "I'm sorry."

Her eyes popped open and she looked bewildered. "Sorry? For what?" Her hands latched on my face, gripping me fiercely. "No, don't be sorry, Joseph. I liked it." She went breathless and her voice dropped to a hush. "Part of me wants to know when we can do it again. I can't—"

She cut herself off, and I didn't like it. "Finish that sentence."

"I can't seem to," her expression was nervous, "get enough of this. I feel like I'm addicted."

My heart was going to race out of my chest. "Addicted?"

She rose up onto the balls of her feet and her lips trailed across my neck. "To you, Sir." My eyes closed and I allowed the sensation of her to surround me. Soft, wet skin caressing mine. Fingertips exploring the contours and ridges of my body. Her mouth licking and nipping at me.

"Come to Hawaii with me."

Where the hell did that come from? It had only been a fleeting thought when I'd noticed her spring break aligned with Conner's ceremony. The sound of water rushing from the showerhead was deafening. I couldn't hear anything else. She wasn't breathing. Noemi's hands tensed on my skin, and she slid down the wall until she was flatfooted. Her eyes were enormous.

"You're going to your brother's thing?"

"You made a good point." I pulled away from the wall and stood straight. "I don't know when the last time I did something for him was, and he's always there for me."

She tucked her hands behind her against the wall, like she was worried she'd touch me and I wouldn't allow it. "When is it?"

"During your spring break." Why did my voice sound so eager?

"You want me to meet your brother?"

Oh, Christ. I hadn't thought this through. "Uh, my parents will be there, too."

I'd thought her eyes were enormous before, but now I was aware she had another level. A voice in my mind screamed to backtrack. She was Mr. Red's daughter. The deeper I got in with her, the harder it was going to be to get out.

What if you don't want out?

"Are you asking me," she said softly, "or is this an order?"

"It's a question." Fuck, was I really doing this? "I'd pay for the trip."

Her gaze dropped down to her toes, then slowly worked its way back up to mine, a hint of a smile in her expression. "Okay." Her smile widened. "Sure."

"Yeah?" I waited for the feeling of terror to seize me, but all I felt was mild warmth. I was . . . pleased.

"Not to be nosey, but your clubs do well? I mean, your place is nice, but the trip won't be cheap."

I gave her half a laugh. "My clubs do all right, and I have investments. Keep in mind, I've been in the financial world a lot longer than you have."

It was her turn to laugh. "That's highly doubtful, Mr. Monsato. You want to compare notes?"

"Here I was, thinking you wanted to get in my pants, not my portfolio, *Ms. Rosso*."

She made a face. "Groan."

I leaned in again, trapping her in my arms. "You should know, it was a question. But if you'd said no, it would have become an order."

"I'm addicted." Her soft voice wrapped all around me. "I'm not going to say no."

Something was wrong with me. I stared at the bank of flickering monitors and felt nothing. No stir of desire or swell of power over commanding this den of sin. Chantal seemed to be having the fuck of her life in Room Three. She thrashed against the restraints, reaching out toward the man that was ramming her. Since she had on the blindfold, she couldn't see he was balding, but I'm sure she could tell his gut spilled over his belt.

Sometimes the less attractive men were the best lay, the girls said, and I'd seen plenty of proof. They tried so damn hard, and it made them focused. Eager to please. It was working for Chantal. She wasn't much of an actress. I was happy for her, and that her string of bad luck was finally over. She'd struck out on reaching a deal with the last few johns, and the ones who had stepped up either couldn't find a clitoris or didn't care to.

I'd had half the mind to meet them in the payment room and explain how much better sex was when you weren't only in it for yourself. Maybe I should text Noemi for Ross's number so I could have that conversation with him and save the next girl he was with from lackluster sex.

No, I don't think Noemi would care for that. But I texted her anyway, telling her she was a filthy girl and I was thinking about her. A female voice rang out from above, and I pocketed my phone quickly, like a child caught in the act.

"Who is she?" Payton asked. She stood on the other side of my desk, her expression demanding.

My pulse kicked. "Don't worry about it."

Payton's face took a dubious cast and her voice was pointed. "She's just some starving grad student."

"Yeah."

"Bullshit." In her absence, I'd forgotten just how good Payton was at reading lies. "What grad student owns a five hundred dollar purse, Joseph?"

There was no way Payton would let this go, but perhaps it would be good for me to reveal it and get some perspective.

I trusted Payton. Realistically, she was the closest I had to a best friend. I glanced at my open doorway. "Close the door and I'll tell you."

When it was done, Payton sank down in the seat opposite my desk.

"She's Noemi Rosso."

It was like she hadn't heard me. She seemed to process the information clinically. "Are you out of your fucking mind?"

"Yes." I rested my elbows on the desk and set my head in my hands.

"He'll run you out of Chicago. He'll destroy you when he finds out."

Even I barely believed it. "He won't find out."

Her laugh was skeptical. "Have you seen the way she looks at you? That girl's at least halfway in love."

"Shit, I know." I didn't tell Payton how strong Noemi's power was over me. Couldn't bring it into words. "I'm taking her to Hawaii with me."

Payton shook her head. "You *are* fucking insane, and you're going to crush her."

"It's just an infatuation. It'll pass."

"Are we talking about for her, or you?" She leaned closer and my body stiffened as she pissed me off. "You think it'll pass because nothing lasts forever?"

"Don't fucking push me, honey."

She shrugged. "It's what we do." Payton leaned back in the seat and crossed her legs, taking a more relaxed posture. "You have to tell her."

"Which part?" I snapped. "That I sell pussy, or that her father's my best customer?"

"Yes." She said it like it was that fucking simple.

"No."

Payton rose to her feet, and it was shocking how hard her expression was. "If you have feelings for her, or see even the tiniest fucking chance of it going somewhere, believe me when I tell you that lying is a really bad idea." She marched to the door, yanked it open, and turned over her shoulder to glance back at me. "It'll break her heart, and I know you're into a lot of shit, but I didn't think breaking was one of them."

The door slammed shut.

chapter
TWENTY-FIVE

NOEMI

Sunlight glared off of the white floor at the ticketing counter of O'Hare's Terminal One. I glanced at the ticket in my hand and wondered if Joseph was either proving a point, or thought I would balk at flying any other way. "First class?"

His expression was casual. "It's a nine hour flight."

I followed him toward the security line, when a man stepped in front of me and made me halt. He wore jeans and a faded sweatshirt that was stretched out, and heat rose in my throat at his sleazy grin. I knew what he was instantly.

"Hey," he said, "aren't you one of Anthony Rosso's daughters?"

"No." I tried to move passed him, but he moved as well, keeping himself between Joseph and me.

"Sure you are. Where you going?"

Joseph realized I wasn't with him then. When he turned and spotted my situation, his face turned dark.

"Nowhere," I said. My annoyance at the stranger only made Joseph's expression scarier. "Excuse me." I bypassed him.

"Who's the guy, Ms. Rosso?"

"Her boyfriend," Joseph snapped. "Who the fuck are you?"

Crap, no, Joseph. "He's no one. Let's go."

I wrapped a hand on his arm, urging him toward the first class security check line. Now I was grateful Joseph had gotten those tickets since the line was empty, and the general one weaved, seemingly endless.

"Oh, really?" The guy's voice rang out behind us. "You've gotta be, what? Twenty years older than her?"

Joseph whirled around, and I put my hands on his shoulders to stop him. "No," I said, my voice firm. "Go." Giving him an order wasn't the best idea, but we had to keep moving, before—

Joseph's hand latched on my wrist and he tugged me through the corded section toward the first checkpoint until we were safely out of the man's view. Hands gripped my waist, steadying me when we abruptly stopped.

"He had a fucking camera." Joseph's eyes were concerned.

"It happens sometimes." I didn't love being startled by paparazzi, but Joseph's hands on me now made it not so bad. "The night we met, there was one waiting for me outside your club. That was right after Becca's meltdown, so it was worse then."

The dark eyes blinked. "That's why you wanted to slip out the back."

I couldn't walk out of his club and be photographed after the fistfight had given me an enormous facial bruise, and it was also why I didn't want to press charges. *Think about the brand, Noemi.*

"If you ignore them," I repeated the words I'd learned long ago, "they don't have anything to photograph. I'm not famous. No one's interested in Noemi Rosso, only what scandal I could bring to my dad's company."

The company that would be mine one day.

Joseph's gaze swept back to the corner where the man

probably lurked, and I could feel the tension in his body in my hands. I didn't want to start the trip off on a bad note. "Are you going to discipline me for giving you an order?"

His attention turned back to me. The concern evaporated and was replaced with a slow, burning heat, and I shivered.

"No, little girl." His lips grazed mine. "Because once again, you want it, and that defeats the purpose. But if you're good, maybe I'll reward you later. And you're wrong. *I'm* interested in Noemi Rosso."

My friends said I was crazy, but also that they were jealous of me. Joseph and I had been together only a little more than a month, and here I was, sitting beside him on a plane bound for paradise, where I'd also meet his family. Seven days with him non-stop, under his command. I was excited beyond belief.

"What are you reading?" Joseph asked when I'd fired up my iPad, waiting for the plane to takeoff. He glanced at the screen and raised an eyebrow. "You're reading the Erwin biography? Is that for a class?"

He'd probably expected some sort of beach read, a break from the dry textbooks I read day-in and day-out. I gave a sheepish smile. "No, I wanted to." Michael Erwin was a tech giant who'd taken his start-up public, and continued to run his business successfully while using unorthodox methods. I'd always loved the well-written biographies. "Hey, it's fascinating. Don't judge me."

"Noemi, I told you I wouldn't do that." He unsnapped the cover of his iPad and tilted the screen my direction.

"You're reading it, too." I laughed.

After dinner, we'd both finished the book and the sun

had set, leaving the cabin dark. I leaned over in my spacious seat, and curled up beside him, launching into a book discussion that lasted another hour. Who'd have thought my bad boy had such a head for finance?

"I don't understand. Why didn't you go to college?" I asked. "You run circles around the people in my classes."

He exhaled slowly. "Well, first off, I'm a lot older than them. I bought my first business when I was your age. And second," he hesitated, "I had cancer. My grades were okay before that, but it was hard to care about the future when I didn't think I'd have one."

I'd been tracing patterns on his knee with my hand, but his words made me pause. My heart hurt. So much of his life had been derailed.

"And third, even if I'd gotten accepted somewhere, we couldn't afford it. My mom couldn't keep her job with all of the doctors' appointments, and I was in and out of the hospital."

"I'm sorry."

"Don't be. I'm doing just fine."

I glanced at his half-empty glass of wine that rested on the tray table of his first class seat. Yes, he was doing all right. I needed something to change subjects. We hadn't talked about his cancer since the anniversary a few weeks ago.

"If you slam that wine," I asked, "could you get drunk enough to tell me the story of how Payton and Dominic met?"

He snatched up the glass and drank a sip, his gaze unfocused as if contemplating. "Payton used to be an escort."

"An escort?" Was this a fancy wine bar term, because the only escort job I knew of was a nice way of saying—

"She was a prostitute. Dominic was her client."

I couldn't reconcile the woman with the concept. Payton was intelligent, beautiful, and confident. The stereotype I had of prostitutes were skinny, sickly drug addicts that stood on street corners wearing cheap clothes and desperation on their faces. Not perfect bodies, high-end clothes, and college educations. She was a hooker?

"I don't understand." I was horrified for her. What had happened in her past that forced her into selling sex for money?

Joseph's gaze watched me like he was studying my reaction intently, and it made me uncomfortable. Was this some sort of test? She was his friend. A good friend, and possibly an ex, so I had to tread lightly. I wouldn't want to talk badly about her, and I liked Payton.

"What don't you understand?" he asked softly. "Why she would do that?"

"Yes." How was that not apparent?

"She likes sex. Why not get paid to do what she likes?"

Was he serious? "Joseph, sleeping with strangers for money is illegal, not to mention, disgusting and dangerous."

The muscles along his jaw flexed as if he were clenching his teeth. "So if she hadn't charged them, then it would be all right?"

"No, of course not."

Warmth faded from his eyes. "Why?"

A warning light blinked in my brain, sensing murky waters ahead. "Because it's like profanity. If you use it all the time, it loses its meaning."

"That's your opinion. Maybe it's just fucking to her, and there doesn't have to be meaning. It's a business about pleasure, not emotion."

Is that what this was between us? Just fucking? "But a girl should have standards."

"You mean, she shouldn't be a slut. She shouldn't give it up to just anyone."

The warning light graduated to a siren, but I ignored it. "Yes."

"Even if she wants to?" Joseph's voice was shockingly harsh. "What if she'd been a good girl up until then? Does that mean she's not a slut if she lets a guy she barely knows fuck her on a table in his restaurant?"

The breath of air I gasped was so sharp it was painful, and I cringed.

"No," he continued. He set down his glass and his hands clamped on my shoulders, straightening them. "I won't allow this posture. You want to judge other people, you should be able to take it, too."

I stared at him at a total loss for words.

"Yeah, society has taught you that she's a slut, but she was careful, and safe, and doing what she enjoyed. She's no different from me, really. And you said you *wouldn't* judge."

My mind fractured. Years of indoctrination had taught me that promiscuous women were sluts and going to hell. Deep down, there was shame inexplicably linked to sexual pleasure. Yet, despite all the years of Catholic school, I thought myself a feminist. Women could do anything men could, including running *Fortune 100* companies. So why couldn't Payton enjoy sex with whomever or how many people she wanted, just like men did?

"I . . . didn't mean to judge." My voice faltered.

Joseph took another sip of his wine and said nothing. Tension radiated off of him.

My fingers toyed with the loose end of the seatbelt as I tried to ease the awkwardness. "So Dominic paid for a night with her?"

"She refused his money afterward."

"Why?"

"I'm told he was the first man to get through to her, and she wanted something . . . real."

Real. Their matching tattoos.

"He took her back to Tokyo and that was that."

Cold dread slinked into my chest and I fought to keep my expression free from judgement. "How did you meet her? Were you one of her—"

"No. We met at a bar."

Perhaps he was being vague on purpose, punishing me. "Was she ever your sub?"

He sort of laughed. "Did she seem overly submissive to you?"

No. She'd submitted to Dominic, but not like I did with Joseph. I let out a sigh of relief. "So you haven't slept with her."

"I didn't say that."

It was before you, I reminded myself, trying to stave off the sting.

"It was a long time ago, Noemi. It was just sex, nobody had any feeling involved. We've both moved on to . . . " his gaze swept down my body and came back up, "better things."

My emotions had been through the wringer, and yet this was a compliment. Payton was provocative and sexually confident, not to mention, gorgeous. He thought I was better than that?

By the time we landed, Joseph's stiffness had drained

away, and we both grinned at each other when we deplaned out into the warm, humid night air, peeling off our layered travel clothes.

"I'm not going back to Chicago until June," I said.

We made our way through the Honolulu airport, which was a collection of buildings with covered walkways connecting them, and followed the stream of people to the baggage area.

For the first time, I heard panic in Joseph's voice. "Shit, I didn't adequately prepare you for this."

"JR?" A deep male voice said. "Over here."

Conner was the photograph aged twenty years. The cute teenager was now a distinguished man, built like a rock but with the same kind eyes as Joseph.

Had I heard him right? "JR?"

Joseph seemed to grit his teeth. "My father is Joseph Michael. I'm Joseph Robert." His hand pressed in the small of my back and eased me forward. "Hey," he said to his older brother.

They embraced in a quick hug and then Conner's gaze turned my direction. "You finally take my advice and get an assistant?"

"No," Joseph answered quickly. "This is Noemi. My girlfriend."

Conner's shoulders straightened with surprise. A huge smile burst on his face. "Girlfriend? Mom is going to lose her shit over this."

Joseph hadn't told anyone who I was, or that I was coming? The sting of disappointment was acute, but his arm was around my shoulders. "It'll make sense once we get there."

After I'd properly met Conner and our bags arrived, the

Monsato men loaded them into Conner's Jeep, and we took off for the rental house we'd share for the next few days with his parents who'd come in from Florida.

We chatted during the drive through the city, talking loudly over the wind whipping in through the open windows. Warm, ocean air and palm trees overhead made me want to revise my earlier statement. Maybe I'd never go back to Chicago.

The house was gorgeous. Pink and yellow hibiscus bushes bloomed in the landscaped yard, and the Jeep pulled up to the circle drive, covered by a stone portico. It was after midnight Central time, but only eight here, and although I was tired from the flight, I couldn't wait to get into shorts and flip-flops, and start my vacation.

His parents were seated on the leather couches in the main room, drinking wine when we came in. They looked relaxed and at home, but when she spotted Joseph, his mother leaped to her feet, her soft face ecstatic.

"You're here!" She hurried to him and crushed him in her arms, her eyes shining with tears. "We're so glad you came."

"Yeah," Joseph's voice was uneven, as if his mother's emotions were getting to him. "Uh, me, too." He gave her a long moment, extracted himself from her embrace, and reached a hand out to me. "This is my girlfriend Noemi."

His mother didn't move a breath. Her eyes didn't blink. Was she having a stroke?

"Girlfriend?" she whispered.

"That's what I said."

Her focus snapped to me, and I felt naked. Her gaze raked down as if seeking every fault and flaw. "My goodness, you're young!"

"Mom."

She waved Joseph's scolding off, and extended a hand to me, giving me a smile that didn't quite reach her eyes. "I'm Carol Monsato."

"Nice to meet you, Mrs. Monsato. Noemi Rosso."

Her voice was almost as firm as her handshake. "It's *Carol*." Her tone was exactly the same whenever Joseph had to repeat something he felt he shouldn't have had to. I pulled my lips back in a pleasant smile that said I understood, and I did. She'd almost lost her son once, so it made sense she would be protective of him.

Joseph's father had a head of salt and pepper hair and a bit of a beer belly, and introduced himself as Joe. He put a hand around his wife's waist. "I know your mother already said it, but we were really happy you decided to join us for Conner's award."

"You have Noemi to thank for that. She convinced me."

This time the smile did reach all the way to Carol's eyes. "Well," she said, "let me show you the house." She gestured to the couch. "I think the sofa pulls out into a bed, JR. We would have booked a house with three bedrooms if we'd known Noemi was coming."

"No need. We'll stay in the same room, Mom."

She shook her head. "No, you're not married. That's not proper. What would her parents think if I let you sleep in the same bed?"

My father would be pissed, but probably because he had no idea where I was. I'd told him I was going to Mexico with some friends for spring break. The first big lie I'd told, and although I felt awful about it, the darkest part of me reveled in being bad.

Joseph's hand tightened around my shoulders. "Do you think putting us in separate rooms will keep us from having sex?"

His mother and I gasped collectively, and I turned to look up at him wide-eyed. Did he really just say that?

"I'm thirty-eight years old," he added.

His mother fought for control. "But you're under my roof."

"Am I?" he said, looking around. "The deposit on my credit card says otherwise."

Holy shit. He'd paid for the house, too? His mother's face flushed red, and I jabbed an elbow into his stomach. "It's fine, I can sleep on the couch."

His expression darkened. "Forget it."

"If you keep being rude to your family, I'm going to prefer it."

His mouth dropped open. Was he expecting me to be a pushover about this? How a man treated his family said a lot about him. Joseph's mouth snapped shut and his expression set.

"I'm sorry," he said sincerely to his mother, "let's try this again. I didn't tell you I was bringing Noemi because I knew this was going to be an issue. Between my work and her class schedule, we don't get to see each other as much as I'd like, so we're going to stay in the same room. If you're uncomfortable, we can find a hotel."

Carol's hands rested on her hips and her eyes narrowed. "Dammit, you're so stubborn."

"Yeah, don't know where I got that from." He accused her with a look.

She threw up her hand, a gesture of giving in. "I'm not

happy about this."

"I get that." Hopefully I was the only one who saw the flash of victory in his eyes.

We dragged our luggage to the end of the hall where an enormous bedroom waited, decorated with stone colors and a Zen-theme. The door clicked shut as Joseph closed it, and I turned to face him, irritated.

"You're right," I said. "You didn't adequately prepare me. Or them."

"I know, I'm sorry. I . . ." he scratched the back of his neck, "don't really know how to do this."

"Do what?"

"Introduce someone to my family."

He hadn't done it before? "For starters, maybe don't tell your mom we've had sex."

"She's not an idiot, Noemi."

I turned and unzipped my suitcase, rifling through the clothes for my flip-flops. "I didn't say she was. You're just not supposed to talk about sex with your parents. Let them live in the fantasy-world, if they want to, that you're waiting for marriage. Don't give them proof that you haven't."

"Stop," he commanded. I hadn't heard him approach, but suddenly arms were around me, pulling me back up against his hard chest. "I'm sorry. I wasn't thinking about the situation I put you in." His lips trailed open-mouthed kisses along my neck. "All I can think about is waking up next to you tomorrow morning."

We still hadn't truly done that, since he worked too much and I had several projects due before break. The idea made my knees soften and my eyes flutter shut. God, his effect was like a rip-tide. Too strong to fight, better to give in.

"So the question is," his voice filled my ear, "will that be on the couch, or here? Because that's going to fucking happen. I stay wherever you stay."

A button was unsnapped and my zipper tugged down. His hand slipped inside the front of my jeans, rubbing me through the cotton of my panties. Heat flowed through me, pooling between my legs.

"Where are we staying, Noemi?"

"Here," I said on a hurried breath.

"Good." Fingertips grazed my clit and then were gone. I angled my shoulders to look up at him, stunned that he'd stopped. Joseph wore an evil, sexy smile. "Did you need something, little girl?"

"I liked what you were doing, Sir."

A noise of satisfaction rolled out of him. "Me too, but my parents are waiting for us to have dinner, and I know you want me to stop being rude."

He'd turned me on in a heartbeat, and I could see the pleasure he took in leaving me unfulfilled. "You suck."

He smirked. "Think carefully about what you say next. I can give you orgasms, baby girl, which means I can also withhold them."

I kept my mouth shut, and later that night, he didn't have to.

chapter
TWENTY-SIX

JOSEPH

It was hot in the large airplane hangar, and they had the doors wide open. We sat in the uncomfortable metal folding chairs that had been set up for the ceremony and faced the plane my brother flew on training exercises.

It wasn't a huge event, maybe one hundred and fifty people in all. The pilots in Conner's squadron and their extended families, plus a few commanders and captains who had come in for the ceremony. I watched my brother in his spotless dress-white uniform accept the plaque and smile while he shook hands and posed for photographs. Something swelled in me at this. I was insanely proud of him, and as soon as I got a moment to tell him, I would.

We mingled with the lieutenants and ate the catered lunch at white linen covered tables as jets took off from a nearby airstrip. At one point, I curled my hand around Noemi's. I'd never been much of a hand holding guy, but there were far too many men wearing what my brother called the "panty-dropping suit" at the event. They gazed at Noemi like she was the most beautiful thing they'd seen.

Not that I could blame them, but she was mine.

We'd taken a family picture beside the airplane, only to have my mother call Noemi into the next shot. She'd been a huge hit with the folks, beating my father at pinochle and cooking dinner with my mother. Mom was notoriously hard on the women my brother brought home, and yet she let Noemi help. If anything, she seemed grateful.

It was insanity being with Noemi. Insanity I enjoyed, like the out of control feeling when she smiled at me, or her desperate pleas for more, late at night when I was inside her.

We woke up together in the big bed, and sometimes I'd pin her wrists behind her back while I fucked her hard, whispering what a dirty girl she was, while my other hand covered her mouth. "Don't get too loud, filthy girl," I'd say. "Don't want my parents to hear what a slut you are."

She stole the markets section out of my newspaper every morning at breakfast, even though we had Wi-Fi. In the afternoons, we'd walk to the beach to go snorkeling, or swim in the pool in the back of the house, and holy fucking God, Noemi in a bikini. The best was when the bikini came off and the tan lines remained, her pale and contrasting golden skin that only I got to see.

Our time flew by, and I wanted everything to slow the fuck down. Suddenly it was Friday and we were back at the airport, saying goodbye to my parents and brother, getting ready to board a puddle-jumper to Hilo on the Big Island.

Once again my mother threatened waterworks and it got to me like it always did, twisting me up in an uncomfortable way. She'd fought me so hard when I'd wanted to give up on the darkest days of my cancer. She'd fought *for* me, and I would forever be indebted.

"I have a serious question for you," Noemi said when we were seated on the tiny, cramped plane. "Would your brother let you borrow his uniform?"

I laughed, enjoying the gleam in her eye. "It's doubtful. Why? You like a man in uniform?"

"God, you would look so sexy." She shivered at the thought. "We know how much you like giving orders." But her expression soured. "I can't believe it's Friday already. It feels like we just got here."

"Our trip's not over yet, though." We'd planned to go to the active eruption site in Volcanoes National Park. We'd both been to Hawaii before, but never to the volcanoes.

It had been a good idea, but the execution failed miserably. The caldera of the volcano had retreated back inside the crater, so we could see the steam from the lava flow, but no actual lava. Impressive, but still disappointing.

As we stood at the railing of the visitor's center overlooking the massive crater, my phone rang. The restaurant I'd booked for dinner had had a kitchen fire during lunch, and was now closed for repairs. So our final dinner in Hawaii was fast food that we had to drive thirty fucking minutes to get to and back, because I'd booked a cabin in the forested part of the park. We weren't ready for it to be so unseasonably cold, nor were we prepared for the drenching thunderstorm that began right before check-in.

The tiny A-frame cabin was referred to as a yurt. It had electricity, meaning one outlet high on the wall over the bed and a single dim bulb at the apex of the roof. No running water—the bathrooms were six cabins down the path from ours.

We'd made it inside the cabin with our suitcases and managed to stay somewhat dry, but it was sixty degrees in the yurt without heat, and the temperature was dropping. Noemi stared at the lumpy, ancient-looking bed, which was the only thing in the room, and back to me.

She laughed, a deep throaty sound. I could barely hear

her over the rain pounding against the roof and the triangle-shaped windows at the eaves. "What is it?"

"I kind of have to pee."

"Shit. Me, too."

We were going to get soaked, but there was no helping it, and we dashed together through the cold rain, splashing in puddles as we made it to the bathroom, and then repeating the journey back to the yurt afterward.

Lightning slashed across the night sky, and thunder rolled through the trees as I unlocked the door and let her inside.

Her teeth chattered. "I get cold easily."

"Let's warm you up then." I pushed back her strands of damp hair and lower my mouth to hers. The lightning cracking outside didn't have a thing on us when we were kissing. The sparks made my hair lift from my skin. Her hands fumbled with her shirt, stretched it over her head, and there was a sopping noise as she threw it to the floor. She came back to me, hungry.

Her skin was covered in goosebumps, and this wasn't a tremble in her body, this was shivering. I yanked off my soaked T-shirt and jeans, and pulled back the fluffy, white comforter while she struggled out of her pants.

The light switch snapped off, plunging us into darkness.

A low creak came from the bed as she got in and slid noisily over the sheets, making room for me to follow. I folded her in my arms and her rain soaked skin was cool in my hands. Bright light filled the cabin for a microsecond, and the boom of thunder was so loud the reverberations rattled the windows.

Noemi's hand was on my chest and her head tucked

into the crook of my neck. She vibrated and chattered from the cold. Was the comforter not on her right? I pulled it tighter against us, urging her closer, although it wasn't really possible.

Her mouth was on my throat, teasing soft kisses, and I turned my head into her kiss. Heat flamed between us. The storm had interrupted my rhythm and I was sluggish about starting the game we usually played. Maybe it was the fact I couldn't hear her breathing over the pounding rain and only saw her in flashes of the lighting. My fingertips traced the edges of her damp bra, and I wanted it gone. All of her skin needed to be pressed to mine.

She deepened the kiss, filling my mouth with her sweet tongue as she shifted under the thick comforter and climbed on top of me. The bra. It had to go, fucking now. My fingers curled around the band at the back, undid it, and tossed it aside. Her hard nipples scraped over my chest and I groaned with satisfaction.

"I fucking love your—"

She put two fingers over my lips, silencing me, and replaced them with her mouth a moment later. There was a disconnect in my brain. Who the hell was in charge? Yet her kiss kept my urge to dominate at bay. I clasped a hand on her breast, filling my palm with the weight of it, and gently squeezed. It made her tongue plunge deeper in my mouth.

Her hips shifted and pleasure washed upward from her teasing as she ground herself on my cock. Now the fucking underwear had to go, too. I slipped a hand under them and closed my fist around the band at her hip, tugging. "Get these off."

She rolled off of me. The cover shifted as she did as

asked, and I yanked my boxer briefs down, kicking them away. I rose up on my elbow and turned to her, but her hands were on my shoulders, pressing me back down so she could straddle my lap.

"You think you're the boss tonight, little girl?"

"Ssh," she whispered in my ear, and her bare, wet pussy slicked across my hard cock. My mind emptied. All I could think about was the sensation and how I wanted her to do it again. The comforter wrapped around us like a cocoon, but she wasn't shivering anymore. Her hands scooped under my head, tilting me into her kiss that was a thousand times better than anything else I'd had. She'd fucking ruined kissing. I'd asked if she wanted me to ruin her, and she'd done it to me. No one would match up after her.

My hands skated over the curves of her bare back, my fingertips skimming the hollow of her spine and working lower, until I gripped a handful of her ass. I lifted her, trying to urge her to take me inside. I'd had plans of burrowing beneath the covers and kissing her legs until her knees shook and she begged me to go down on her, but now I was impatient. I wanted . . . that connection.

"Fuck, get on me," I demanded, my voice strained with need.

"No more talking."

What? "Excuse me?"

"It's not an order, Joseph," she said softly. "Tonight it's a limit. No words."

Annoyance rolled hot through me, coupled with unease. Why would she do that? She loved my filthy mouth. Her body slid against mine once again and I bit down on my tongue. Keeping my mouth shut was going to be fucking impossible.

But it was a limit.

I would have to try.

Noemi rose to sit upright, and finally, after a lifetime of torture, positioned my cock so it was right at her entrance. My breath stuck in my lungs as the lightning flashed, flooding the room with the perfect image of her naked body on top of mine, my hands clenching her hips. We moaned together as she slid down on me, all the way to the base.

The darkness was like a blindfold, and the loud, driving rain was the dominating sound, drowning out almost everything else. But as she began to move, the bed creaked. Her tight, hot body gripped me and I dug my fingers into her skin, like I needed to hold on or I'd lose my damn mind.

She rode me, slow and deep, her knees clenching around my rib cage and her hands pushing on my chest for leverage. I needed it faster, or slower, I didn't fucking know anymore. Only that I had *need*. An unsatisfied ache for something, and each of her thrusts seemed to promise relief.

Her heart was pounding beneath her heaving breasts, I could feel it. I could taste her desperation in her frantic kisses, like she had that same need I did. Restless and urgent for the remedy.

Her hands laced with mine and she pushed them until the backs of my palms were against the pillows beside my head. I inhaled. This wasn't what I allowed. Her on top and in control. Setting the limits was one thing, but she was pushing me . . .

Wasn't that what I did to her? Pushed until we discovered something new? I squeezed my grip on her fingers, but remained, forcing myself to endure the submissive position.

Her undulating body had my pulse roaring in my head. Soft, warm breasts flattened against me when her tongue was tangled with mine again, her damp hair falling in my eyes.

The burn inside me grew to an inferno. I needed more, I needed her to . . . I needed . . .

I kept our hands twined together as I sat up, forcing her upright, and twisted her arms behind her back. My mouth slammed into her throat and from beneath, I drove up into her. The legs around me shook. Her whole body trembled as I plunged inside and retreated, faster and faster until we were gasping loudly for breath, drowning in each other.

Her head tipped back and I set my forehead against her neck, fighting the swell inside as we connected again and again. Humid air dragged through my lips. I released one of her hands and it was instantly on my head, holding onto me, her fingers clutching hard in my hair.

The thunder boomed outside and shook the walls, but we didn't slow down. It just kept building, and building.

"I love you," she cried. "Oh my God, I love you."

Her orgasm burst. It tore from her mouth and her body, shattering all around it, sending me over like a shockwave. Unimaginable pleasure sliced me into a million pieces and everything poured out into her, maybe even my soul.

A single breath.

Then another.

Her shuddering slowed to a stop as the fire in me was finally satiated, and dread replaced it.

I love you.

It echoed in my ears and had sent me soaring, but I hadn't said it back. Confusion swirled and the words stuck in my brain, which was unable to manage anything. Noemi

Rosso was in love with me.

Holy. Fucking. Shit.

She climbed off and lay down, pulling the covers up to her neck. Her hand searched for mine, located it, and tugged me. I complied, spooning against her, but I couldn't breathe. What the hell was I going to do?

"Noemi," I whispered over the rain.

"Ssh, I said no talking."

Christ, I didn't sleep at all.

chapter
TWENTY-SEVEN

NOEMI

I woke up alone. I lay on the sagging mattress and tried not to cry. What the hell had I done? I'd gone and screwed everything up by opening my stupid mouth.

At least it wasn't a lie.

I was hopelessly in love with Joseph. I felt like I could walk into a room filled with a thousand Paytons, and he'd only see me. I was inexperienced, but I wasn't naive. I was sure he'd run screaming away if I used the L word, and apparently, I had been right.

I dug clothes out of the suitcase and pulled them on slowly, my body all out of sorts. Like I was hungover from what we'd done last night, or going through the beginning stages of withdrawal, which made more sense. I'd told him I was addicted.

Joseph sat outside on the top of a picnic table and his feet on the bench, his broad back turned to me, but I could see he was talking on the phone. Two Styrofoam cups rested on the table, steaming into the morning air. One was his coffee, and the other water, with an unopened tea bag pinned beneath it. Those little details got to me, something as simple as him remembering I preferred tea to coffee, or discovering a new bottle of my brand of shampoo in his shower.

My heart ached for him, and worse at knowing he didn't feel the same. I foolishly hoped someday he would. A deep breath filled my lungs and I plastered a light, pleasant expression on my face so as not to give away the turmoil inside. I'd pretend like nothing happened.

A stick cracked under my foot as I approached, and he turned. "Okay, I need to go. Thanks," he said, pressing a button on the phone, and pocketed it. "Sorry, I had a work call and didn't want to wake you."

"Good morning." It came out too bright and not at all natural.

Joseph's gaze turned suspicious. It was terribly awkward, standing across from him after I'd put myself out there and not gotten the response I'd wished for. He clearly cared for me, I knew that, but it was still tough to swallow.

"Is that for me?" I pointed to the cup, but as I reached for it, he trapped my hands.

"Don't you have a good morning kiss," he said, his eyes like pools of black ink, "for the man you love?"

Oh, shit. When his mouth took mine it stole all the air. His hand cupped the back of my neck, molding to hold me better as soft lips moved against mine, igniting heavy, thick desire between us.

"Are you mad I'm so stupid?" I asked.

His mouth was carving a path along my jaw, but froze. "What?"

"You said I was too smart to fall in love with you." It was hard to keep myself held together when he was only an inch from me.

He chuckled and the mouth continued to its destination, landing at the edge of my ear. "Yeah, I'm furious. Can't you tell?"

My legs refused to act like legs, and I put my hands on

his bent knees to steady myself. The world was spinning, and he kept me upright.

"When the time is right," he whispered, "when I know exactly how and when to say it . . . Can you give me a little more time?"

I let out an enormous sigh of relief that shifted into amusement. "Are you telling me to *wait*?"

Good lord, his smile did not help my weak legs. "Yes, little girl. It will come out of my filthy mouth."

Our flight didn't leave until two, so we drove into Hilo and strolled through the touristy section of downtown to kill time, eating ice cream cones under the palm trees on a beach. I watched the bright blue waves lap at the black rock shoreline and tried to enjoy my last few hours here before going back to wintery Chicago, and final exams.

"God, it's so beautiful." I put my hand on his leg. "Thank you for bringing me."

He smiled. "Who should be thanking who? I'm here on a beach, trying to keep myself from getting hard watching you eat your ice cream."

I licked the cone in what I hoped was a suggestive and not just weird manner.

It seemed to work, but then his expression turned sincere. "Thank you for saying yes."

"When we get back, we should have dinner with my dad. I don't like sneaking around."

Joseph's body went stiff. "Yeah. I'm going to need a few weeks with that."

"What? Why?"

His expression was almost a scowl. "I've . . . got something to wrap up first."

My heart beat faster with anxiety. "Oh, no. Are you doing a deal with Katzenberg?" *Stay out of it, Noemi. He knows what he's doing.*

"Something like that." He stood and tossed the remainder of his ice cream away like he'd lost his appetite, and held his hand out to help me up. "C'mon."

We wandered through jewelry shops and art galleries, and I paused when I saw a framed photograph of a yellow hibiscus against the black lava and ocean in the background.

Joseph lingered behind me. "You want to put that in your bedroom. I'm thinking over the six-drawer dresser?"

"Yes." I shook my head in disbelief that he'd know that.

"You should. It'd look great there."

If I bought it, every time I saw the picture I could remember this trip with *him*. I dug my wallet out of my purse, but my heart sank.

"I can't." Embarrassment warmed my cheeks. "My financial manager will see the Hawaii purchase and he might pass that along to my dad."

I had my own money, in a sense, as I had stocks in the company and other investments, but my credit account came from my father. One year Becca's spending had gotten out of control, and the financial monitor had been installed to curb that.

Joseph gave me a smile. "Ah. Okay, I'll get it for you."

"No, no, you can't do that. It's almost three hundred dollars."

His laugh was like it wasn't any big deal. "Noemi—"

"I'm serious. I'm not comfortable with it after all the money you've already spent on me."

He stared at me like I was being silly. "But I want

to do this."

How could I explain my irrational logic? Joseph was wealthy and older than me, and I'd already opened the door to a slippery slope. First it was fancy trips, then artwork, maybe next it'd be jewelry. I'd never want a sugar daddy. "No, thank you. I've changed my mind, the proportions are wrong. That dresser's really big."

His gaze was skeptical. "You're sure?"

"Yeah. It's a nice image, though."

Joseph glanced at his watch. "All right. We should get going."

We walked to the rental car but as we got close, he pulled to a stop.

"Fuck, I think I set the keys down at the counter when we got ice cream."

We had to divide and conquer, and while I retraced our steps through the different stores in search of the keys, Joseph went to the ice cream shop. His text came through ten minutes later that he'd found them on the beach, where they'd fallen out of his pocket.

"That's disappointing," I said when we were seated in the car. "I was kind of hoping we didn't have to go back to our real lives."

He grinned. "Me, too."

We'd been back two days before a nasty head cold hit me. Either I'd picked it up flying back, or the weather change had taken its toll on my sinuses. I couldn't get out of bed, and slept through class for the first time in years, but I was too miserable to care.

It was late afternoon when I sent a text to Joseph.

> You're still not sick?

No. How are you feeling?

> Awful.

You want anything?

I was torn. I wanted *him*, but the stronger part of me knew he needed to work. I'd gotten a solid week of his time, and now he was way behind with his businesses.

> No thanks.

It's no problem. I sent Payton your way with something to make you feel better.

> I look like hell.

You probably look sexy as fuck surrounded by all those used Kleenexes and smelling like Vick's.

I'm jerking off thinking about it, filthy girl.

I laughed and the sound echoed in my empty apartment.

THREE *little* MISTAKES

Thirty minutes later the front desk called to let me know Payton was on her way up, and I dragged my feet to the front door.

"Hi," I croaked out.

Payton was as stunning as the first time I'd seen her. Her boots clicked across my entryway when she entered, a large, flat package wrapped in brown paper tucked under her arm.

"Sorry for, you know, this." I gestured to my flannel pajama bottoms and sweatshirt that had seen better days.

"Are you fucking kidding? You're fine. He said you were pretty sick." She untucked the package. "Joseph told me this goes in the bedroom."

I didn't need to peel back the paper to know what was behind it. I followed her down the hall and was irritated and delighted at the same time. Payton laid it down on my bed, opened the thick paper, and revealed the framed picture I'd wanted to buy in Hawaii.

"Pretty," she said.

"That asshole told me he lost the keys. He must have gone back and gotten it."

"He bought you artwork." She smiled. "Yeah, what an asshole."

"I told him not to."

Her expression was amused. "How'd that work out for you?"

I sank down on the bed and watched her prop the frame up against the wall. It wasn't hung yet, but I could already tell the proportions were perfect.

"I love him," I blurted out.

"Do you?" She asked it like she was curious. "You love

all of him, even the not-great parts?"

I wondered what exactly she meant, but a knock came from my front door, making both of us jump. I sighed. Joseph had taken back Ross's key, but I'd forgotten to remove him from the list of visitors who could come up unannounced. I left Payton in the bedroom and moved down the hallway. My body ached as I pulled the door open.

My father stepped inside, his eyes filled with concern.

"Hey." I smiled widely. He *never* came to my place. "What are you doing here?"

"You cancelled dinner tonight because you were sick." He had a black wool jacket on over his suit, like he'd come straight from the office. "Honestly, Noemi, I came to see if that was true."

"Why wouldn't it be?"

"Where were you last week, young lady?"

Oh, shit. The medicine head made the effects of being caught in the lie worse, and I latched a hand onto the couch to support myself. "Uh . . ." It seemed pointless to dig my hole deeper, and really, what was the big deal? I was twenty-three. I hadn't done anything dangerous or illegal. "I went to Hawaii with my boyfriend. I'm sorry I lied to you."

"Shit."

The air in the room plummeted twenty degrees when Payton's voice rang out. She stood in the hallway, her face paper-white and her wide eyes pointed at my father. His expression was blank, which I hadn't seen before. He was an emotive man, so it was bizarre.

"Dad, this is my friend, Payton."

Neither of them moved at first, but Payton finally marched forward and held out her hand. He took it.

"Nice to meet you, Paige," he said.

"It's Payton," she corrected, but her voice was tight, the last syllable dying on her tongue. She pulled her hand back quickly and adjusted the sash on her coat. "I should get going, Em."

"Wait a minute," my father said. "How did you two meet?"

Crap! Joseph had asked me to give him a few weeks before introducing him to my father. I needed an alternate story that didn't involve Joseph. "Her fiancé's a VP at Chase Sports. I interviewed him for a paper I had to write."

I was fairly pleased with the plausibility of my lie, until Payton looked like I'd punched her in the stomach.

"I have to go," she said quickly, her gaze dropping as she hurried out the door, not saying goodbye to either of us.

She'd gone awkward at the sight of my father, but it happened occasionally. People were star struck by Anthony Rosso, who had no business being called a star. He'd only been in a few episodes of a TV show that aired several years ago, and hadn't rated high. Plus, he was wealthy and had power, but he was still just a man.

"You must make her nervous," I said, expecting him to be offended by her abrupt exit.

"What's her fiancé's name?"

What on earth? "Why?"

"We have a lot of money, and some people might want to take advantage of you."

I sank down on the couch, woozy. "Dominic's a VP at Chase, I don't think she's hurting for money."

"Are you okay?" The concern was back in his voice.

"Yeah, but this cold is kicking my butt."

As he went into the kitchen, his phone chimed. He came

back carrying a glass of Kool-Aid and put his arm around me, helping me stand.

"I should be kicking your butt for lying to me. Why'd you do that?"

"Can I tell you I'm sorry, that it's a long story, and explain it some other time when my head's not pounding?" The thought dawned on me as we moved toward my bedroom. "How'd you find out?"

"Ross called." I stared at him with disbelief. "Hey, I'm as surprised as you. He was hoping I knew someone over at the accounting firm he's interviewing at. When we got to talking, he mentioned you were dating an older man, and you hadn't gone to Mexico with your friends."

"Fucking Ross."

The profanity shocked him and he almost dropped me on the bed.

"I'm told this boyfriend has a tattoo, Noemi. You know I think tattoos are an intelligence test, and if you have one, you've failed."

"Don't judge him," I scoffed, curling up under the covers. "He's smart."

My dad gave me a soft smile. "Of course he is. He's with you, isn't he?" He set the Kool-Aid on my nightstand and his phone chimed again. "I can't push my meetings much longer. You need anything before I go?"

"No, thank you." He smoothed a hand over my forehead. "I'm sorry I lied, Dad."

"I know you are. Call me when you feel better and you can tell me about your new, dumb, yet smart man."

"Ha, ha. I'd have to get you on the phone first."

chapter
TWENTY-EIGHT

JOSEPH

I could not get Anthony Rosso on the phone. I'd been trying every day since we'd returned from Hawaii. At first, I kept my name out of it. Rosso was a cautious man, and I was sure he'd assume I was trying to scam or blackmail him.

All I wanted was to give him some warning about what was in the works. My name got me past the first line of defense—the administrative assistant who would win the gold fucking medal if brushing people off was an Olympic sport. Today I had a new person.

"Mr. Monsato," a male voice came on the line. "What is it you want to speak to Mr. Rosso about?"

"A private matter."

The man's voice turned rough. "I know who you are, cut the bullshit. What do you want?"

I gnashed my teeth. "It's personal."

"I can pass it along, but you won't be speaking with him directly."

"That's not going to work for me—"

"If Mr. Rosso decides to visit your establishment, you can speak to him then, but don't call again or you'll regret it. Goodbye."

I set my phone down on the restaurant table and glared out the window. I could feel time slipping away. After the man at the airport, and Payton's run-in with Rosso at

Noemi's place, it was as if every moment was another opportunity to fuck up my plans.

Payton breezed into the crowded restaurant and I gestured her over. She slipped her sunglasses into her purse, took off her light jacket, and collapsed into the seat.

"You're late," I grumbled.

"Oh my God, by a whole two minutes. Gimme a break." She straightened in her seat and grinned at me, and her whole attitude was annoying.

"What?" I snapped.

"I can't believe you're doing this."

Me, too. "I don't see another option. The scandal, if it ever got out, would ruin her."

"But you love that place. And, Joseph, the *fucking money*."

"Nothing lasts forever."

I'd loved the blindfold club. Interviewing the johns and selecting which girl was best to pair with them to maximize my profit was a game I would miss playing. The money was amazing, but I'd also invested wisely and had three other businesses to run. My mind had been made and my decision was firm. I could walk away from the club and be fine, but if Noemi were linked to it through me, I'd never forgive myself.

And I wasn't ready to let her go.

"Last chance," I said to Payton, "if you want to make a bid."

She shook her head. "Dominic tolerates me working there, but owning the place? I don't think so."

"Besides, you're having so much fun with all that freelance copy writing you're doing."

"Ugh, don't remind me." She drank a sip of her water. "Don't worry, I'm sure he'll do great as the new Joseph, and

I'll be there to help."

Julius arrived at the restaurant ten minutes early, wearing an anxious expression above his hulking form, but he relaxed a little when he spotted Payton with me. He'd always liked her, and they had a great, platonic chemistry.

"What's going on?" he asked, and I motioned to the seat beside Payton. "Something bad happen you wanted to talk about?"

"No," I said. "Something good. You've been working for me since the club opened. You know how it operates, you've handled the tough situations, and you always know what's going on."

"Uh, thanks."

"Do you want to make more money?"

"Sure. You giving me a raise?"

"A promotion." I took a deep breath and exhaled it out. "I'd like to sell you the club."

"Say what now?" Julius looked from me to Payton, confusion streaking his expression. I gave him a moment to see I was serious and let it sink in. "I don't have that kind of money."

So he was interested. Good. I pulled out a manila envelope containing the formal offer, which sold the wine club front of the business.

"I'd like to offer you a structured deal. Descending percentages of the profit going to me for the next few months as you transition in." The paper trail would be a mile long, funneled through wine brokers and expense accounts, to offer me maximum protection if it was busted during that time.

"Take these and read them over, let me know if you have any questions."

"Yeah," he said instantly. "Where you going, and why not her?"

"He's going legit," Payton answered. "And I can't run it because men don't trust women who look like I do. The owner needs to be male."

Payton made a good point, and Julius would be prefect. Men assumed Payton wasn't smart because she was beautiful, and plenty assumed the same of Julius because he was an enormous bear of a man. Bouncers and escorts weren't supposed to have brains, and it was a hell of an advantage.

"You and Payton together?" I said. "You two will bleed the wealthy men of Chicago dry."

It had been a lot of fun doing that, but nothing lasted forever.

Noemi had recovered from her cold by Friday afternoon. I hadn't seen her all week. It had been one errand after another—lawyers, banks, and the usual day-to-day with my legitimate businesses that dominated my time. She was busy too, catching up on her classes she'd missed while sick, and studying for her finals.

Our Tumblr account was . . . active. She'd been posting a lot more than five clips a day, and I teased I'd created a monster. I loved it, but my right hand was ready to blister.

Hawaii had done a number on me. For the first time since the cancer diagnosis, I could imagine a future. I'd lain in the sagging bed in the yurt, listening to the driving rain, held a sleeping Noemi, and I could picture doing it again when we returned to Chicago. After. Giving up my club would keep that future possible.

She hadn't said those three words again since that night, not that I could blame her. But the asshole in me wanted to hear them again, and again. I needed them. Fuck, I needed her.

She answered my call right away. "Hey, you."

"Where are you, baby girl?"

"In a cab. I'm feeling too lazy to walk to the CTA station and wait. Why, what's up?"

"Let's grab a quick dinner. I'd like to see you." While that was certainly true, what I wanted to do was explain I was selling the wine club, and after this weekend when I was officially out, I'd tell her what it really was. It needed to happen before our relationship went any further.

"Oh. I've got a meeting with my advisor at four-thirty, and I don't know how long that's going to go. Plus, I still can't breathe through my nose. I might pass out on—Shit!"

There was squeal of brakes, followed by an enormous crash and Noemi's distant scream cut through the phone.

My blood turned to slush. My heart froze into ice.

"Noemi?"

In the background, there was a male voice, heavily accented, shouting about a crazy asshole driver.

"Noemi?" I yelled. Holy fucking shit, that scream was the stuff of nightmares.

Fumbling noises echoed, and a hurried breath came on the line. "Joseph," she said, "I'm here. I'm okay."

"What the fuck just happened?"

"Somebody pulled right out in front of us. There was no way to stop in time."

My freehand balled into a fist. "Jesus Christ, are

you okay?"

"Yeah, yeah. I mean, I banged my face into the divider, but I'm all right." She exhaled a long breath as if trying to calm herself. "Excuse me, sir, are you okay?" I assumed it was to the driver, and I waited impatiently for her to come back on the line.

"Where are you?" I demanded.

"I . . . hang on." There was more discussion between her and the driver. "We just got on Broadway."

I snatched up my coat. "I'll be there in twenty minutes." Fuck, if I was lucky. Traffic across town was going to be a bitch.

"Don't do that, I'm fine." A car door creaked opened and banged shut, and the wind whistled through the phone. "We weren't going fast and the taxi's barely damaged."

"You cannot leave, miss," the male voice said. The taxi driver sounded upset, and I didn't appreciate his sharp tone with her.

"Joseph, don't waste your time. The police will already be gone by the time you get here. I can grab another cab."

I was out the door and hit the key fob to unlock my doors. "I wasn't asking, Noemi."

"Seriously, this is silly."

"The fact that you think I'm going to budge on this is silly."

She sighed, a long and exasperated one. "Fine. See you in twenty minutes."

My hands clenched the steering wheel so hard on the drive over, they ached, and I'd apparently hit the road right as the motherfucking asshole parade started. Thank God she was okay. The scream played on a loop until I finally spotted her. I didn't care I was double-parked or that the engine was still running. I sprinted up the sidewalk and swept her into my arms, examining her for any signs of injury.

"I said I was fine," was the greeting she gave me, her expression irritated. "See? Not even a bump."

"Yeah, well, you're tough," I said. "I've seen you take a punch like a champ."

She gave me a lopsided smile. "Can we get going now?"

I led her to my car and pulled open her door. What a pair we made, me in one of my finest suits and her in jeans and fluffy boots, complete with backpack. The circumstances were shitty, but regardless, I was happy to see her.

When I got back into the driver's seat, I noticed her rubbing her neck. "Does it hurt?"

"It's just stiff."

"Maybe I should take you to the emergency room to be safe."

"For the millionth time, I'm okay. It's a little whiplash. I need twenty minutes in a hot shower and I'll be good as new."

I eased out into traffic and put my hand on her leg. It wasn't an attempt to dominate or control, it was to satisfy my need to touch her. To connect.

"My shower is better. It has a pulse setting."

She fiddled with her backpack straps. "No, I can't go to your place. I need to change before my advisor meeting."

"You were just in a car accident. Give me the advisor's name and I'll reschedule for you."

She let out a noise of annoyance. "Can you try not to control me right now?"

I wasn't actually trying to. "Sorry," I said, my voice plain, "but that's not something I can turn off."

Her irritation seemed to increase ten-fold when she realized I wasn't taking her home. "I said I couldn't go to your place. Come on, Joseph."

Frustration tightened every muscle in my body, and it slipped out. "Hearing you scream scared the shit out of me. Can you humor me?"

Her statement was flat. "I thought you liked hearing me scream."

Christ, was she serious? Her horrified, painful cry was a world away from the loud gasps of pleasure I enjoyed pulling from her. "No, never like that."

She didn't protest anymore, in fact, she was absolutely quiet the rest of the drive. I could tell her neck was bothering her and I wished I could do something to help. I felt fucking powerless, and I *hated* it.

Once we got to my place, Noemi pulled off her coat and headed straight for my bathroom, her body language making it clear she wanted space. If it had been another circumstance, I wouldn't have allowed her distance or lack of communication, but I sensed not to push.

"Do you need anything? Want me to come in with you?" I asked.

"No." Her voice was firm. "You seriously think I'm in the mood right now?"

"I didn't mean I wanted to fuck you." I fought to stay in control of my emotions. "I was asking if you wanted help."

She tried to shake her head and winced. "I'm sorry. I don't mean to be a bitch."

"You don't have to apologize. You want to get in alone, I understand. Call for me if you change your mind."

Without a word, she vanished into the bathroom and

closed the door.

I took off my suitcoat and hung it in the closet, then went to the living room and sat down with my iPad. There were work emails to go through, schedules of upcoming shows to approve, and a request for a new sous chef to be hired at the restaurant. My mind wandered as I tried to read them and work, but the girl in my shower was always my focus.

I was in love with her.

The sickening sound of the crash had snapped my heart into two, and her voice afterward had sewn it back together, a piece of her inside. I was supposed to wait. I wasn't supposed to tell her until she knew all of who I was, but I couldn't. Life was too short. My feet carried me swiftly to the bathroom door, my heart racing.

I knocked my knuckles on the wood. "Noemi?"

"Fuck off."

What the hell? "Excuse me?"

There was no answer.

The only sound was the constant stream of the shower running. I grabbed the doorknob and turned, only to discover it was locked.

"Noemi, answer me."

But she didn't.

"Open the goddamn door."

Still nothing. My airway cut off and I stared at the doorknob, hurrying through my options.

"Open the fucking door, *now*."

My blood pressure roared in my ears, right along with the sirens telling me to get inside the bathroom by any means necessary. Something was very wrong, and I didn't have time to figure out where the key was. I lifted my foot and kicked just to the side of the doorknob, putting everything I had into it.

The doorjamb splintered and broke from the wall as it gave way and the door swung open. I hurled myself into the bathroom across the tile, straight to the fogged glass door, and yanked it open.

She was sitting naked on the floor of the shower with her back against the wall and her knees pulled to her chest, the water cascading down her head and drenching her. When I opened the door, her head tipped back and she glared up at me with fire I'd never seen from her. But that wasn't what sent my heart to my feet.

Her left eye wasn't the hazel color I loved—it was enormously black, her pupil blown to hell.

chapter
TWENTY-NINE

My knees splashed to the tile and water soaked into my pants as I knelt beside her. "Shit, Noemi!" I tugged her into my arms, but she fought me.

"Leave me alone!" Her hand lashed out, and the sting against my cheek was shocking.

"Oh, fuck, baby girl," I wrapped my hands around her wrists, urging her to stop. "Jesus, please." She struggled against me as I dragged her from the shower. Noemi was gone. This was some wild, vicious creature.

Adrenaline made my hand shake as I dialed 911 and spat out my address, explaining what had happened. I was sick to my stomach, yelling at them to send someone immediately. I was sure I used profanity in spades, but I was out of my mind with fear, and everything was moving too fast.

"Please, Noemi," I begged, trying to get a shirt or pants on her.

"Stay the fuck away from me!"

I had a black robe on a hook and yanked it down, and she left me no choice. I twisted her arm behind her back and forced her into it. Her cry of pain was a knife in my chest. The robe was too big, but at least she wasn't naked or wet anymore. I locked her in my arms as she bucked against my hold, and I whispered to her. I begged her to calm down, told her she was going to be all right, and that she was safe with me.

"I love you," I said, feeling broken.

She didn't acknowledge it. Karma was a cruel bitch.

It was a blur after that. At some point I'd moved her to the living room and propped the front door open, and paramedics arrived. I stood to the side as she was strapped struggling to a stretcher, and followed alongside her, all the way down into the ambulance, past the people gawking on the sidewalk.

I sat on the bench by her head and put my hand on her shoulder, trying to stay out of the medics' way, but desperate to do something besides answer the medics' questions about her head injury, which I hadn't witnessed. I should have fucking made her go to the emergency room. My job was to keep her safe and I'd failed her spectacularly.

"Fuck you," she spat out, but whether it was to me or the paramedic placing an IV in her arm, was unclear.

"Which hospital are we going to? Cook County?" I asked the guy who didn't look much older than she did, but he was far more calm and in control than me. He slid the needle into her vein easily, while the ambulance took a corner hard. I had to brace a hand on the side to stay steady.

It felt like a lifetime before we reached the emergency room bay, and I was escorted to the waiting room. I fucking hated hospitals. The smell of disinfectant, the noises, and the chill that hung in the air. I shivered, still damp from pulling Noemi from the shower, and I never grabbed a coat. I stared at the phone in my hand, too confused to remember what I was supposed to do. Shit. I scrolled through the contacts and hit send.

"Rosso Media Group, this is Kristen."

"I need to speak with Mr. Rosso, and it's urgent."

"Who's calling, please?"

"Tell him his daughter is in the hospital. Cook County's ER."

My finger tapped "END CALL." Who knew what was going to come out of my mouth if I stayed on the line? I folded myself into one of the nearby chairs and pulled up my Internet browser. *Jesus, let her be all right.* I wouldn't get immediate answers from the hospital staff, so I began to research what was most likely happening to her.

It was two hours, the longest of my life, and I shot to my feet when the desk called for the people waiting for Noemi Rosso. The nurse guided me through the corridors of triage rooms, until knocking on one and pushing it open.

Noemi rested in the angled bed, wires and tubes snaking out to her monitoring equipment. The sight was a punch to the gut and I willed myself not to double over. And then, relief swelled and burst inside me when her eyes blinked at me with recognition.

"Joseph," her voice was concerned, "what the hell happened?"

I hurried to her bedside as the nurse lingered at the doorway. "The doctor will be with you shortly." The door thudded shut as she left.

"I don't remember how I got here," Noemi said, her gaze scanning the room and returning to me.

"Do you remember the car accident?"

"No," she gasped. "Is your overpriced car okay?"

It took me a second. "No, my car . . . you were in a cab. You don't remember that?"

Her gaze dropped down to her hands in her lap and the medical bands around her wrists. "No. I remember being in class, and—that's it. What happened?"

I took her small hand in mine, then explained it as quickly as possible, my fingers stroking hers gently. I told her what I'd heard on the call, how she'd argued about coming to my place, and how I'd pulled her from the shower. "I'm so sorry, Noemi."

"For what?"

"I should have made you go to the hospital. And I should have fucking noticed something was wrong sooner."

"Stop it," she whispered. It was so unnerving to see her eyes at different pupil ratios, but she was talking again. She sounded like herself. "What would have happened if you'd let me go home like I wanted?"

The thought had occurred to me soon after I'd taken a seat in the waiting room and I'd driven it away. "I don't want to think about that. How are you feeling?"

"My head hurts. A lot."

I cupped her cheek as delicately as possible, and used my thumb to brush away the tear that fell. Then, another, until there were too many.

"I don't know why I'm crying." She wiped at her face, horrified. "I can't stop."

"It's mood swings. It's okay."

There was a brief knock and the doctor came in, a short, frumpy woman with a no-nonsense hairstyle and matching attitude. She went over the MRI results that didn't show any bleeding, but wanted to admit Noemi for observation for at least another day until the symptoms were gone.

"Plenty of rest," the doctor warned, then looked at me. "She's going to have periods where she's confused, or dizzy, or irritable. We'll monitor the swelling and hopefully she'll be back to full cognitive function in a week."

"School?" Noemi asked feebly.

The doctor shook her head. "No. You need to give your body time to recover."

Disappointment washed over Noemi, but if she tried to push herself with this, I'd make it an order. The asshole in me found the concept of spending a week in bed with her appealing. Maybe a little torturous, but I could deal.

The doctor left when all of our questions were answered, and I sat beside Noemi on the bed, waiting for the nurses to come move her to a room upstairs.

Her voice was soft and warm. "I feel like I haven't seen you in forever."

I gave a sad smile. "I know. There are easier ways of getting my attention, little girl." I leaned over the bed, ignoring the beeping machines that reminded me of a time I never wanted to think about, and set my lips cautiously on hers.

Behind me, the door swung open. I wasn't about to let the nurse interrupt this moment between us. A man cleared his throat, and she broke off the kiss to glance at him.

"Dad."

My lungs refused to work. The moment was inevitable. I'd expected him hours ago, when I could have explained to him privately, but he never fucking showed up.

"I was on my way to New York when they called, and I had them turn the plane around," Rosso said. "This is the boyfriend?"

I watched her face as she smiled at me and then glanced to her father, and I hoped it wasn't the last time I'd see her look at me that way.

"Yes," she said. "This is Joseph Monsato."

I rose and turned, my gaze finding him quickly. His

mouth hung open and eyes filled with pure disbelief. All the emotions ran visibly through him, competing for dominance. Confusion. Anger. Fear. The perfect blend rose to the surface and his hands clenched into fists.

"What the *hell* are you doing here?" he demanded.

"We should talk outside."

"Get the fuck away from my daughter."

"Dad," Noemi said. "He's my boyfriend."

All that did was make him angrier, and his swift approach had me preparing for a punch to come flying my direction. He didn't know me outside the club, and didn't know me well there, either. He had to assume I was scum, unworthy of his daughter, which was true.

"Please," I said, although I put force behind my words. "Let's talk outside. Noemi has a concussion."

His face was flushed as he grabbed the front of my shirt and hauled me into his face. "Did you do that to her?"

"No."

"Dad, stop! He saved my life!"

Her panicked words brought him to a halt. Wild, dangerous eyes glared at me. Hazel, like hers.

"I was in a car accident in a cab," she continued, "and he came and got me. If I'd gone home alone, I'd probably be dead."

There was a stab of pain in my chest at her words, and Rosso turned, shoving me back. He positioned his body between us, trying to block her from view.

"Get out," he ordered.

She was breathing hard and her head had to be pounding terribly. "What is going on? Are you that upset because of Katzenberg?"

Rosso glanced at her, confused. "What?"

"No, Noemi." My voice was resigned. "This doesn't have anything to do with Katzenberg." I should have told her, right from the start.

"I don't understand," she said.

"I don't, either," Rosso snarled. "Do you know how bad it would be if this got out, Noemi?"

"No. She doesn't know." I moved to the right so I could see her. "I'm sorry. I was going to explain."

Her expression was cautious. "What don't I know?"

"He runs a whorehouse." Her father sneered. "That's where all his money comes from."

I glared right back at Rosso. *Most of it's yours, asshole.*

"Or so I'm told," he added, his voice wavering, but I doubt she noticed.

Her first reaction was this was a joke. Her lips curled into a faint smile, the word *ridiculous* probably on her lips, but the smile slowly died when I didn't deny it. She stared at me, silently demanding my rebuttal, but I had none I wanted to do in front of her father. *Please, baby girl, let me explain. Don't judge me until you hear all of it.*

There was no upside to revealing how her father knew about the blindfold club, other than bringing him down with me. Petty revenge, but she adored her father. I didn't want to hurt her more than I already had.

Her voice was severe. "Joseph. What is he talking about?"

I kept my posture stiff despite the desire to sag my shoulders. "My wine club . . . it's a front."

Jesus, this was too much to put on her damaged mind. Her eyes blinked and tears rolled down her cheeks, but there was no soft cry. Her shoulders didn't move. She brushed the tears away like they were a minor nuisance.

"Payton," she said, her voice barely a breath. "You . . . Oh, God. She was one of your whores?"

That was a word we didn't use at the club, an unspoken rule. When Dominic said it to Payton, it had made my blood run cold. "She worked for me, yes." My gaze burned into Rosso, who refused to meet it.

"You're a . . ." the word came out sounding foreign, "pimp?"

"Let me explain to you, alone."

Rosso shook his head. "No. Get out before I have you removed."

Her expression turned hard and cold. "Answer the question."

It wasn't the title I liked assigned to me. I oversaw negotiations between clients and service providers, often in excess of thousands of dollars, but when you boiled it down, I was just a guy selling pussy. "Yes."

"How could you not . . ." She swallowed hard. "Do you love me?"

"I—" Yes, but under her father's terrible scrutiny, I struggled. I did not want to say that to her for what would be her first time, while in this situation. I went with the first thing I could, a terrible, little mistake. "I care about you so much."

Her face crumbled and her head turned away from mine, a soft whimper of pain at the action, and it was crushing. Watching the effect of my mistake as it destroyed her, destroyed me as well.

"Please go."

"You're going to let me explain," I said, desperate.

Her choked voice just got it out. "No."

"Noemi," I growled. "Just wait a minute."

Her head lolled back, and eyes full of fire stared me down. "No. Stop. You said it was a word you'd always respect. Leave, Joseph."

"Please, think about this, baby girl."

"I am." Her voice was colder than steel. "I'm thinking about the brand."

Everything was hazy as I rode in the cab back to my apartment. I wanted to believe it wasn't real, but then there was the fucking bathroom door I'd broken down, all askew and wood splinters on my tile floor.

My club was gone. Tonight Julius would run things from my office with Payton's assistance—no, he'd oversee the business from *his* office. And Noemi was gone. The icy cold judgment in her eyes was too much. I couldn't push her. She was injured and her emotions were scattered. When she got better, she'd come back to hear my side, I convinced myself.

Nothing lasts forever.

I wanted to punch the wall, but instead I went into the bathroom, my feet crunching on the dust, and began to clean up. I was exhausted, both emotionally and physically, and everything ached. My throat burned and I put my hands on my neck to massage the—

Holy.

Shit.

My stomach bottomed out. No. *No.*

My hands shook as I set them on the counter and leaned over the sink, bringing my face close to the mirror.

As I turned my head to the side, it forced the small, little lump to protrude on my neck.

A swollen lymph node.

chapter THIRTY

NOEMI

I hadn't spoken to Joseph in twelve days. He called at least four times daily, but that lessened to three after I'd been out of the hospital a week. The scene in the emergency room haunted me. *"I care about you so much."*

Not enough to tell me the truth, though.

I'd thought Sensible Noemi was dead. I hadn't heard from her in weeks until that afternoon. She roared back to life when Joseph's secret was revealed, taking control back. If Joseph's brothel had been discovered, my bad boy would have gone to prison, and it would have ruined me. No one wanted a CEO who was involved in that kind of seediness. Public opinion would have deemed me too stupid to know what he was doing, or worse, in on it with him.

He sold sex.

I hated him and I loved him. He'd said I was too smart to fall in love, but no. Obviously I was incredibly stupid and a fucking fool. He'd made me a disappointment in my father's eyes, too.

Joseph was persistent, I had to give him that. When the front desk wouldn't allow him up, he said he'd wait, and they had him removed. He kept coming back, and my father got involved, telling security the next time Joseph appeared, to call the cops.

I missed him and his filthy mouth terribly. Part of me

wished I could go back in time and take the El that day instead of the cab that had set this all in motion. I'd be blind to what Joseph was doing, but I'd be with him. Ignorance was bliss, right?

The picture from Hawaii had been shoved in the back of my closet, buried under sweaters I didn't need because it was finally warming up outside. I couldn't bring myself to throw the frame out or give it away.

My concussion symptoms faded and I was over them. The mood swings were bad, but the foggy memories were cruel. Sometimes I had to be reminded why Joseph wasn't around. I was given extra time on my final exams, but I hadn't felt I'd done well when I sat for them. Underprepared, and exhausted, and distracted. For the first time in my academic career I hoped for a B.

My last final was over by mid-morning, and I pulled out my iPad, wanting something mindless. I needed to release the tension I'd been holding inside. I'd do anything to make myself feel better, even if it was for five, sad minutes.

I wasn't ready for it, but I should have known. I wouldn't take his calls or see him, and blocked his email, so Joseph had been reaching out to me on Tumblr. Our feed was full of GIFs and images. Apologies. Requests to communicate. A simple graphic that said "I need you." Five a day since I'd sent him from my hospital room.

I bawled my eyes out like a big baby. It wasn't the release I wanted, lying fully clothed in my bed in the middle of the day, but it worked and I cried myself to sleep.

My phone rang, waking me, and it was the front desk. "I have a Payton McCreary downstairs," the clerk said. "Would you like me to let her up?"

I didn't know, and my pause was so long, the clerk got worried.

"Are you still there?"

I scrubbed my face, erasing the tracks of dried tears away. "Send her up, please."

Payton stood cautiously in my doorway and it was an interesting sight, seeing her confidence flagging. "Hi. Thanks for meeting me."

"Come in." I motioned inside. I willed the flashes away of my night with her. I didn't need any more reminders of the man I'd left, but I couldn't stop myself. "You want something to drink?"

Her gaze surveyed the apartment as if looking for something and she seemed satisfied. "No, thanks. First things first, how are you? Like, physically?"

"I'm better." I strolled to the couch and sat, and she followed my lead, sinking down onto the soft cushion. Tension appeared to have her wound tight as a spring, and it made me suspicious. "Did he send you?"

"Joseph?" She shook her head. "No. Fuck, he'd shit a brick if he knew I was here."

I didn't want to be rude, but it sprang from my mouth pointed. "Why are you here?"

"I need a favor, but also to make sure you have all of the information."

My eyes burned. "There's *more*?" How much worse could it get?

"Yeah." Irritation trickled in her voice, and she made a face as she tried to squash it. "He started the blindfold club a few years ago, when he brokered a deal between me and a guy that needed to stay anonymous." She glanced at her nails. "Pretty sure that guy's office is in D.C. now."

I didn't care to hear about Payton banging some politician, but stayed quiet.

"The business grew from that, and Joseph . . . he enjoyed the power. The clientele list is like a who's-fucking-who of Chicago's wealthiest people. Some of them are in the legal system and the rest think they're above it. No one cares about the legality."

"I don't need to know this."

"Yes, you do. You need to understand how much he loved what he did. The club put him in position to negotiate with extremely powerful people. Nobody was getting hurt. The women who work the club are there by choice, because they love sex and money, and Joseph keeps them safe. They can walk away at any time, just like I did."

Was I supposed to be impressed that he ran his high-class whorehouse with professionalism? "What is your point?"

"He fucking *loved* his club. The power and the money, and he gave it all up, for you."

I scowled. "When I found out."

Payton's voice was weighted. "No. He sold it a week before your accident. He'd called me from Hawaii to put it in motion. He was going to tell you, Noemi."

Disorienting thoughts floated in my mind like a static-filled radio. He'd sacrificed his most lucrative business for me. He'd been the one to call my father and stayed by my side, even when he knew it risked outing him.

"He lied to me."

Payton's blue eyes turned cloudy. "You're going to have to trust me when I tell you that no one knows what that's like better than I do. Yeah, he lied and it fucking sucked. He was trying to make it right."

I threaded my fingers through my hair, not sure what to say. I hadn't given him a chance to explain. Sensible, judgmental Noemi was in charge.

"He told you I worked as one of his girls, but did he ever mention Mr. Red?"

I shook my head.

"He was the last client I saw before Dominic. Mr. Red was a regular I had almost every week."

I stood up too quickly and got lightheaded. The last thing I wanted was to hear about the men who paid for sex. "I don't—"

Payton was on her feet instantly, as if ready to catch me. I'd gotten so woozy, I swayed.

"He's a nice guy. I was way too much for him, but that's neither here nor there. He was sweet, and lonely because his wife wouldn't touch him."

"Oh, God, he was married." *Stop being so naïve. Most of them probably were.*

"Mr. Red fell in love with me, hard. He wanted to leave his wife, but I didn't feel the same. When I went to Japan, he searched for me everywhere. He wasn't real delighted when I returned engaged to someone else."

Her gaze turned away from me and she peered out the window, watching the afternoon sun collide with nearby buildings.

"Mr. Red ambushed Dominic at his office two weeks ago."

I sucked in a breath. "What?"

"Dominic knew he had to be careful. Even after I left, Mr. Red is still the biggest customer at the blindfold club, and he's powerful, too."

The lovesick man had confronted Dominic? I envisioned the worst. "What happened?"

When her face turned back to mine, she blinked something away. Tears?

"Mr. Red wanted to see Dominic, to make sure he was a good man. Like, worthy of me. He told Dominic he'd destroy him if he broke my heart."

"Oh." The word stuck in my mouth.

"I'm telling you this because people can do things you don't like, or things that seem wrong, and still be good people. If you love someone, you love them, mistakes and all." She took an enormous breath, and her expression shifted to fear. "Now I'm going to ask you, what's the Italian word for red?"

What?

The world came to an abrupt stop.

"Holy fuck." I banded my arms over my stomach, trying to hold myself in one piece. *Rosso*.

My father had paid for sex. He'd *paid* Joseph. Payton hadn't been star-struck when my father had come to my place, she'd been terrified, and . . . oh, God. I'd been the one to give him Dominic's name.

How could my dad give me those looks of disappointment? He'd cheated on my stepmom. He'd bought prostitutes. He sure the hell wasn't thinking of the brand, week after week when he went to the club.

"You think less of him, I'm sure," Payton said. "Joseph refused to tell you because he wanted to protect you. He didn't want you to see your father as . . . just a man, who was lonely and desperate. But now that you know, you still love him, right? Mistakes and all?"

It wasn't a fair question since I was reeling from the bombshell that I should have seen coming. I was incredibly disappointed, but yes. He wasn't just family, he'd been the most important person in my life for so long. I'd love him no matter what.

When I nodded, her voice was strong. "Then you can still love Joseph. You can get past this. You're going to need to, because now is when I ask for the favor."

I felt weak and emotionally drained, and lowered back to sit. "What is it?"

"Joseph's sick."

It stung and knocked me back. My brain couldn't interpret. "What? Sick how?"

"Sick," she said, the word weighed. "He thinks maybe it's just a physical reaction to losing you. He won't go to the doctor. He's really fucking stubborn."

The room emptied of air. I dug my nails painfully into my thighs, needing something to hold onto. No, he couldn't be. He'd been cancer free for twenty years.

Nothing lasts forever.

"I've been trying to convince him, but I'm getting fucking nowhere." The couch shifted as she sat beside me. "Joseph doesn't take orders from anyone."

My eyes burned with unshed tears but I tilted my head back to drain them away. "You think he will from me?"

"I do." Payton's expression hinted at her concern. "He loves you. I think he'll do anything you tell him to, even if he's scared. And maybe he won't listen at first, Noemi, but you still gotta try. Please?"

Of course I was upset with what he'd kept from me, and

Payton was wrong in her belief that he loved me, but this trumped everything else. "Yes."

She looked relieved.

I climbed to my shaky feet and reached for my jacket. I didn't want to waste any time. "Will you drive me?"

Payton launched to her feet, not missing a beat. "Let's go."

chapter
THIRTY-ONE

I rode in Payton's Jaguar and tried not to think about where the money to buy it had come from. We passed Joseph's Porsche in the parking garage as she searched for a spot, and the overpriced car put flutters in my belly.

He was inside his apartment.

And he was sick. The interior of her luxury car seemed impossibly small and I couldn't find any air to breathe. I followed slowly behind her through the garage as we made our way to the elevator, stalling. I needed to organize my thoughts.

The inside of the elevator felt worse than her Jaguar, and shrank with every floor we climbed. Sensible Noemi was angry. *Just because he's sick, doesn't make what he did okay. Think about the brand.*

The other side, the one Joseph had brought to life, was anxious to see him again. She was desperate to get another fix. My heart clogged my throat when Payton knocked on his front door.

"It's Payton," she said loudly.

Footsteps pounded closer and the door swung open, revealing a shirtless Joseph, unshaven and hair disheveled. I swallowed hard. His eyes were sunken and he looked tired. His angry expression was directed at her. "Give it a fucking rest, I already—"

His mouth snapped shut as his gaze found mine.

"I told her." She announced it like it wasn't a big deal. "I told her about Mr. Red, too. I figure you're already pissed, and she needed to know."

Joseph's dark eyes went wide, and his gaze swung back to her. "What the fuck, Payton?"

Her face turned hard. "Don't give me any shit. If the roles were reversed, you would have done exactly the same, and I told you, I don't like lies. Stop being a pussy and go see the doctor." Her head turned to me. "You want me to wait for you?"

"No." It was hard not to keep looking at him. "I'll grab a cab."

"The fuck you will," he snapped, probably overly sensitive about the accident. His face softened and turned apologetic. "I'll drive you home when you want."

My voice was hesitant. "Oh, okay."

I didn't like the awkwardness between us, but the lie was a wall forcing me back. A wall he'd built.

Payton gave me a nod and turned to leave.

"Wait," Joseph said. "Thank you."

She gave him a pleased smile. "You put me and Dominic together. Somehow you knew when you interviewed him, he was what I needed." Her gaze on me was warm. "You and I are a lot alike, Joseph."

She thought I was what Joseph needed? I watched her head down the hallway, and risked a glance back to him. He was still shirtless and tattooed, and the man I loved. Possibly sick.

"Come in." He stepped back from the doorway and gave me space.

There was a blanket and his iPad on the couch, and CNN was on mute on the television. Around his coffee table were boxes of snacks, like he'd been camped out there a while. The half empty glass on the table was a bright red drink. Kool-Aid.

How long had he been sick?

"I'm sorry." His voice was solid. "I should have told you, but . . . No, I just should have told you."

"Yes," I said quietly.

"I was worried once you knew, I was going to lose you." He drew in a deep breath. "Did I?"

I couldn't answer the direct question. "Go see the doctor, Joseph."

His eyes narrowed at my tone. "No."

"No? How can you say no? Are you scared about what they'll find?" A fire built inside me that quickly flared out of control. "Because you're going to be fine."

He put his hands on his hips. "Oh, yeah? How do you know that?"

"Because I *want* you to be, and I told you, Rossos always get their way."

A hint of a smile curled on his lips. Even tired, he was so beautiful. "I don't have cancer."

"That's what I'm saying, but you need to—"

"I don't have cancer," he repeated, firm. "I have mono."

What? I stared at him.

"She wore me down. I went yesterday afternoon, and the monospot test confirmed it."

It was ironic that this word brought me joy. "Mono." *He was okay.*

"My swollen lymph nodes are already gone. How are you feeling? I've been trying to talk to you, but communication has been pretty one-sided."

It had been. I'd been holding a grudge, which I hated, and because of it, he'd gone through this cancer scare alone. I should have been there for him.

"I feel . . ." Awful? Like I shouldn't have judged him without hearing his side? "I feel like I don't have mono."

He nodded. "The doctor said you probably don't. It's highly contagious, but at the same time, the stars have to align just right for someone to come down with it." Joseph made his way incredibly close to me, and I stared up into his gorgeous eyes. "I thought I'd never see you again."

My voice was breathless. "Yeah, well, nothing lasts forever."

He cupped the back of my neck, which held my gaze on him, as if there was anywhere else I'd look.

"Nothing lasts forever," he repeated, "except for the way I feel about you. I love you, Noemi. I think I've been in love with you since the night you insulted my car."

I sucked in a breath, and laughed at the same moment tears welled in my eyes. "It *is* overpriced."

He loved me. The words had rolled out of his filthy mouth with no trouble, with no hesitation. Payton had been absolutely right. I loved Joseph, mistakes and all.

"I love you, too," I said. "Even if you pay too much for a ridiculous status symbol."

His thumb brushed on my cheek as he leaned in, then froze. "I want to kiss you, but I should remind you I have mono."

A smile broke on my face. "I don't fucking care."

His lips met mine, urgent and desperate. I gasped against his kiss, my body sighing with relief to have him back. He was okay. He was kissing me, and I could not get enough. Sparks showered down from his mouth pressed against mine, claiming me as his.

"Such language," he whispered.

"You're a terrible influence on me."

His expression said he wasn't sorry about that. "I won't keep anything from you again. Do you forgive me, baby girl?"

My hands slipped into his hair, tugging him back to me. "You know I can't say no. You've got me addicted."

"We're both addicted, and I plan to keep it that way. Now get in my fucking bed so I can sleep with you."

Whether he meant sex or just sleeping didn't matter. I followed his order gladly.

FOUR MONTHS LATER

JOSEPH

This was going to be the most awkward dinner of my life.

Eight months ago I would have sold my Porsche for the opportunity to have dinner with Anthony Rosso. Now I wished he wasn't here. His glare from across the table wordlessly repeated, *"You will never be good enough for my daughter."*

Yeah, I was aware. But she loved me anyway.

Noemi had forgiven me, both my big and little mistakes. Each day we were together was another day she chose to be in defiance of her father. She shrugged off his hypocritical judgment, and it was impressive.

Rosso glanced at his phone on the tabletop, and a hint

of excitement glinted in his eyes. "She's here."

We rose as Claudia made her way through the restaurant to the table, a bright smile on her lips. Like all the women who had worked for me, she was young and beautiful. As she planted a kiss on Rosso's cheek, I wondered who around us at the restaurant instantly labeled her a gold-digger based on the age difference and the fact that he was the richest man in Chicago.

They'd be wrong, though. Claudia had plenty of money. Not just his, from their time together at the club, but from her day job as an attorney. She'd been a junior assistant at the corporate law firm I often used when I discovered her years ago.

"This is my daughter, Noemi," Rosso said.

Claudia extended a hand across the table and shook Noemi's. "Claudia. It's nice to finally meet you."

Noemi had a pleasant look on her face. I could tell she felt awkward, but she did a great job masking it. "Yeah, you, too."

Rosso wouldn't introduce me. Not because Claudia and I already knew each other, he wouldn't do it because it would require him to acknowledge my presence, or my attachment to his daughter.

"Hey, Joseph." Claudia's tone was light and casual.

"Good to see you."

She turned to Rosso. "Did you order some wine, Tony?"

He nodded and held out her chair, which she slipped into. Once we were all seated, tension gripped the table. It wasn't just uncomfortable, it was fucking painful.

"What a relief," Claudia said abruptly. "I was worried this was going to be horribly awkward."

THREE *little* MISTAKES

Noemi let out a tight laugh, and some of the tension dissipated.

The night after Noemi had been admitted to the hospital with the concussion, Rosso had gone to the blindfold club, demanding to see me. Payton had relayed the story, how shocked he'd been when he learned I'd sold the club to try to be with his daughter.

Since she was smart, Payton convinced Rosso to have a drink while Julius called Claudia to get her ass to the club, and she came *running*. How had I not picked up on it? She'd been exclusive to Mr. Red for more than a year.

He'd gone into Claudia's room, only she wasn't naked and bound to the table like usual. She'd been clothed and sitting in the chair, wearing the blindfold to protect his identity. With what had happened, everyone was concerned Mr. Red wouldn't be back, and Claudia confessed she didn't want to lose him.

Not his money, but the *man*.

She was in love with him, and neither one of them knew the other's real name.

Rosso had been fucking Clare, but when he took off her blindfold that night, he fell hard for the woman beneath it—Claudia. His divorce papers were only a few weeks old when he'd been photographed at a romantic dinner with Claudia.

Noemi's father didn't visit the club anymore, but he didn't come after it to try to tear me down, as he had no reason to do either. Julius was still mining Rosso's connections and finding new clients. Business remained strong, and I was pleased about that, even as my structured deal ran its course and I was no longer affiliated.

I stared at Rosso's hazel eyes. Perhaps he'd never get

over who I was, but nothing lasted forever. *Just that one thing,* I reminded myself. I'd have to get Silas to work it into the tattoo.

I glanced down at the delicate hand that was encased in mine, resting in my lap, and back up to her. A smile broke on her gorgeous face.

Noemi Rosso. My girlfriend, my submissive, and the fucking love of my life.

chapter
THIRTY-TWO

NOEMI

When the Porsche pulled up in front of my apartment building, I hurried out into the August heat that was thick as a wall even though it was nighttime.

"Whoa," Joseph said when I slid into the passenger seat, his gaze lingering on my dress. "Where'd you find that?"

"A thrift store over on the south side. Isn't it totally rad? Gnarly?"

He gave me a half-smile, laced with seduction. "It's something."

"Look at you, Don Johnson." He had on a pale grey sports jacket with the sleeves pushed up, and a salmon colored shirt beneath. Gorgeous no matter what decade we were dressed for.

"I'm surprised you know who that is." He put the car in motion when my seatbelt was on. "Why is your generation so obsessed with the eighties? You weren't even alive."

I grinned. This whole thing had been my idea to energize sales at Dune. 1980s prices on a few featured cocktails while eighties music filled the club, once a month, and dress-up was encouraged. Joseph had found a DJ that was phenomenal at remixing all the Culture Club and Flock of Seagulls with driving bass to keep it fresh and the dance floor packed. Last month had been the trial run, and sales were through the roof.

Tonight we'd decided to see the success for ourselves.

"The eighties seemed like they were awesome," I said. "God, the big hair. How much cocaine did you do?"

"Ha, ha. I was in elementary school."

My dress was killer, but also itchy. A tight bodice of midnight-blue satin that was covered with black lace. An off-the-shoulder neckline which exploded into the prerequisite puffy sleeves, and a bulbous, tiered skirt that stopped at my knees. I'd teased my blonde hair up and wore it over one shoulder, then layered on the heavy eye makeup.

When we arrived at the club, there was a line. It was only a few people, but it was the first time Dune had had a line this summer. I took Joseph's arm and we breezed past the bouncer straight into the club.

We'd only been there a few minutes before the text message came from Payton, telling me Dominic and she had arrived with their friends.

"This is Logan and Evie Stone," Payton said, introducing the attractive couple. The woman wore a ghastly floral print dress that was perfectly eighties, and pronounced her pregnant belly. She gave me a warm smile as she shook my hand.

"I'm Noemi Rosso. Do you know Joseph?" As soon as I asked it, I wanted it back. According to Payton, these were her and Dominic's closest friends. It seemed likely Joseph would know them.

Evie's smile was weird. "Uh, yeah. We've met."

Logan's arm squeezed his wife to him. "What do you want to drink? Apple juice?"

She nodded and flashed us a guilty smile as he went to the bar. "It's the only craving. I need apple juice by the gallons."

Payton adjusted her hot pink leg warmer. "Did Logan

give you any lip about coming? It's a school night," she teased. I'd been told the pair worked together at a design firm. The reality was school wasn't starting for another few weeks. My final semester before graduation.

Evie made a face. "I guess you didn't hear him and Dominic planning out their matching outfits."

"We did no such thing," Dominic said. "Logan asked me for advice. I'm older, wiser, and much more hip."

Payton snorted. "Says the man who just used the expression *hip*."

I leaned back against Joseph, enjoying his arms around me, feeling like I belonged here.

We danced, and drank, and Joseph admitted the theme night was fun. He still didn't quite get why all the twenty-year-olds were so enamored with the decade, but it didn't matter. Liquor sales were double what they normally were.

Logan and Evie couldn't stay long, claiming they had a managers' meeting early in the morning. Payton and Dominic took off right after them, and Joseph led me upstairs to his office. We'd finally had sex on his desk last month, something we'd both been wanting since that time I'd turned him down.

"Such a fucking cock tease," he'd whispered. "My balls were blue for a week afterward. You made me crazy."

"Aw, poor baby," I said, sarcastic.

"I'll do the same to you, little girl. Make you want it so bad you can't see straight. Have you begging for me."

Of course he'd made good on his threat.

So now I stood in his office, floating in that happy place between sober and full-on drunk, staring at my perfectly imperfect boyfriend and Dom. His eyes were playful, and yet it made my mouth go dry. His effect over me only strengthened over time.

"Go out on the balcony," he said. The mischief in his expression was sexy, and anticipation heated me.

The balcony was as small as a closet, a half wall with a railing to keep drinks from going over. I glanced down at the main level and the sea of people undulating on the dance floor. Joseph stood behind me, his hands on my hips.

"Are you wearing panties under this ridiculous dress?"

We'd played this game enough times I finally knew how. Perhaps I even knew how to beat him at it. "Yes, Sir."

"You know I don't like it. Take them off."

No one could see us below the waist. I reached under my skirt and pushed my panties down to my ankles, stepping out of them. I asked it innocently and surprised, although it was what I hoped for. "Are you going to fuck me here, Sir? Where someone might see?"

He didn't answer. Joseph stood beside me, turned, and sank down to sit with his back against the half wall.

"Get that skirt up and show me your pussy."

I stared down at him and dragged the layers of the skirt up slowly until I had it clutched in my hand at my waist, my lower body completely exposed to him, and hidden from everyone else.

"Fuck," he groaned. "Come here."

A smile warmed on my cheeks. I stepped over him, positioning the juncture of my legs right in front of him, where I was bare and wet.

The railing was cool in my hand when I latched onto it, needing to hold on when Joseph's tongue licked me. The soft wetness teased, and pleasure made me shudder. His hands were firm on my ass, holding me steady while he fucked me with his mouth.

"God, yes." I kept my hooded gaze on the crowd below. Could they tell what was happening? I moaned when his tongue swiped hard and fast over my sensitive clit. He knew exactly how to touch and taste me, and yet he never seemed to want to stop learning. Joseph wanted to study my body and push me to new heights.

The tremble began in my legs, shuddering along my high heels. No longer was I shy about what I wanted or needed. My requests for more, verbal and non-verbal, turned him on like nothing else.

Heat swelled like a crescendo, raging hotter until I couldn't think about anything else but the orgasm he was about to give me.

"Fuck." I subtly shifted my hips in time with his mouth. "Right there. Oh, God, go. Go, go, go . . ."

I cried out. Not too loud to be heard below, but loud. My grip on the skirt fell away, and my hand tangled in it as I grabbed the top of his head, holding him as I came in a rush. Bliss exploded and my legs almost gave way.

"You liked that, baby girl? Riding my tongue and coming on my face?"

"Yes, Sir," I said between pants. "I loved it."

I clung to the railing, bent slightly at the waist, when he stood. I closed my eyes as his zipper was undone. *Yes.* Strong hands pushed the skirt up, and he smacked my bare ass. "I told you to keep this up."

Fingers trailed down through my slit, and I twitched, oversensitive from my orgasm. He continued to tease and torment. I kept thinking at any moment he'd plunge deep inside me, but it didn't happen. The waiting was killing me. "Please," I whispered.

"Tell me what you need."

"Your cock inside me. Oh, shit, Joseph, please."

"This?" He ran the velvety tip of his cock over me, sliding between my folds.

I hissed through clenched teeth. "Yes, Sir."

The push of his body inside mine voided my mind. His hands were tight on my hips, and it felt like he was everywhere. Inside and surrounding me. He groaned, low and deep, as he entered and buried himself to the hilt.

"Look at them," he ordered. "Those people down there don't have any idea how hard I'm about to fuck you." His words were a blast of heat. "But you do, don't you?"

"Yes, Sir."

"You've been posting some rough stuff recently. You want it rough, Noemi?"

Not only did I want it, but I felt like this was one of the areas where I could push him. "Yes, Sir."

He gave me his first thrust and I moaned. He leaned over so he was close. "And what about the bartender down there? He can't keep his eyes off of you whenever you're here. You want me to invite him up next time? I'm sure he'd love to have you suck his cock while I fuck you."

"Oh my God."

"Your body says you like that idea." His voice was all sin as he thrust again, deeper. "You're a filthy slut, and I fucking love it."

It was a starting pistol on him, and his body slammed into mine. Jarring blows that rattled my teeth and had my body singing with pleasure. I bent over further, leaving the skirt hiked up around my waist, and gripped both hands on the railing. My biceps strained against his furious pounding, taking each impact as I begged for more.

We didn't last long on the balcony. Maybe Joseph was worried we'd get caught when I got too loud. He pulled out of me and shoved me stumbling back into the seclusion of his office. I didn't get a chance to catch my breath. He charged at me, throwing me against the desk.

Holy shit. The temperature of the room climbed a thousand degrees. I pushed up on my hands, only to have him slam me back down, my face against the desktop. His cock impaled me in one hard move, draining air from my lungs.

Oh my God, I loved it. He took what he wanted, and I gave it gladly. His hips ground into mine, slapping a furious rhythm, his thrusts tapping me closer to another orgasm. My fingers curled into fists and my eyes shut.

We banged into the desk so hard, it hurt, but I liked the pain. I liked listening to the desk thump and move across the floor as Joseph rammed into me. I cried out when my head yanked back painfully, my scalp smarting from his grip in my hair. He bent me back until I thought my spine would snap. My eyes flew open to stare up at him, who stared down at me. His eyes, his mouth, his hands, and his cock had claimed every inch of my body, and his soul owned my heart.

His lips closed over mine. The kiss was fire. Sin. Love. It branded me forever.

His other hand wrapped around my throat and he gazed at me unblinking while the fingers tightened. We hadn't done this since the belt around my throat. I hadn't stopped him then and I wasn't about to now. His grip grew stronger, and blocked off my windpipe.

I studied the dark eyes and learned every fleck of caramel in them as things grew hazy outside the focus of my vision.

Air, my body demanded, but I wouldn't use my safe word. I was safe with him, and he knew what he was doing. I couldn't keep my hands in fists anymore, my muscles refused to respond.

He grew dim and the tremble seized my body, just as the unavoidable fight response reared up. I needed to breathe. Fuck, I needed to breathe. The hand on my throat was too tight, too strong. My eyes fluttered closed as I went weak.

The hand released me, and as air poured into my body, it brought ecstasy with it.

"Fuck, fuck!" I screamed. I convulsed in his embrace, swept away in orgasm.

"Yes," he groaned. He shuddered and pulsed inside, his tempo slowing as he came violently.

It was like we were standing on a fault line, we swayed and shook. I rode my way back from indescribable pleasure on his cock that was deep inside, still jerking in the aftermath of our mutual climax. Mind-numbing. I collapsed onto the desk, my body spent.

"You okay?" His lips trailed a line of kisses along my upper back. "Too rough?"

"Mmm, no. It was great," I purred.

He chuckled and returned to his task of kissing all of my exposed skin. "I have a serious question for you."

"What is it?" I stayed on the desktop, waiting to get my breathing back to normal and for my arms to work again.

"Where the hell are we going to put all your stuff?"

"What?"

"The stuff in your apartment."

"Am I leaving my place?" Finally my body would cooperate and I got up on my elbows, turning to look at him.

"Yeah, you're moving in with me."

I shot a skeptical look. "Oh, am I? I happen to like my place. Maybe you should move in with me."

"It's cute you think this is a request," he said, power burning in his eyes that was undeniably sexy. "You think Tony's going to pay the rent if I'm living there?"

No, my father certainly wouldn't. "I wouldn't recommend calling him Tony, *Joe*."

Joseph spanked me playfully. "Move in with me, Noemi. I'll let you decorate the guest bathroom anyway you want."

I laughed. "I want the kitchen, a bathroom, and the master bedroom."

"Oh, we're negotiating?" He helped me turn to sit on the desk and did up his pants. "Kitchen and bathroom, but our bedroom has to meet specific needs."

I shivered. *Our bedroom.* "Deal."

His hands cupped my face and he kissed me so softly my heart swelled to twice its size. "I love you, you know. Forever and beyond."

THANK YOU

To my husband. You are a truly amazing man and father, and I still can't believe I found my soulmate in a hot tub in a foreign country. You are proof that true love stories can be even better than fiction. Thank you for every day, for putting up with my shit, for being so freaking sexy, and for making me the happiest I've ever been. I love you so much.

To my beta readers Robin Bateman, Michelle and Yaya from After Dark Book Lovers, and Ms. "*Yeah, I'm not a huge fan of choking.*" :-) I felt like I sent you ladies a shameful first draft and none of you held it against me. Your feedback was invaluable. Thank you so much!

To my editor Lori Whitwam. I still haven't figured out when to use lie vs. lay, but my overuse of 'that' has improved! Maybe a few more books and I'll finally get it. Thanks for fixing my bad habits and giving me notes that make my day.

To all the bloggers and readers out there who mentioned my work and helped me find new readers. You guys are amazing, and I couldn't do this without you.

IF YOU ENJOYED THE BOOK

Thank you so much for taking the time to read Joseph and Noemi's story. If you enjoyed it, would you be so kind as to let other readers know via an Amazon review or on Goodreads? Just a few words can help an author tremendously, and are *always* appreciated!

ABOUT THE AUTHOR

Nikki Sloane landed in graphic design after her careers as a waitress, a screenwriter, and a ballroom dance instructor fell through. For eight years she worked for a design firm in that extremely tall, black, and tiered building in Chicago which went through an unfortunate name change during her time there.

Now she lives in Kentucky, is married and has two sons. She is a member of the Romance Writers of America, also writes romantic suspense under the name Karyn Lawrence, and couldn't be any happier that people enjoy reading her dirty words.

Find her on the web: www.NikkiSloane.com

Contact her on Twitter: @AuthorNSloane

Send her an email: authornikkisloane@gmail.com

the blindfold club series

THREE **SIMPLE** RULES

THREE **HARD** LESSONS

ONE **MORE** RULE (A NOVELLA)

THREE **LITTLE** MISTAKES

THREE **DIRTY** SECRETS

THREE **SWEET** NOTHINGS

also available

SORDID
A DARK EROTIC ROMANCE